A Pride & Prejudice Reimagining

Happenstance
&
Holidays

Kitty Bennet's Adventure
Book Eight

NEY MITCH

ISBN: 979-8-88653-428-3

Published by Satin Romance
An Imprint of Melange Books, LLC
White Bear Lake, MN 55110
www.satinromance.com

Published in the United States of America.

Cover Design by Caroline Andrus

Dedication & Author's Note

Readers, we're on Book Eight, nearing the middle of the end—but still not quite there *yet*. Yes, I still haven't embraced the idea that brevity is the soul of wit. Then again, I have never been a wit. Despite one's wishes, we are not all Miss Austen, hard as we try to be. Here is an *important note* for you before you delve into this part of the series.

This entry will focus primarily around Rosings Park and Longbourn during the Twelve Days of Christmas, and a little time after. After the book, there is an Afterword, to explain the choices that were made to the reader, if they are curious.

I hope that you like this next installment in the series and are interested in some holiday cheer. I wrote this one with you in mind especially.

You still are the best, alongside those who have always supported me, including Helyn Guy-Roberts, A. K. Madison, Laura Novo, as well as my wonderful publisher, and those who helped me with this book.

Chapter One

CHRISTMAS BELLS ARE RINGING

And to Rosings Park, we arrived.

The ride toward the great house was casually uneventful in every respect. There was no dramatic overturning of a carriage, no highwaymen who came to greet us, and no broken wheel that occurred. The weather was congenial, for that time of year, there was no rain, no snow and soon, we had crossed the difference between the public road, and the hills and woods that belonged to the great lady.

To the great lady that was now our aunt, through marriage.

The great lady who did not approve of my sister's marriage to her nephew.

To the great lady who appeared to be civil, but we did not know just how far her contempt would exert.

"I admit," I whispered to Georgiana as we rode through the trees that abutted the estate, "that I cannot help but predict how things are going to be."

"And how will they?" Georgiana asked back.

"Well, if your aunt is anything like she is described—and I mean no offense, of course."

"I know you do not. Go on, don't mince words with me. I love my aunt, but I know what she is."

"I just cannot help but determine much strained civility, many kind words spoken, but they won't be true. I think your aunt still will groan, secretly, at our presence. I assume that she still cannot forgive us Bennet sisters for either existing, or for meeting your brother. Am I extreme?"

"No," Georgiana answered, so simply and curtly, that I felt an intensity of my confirmation. "You are not."

"Truly?" Enara asked us. "Mr. and Mrs. Darcy have been married for so long now, that I thought Lady Catherine would have recovered from her disappointment."

"Hell hath no fury like a great person scorned," I remarked. "And Lady Catherine's reputation has always stricken me as her being a person who has always had the pleasure of getting her own way in life."

"And whenever someone like that does not get their own way..." Arthur Philips uttered.

"It can lead to a lingering resentment," Georgiana finished his sentence. "Yes, there is always that possibility. I love my aunt. But her pride was hurt, and I cannot determine that it has recovered, since I have not seen her in so long. Hopefully, she has rallied from her disappointment."

"You don't think," I gathered, "that she would ever reach a point where she would be outwardly rude to us? It is just that I cannot help but still believe that she might take her frustrations out on Eliza. She wouldn't...would she?"

"I am sorry to say that I do not know. But there is the possibility that..."

"Yes."

"Yes."

Georgiana did not say it, because she didn't need to say it. The same went for Enara and Arthur Philips. We all were of the same mindset. We didn't need to put words to it to know that the holiday could all end in disaster. That left us to make little excuses for the lady if her tone were ever to prove foul.

As we turned a corner, down the lane, we arrived at a simple house.

"Wait?" I gasped. "Is that Hunsford Parsonage?"

"Yes, it is."

Through windows, I saw two faces produced. First, there was one from upstairs, and the other was from a room that was to the right of the door.

"That's Mr. Collins," I said, gesturing to the man's face on the ground floor. "And that's Charlotte."

I could scarce believe it! After all this time, I was now seeing them again. Naturally, I knew that we were going to encounter them both, but I had prepared to do it when we arrived at Rosings Park and had already settled. But to see them there, through the windows of the parish, had stricken a sharp pang of disturbance within me.

And I could only imagine what Jane and Lizzy were feeling now. Then again, Jane would probably not be feeling anything at all, and Elizabeth would not begrudge the couple either, perhaps. After all, she had been the one to do the rejecting and had acquitted Mr. Collins of any guilt for standing to inherit Longbourn. Also, since she had gone to visit them for a time, which is where she saw Mr. Darcy again, she had little to hold remorse for.

It was only I that might hold any apprehension toward the reverend and his wife. I did not hate them. No. Especially not at this time of year. I merely did not care for them, that was all. And whatever surprise that I felt when seeing their faces through the Hunsford windows, it would soon pass.

It was merely a trick of the moment.

"Isn't that the dreadful Mr. Collins that proposed to Lizzy?" Arthur asked me.

"Yes, he is," I answered.

"I gather that you are not eager to see him again."

"He was not eager to see us when Lydia and Mr. Wickham married. So, I cannot imagine me having to be obliged to be happy to meet him."

"Naturally." Arthur smirked. "I confess to being interested in seeing the man who proposed to my cousin and shall inherit Longbourn. There is something altogether interesting about meeting such characters. They lend sparkle to situations."

I rolled my eyes.

"To be sure. If you find foolishness to be sparkling."

"But I do. Life is only as interesting as the absurd characters that we meet. For they give us things to talk about. After all, if we only say pretty things in life, then we would all be prodigiously dull."

"That's the sad business of it," I inferred. "The only way to truly be worth speaking with, or regarded as clever, is if you are committing to some form of insult—in one way or the other. It's such a spur to one's genius, and morality, that to be preferred company is to be cruel."

"It is a tendency, generally acknowledged," Georgiana said, "that there is a great deal of truth to that statement. A person is the most interesting when they are either the subject of ridicule or doing the ridiculing. Well, Arthur and Enara, if you want absurdity to amuse you, Mr. Collins will offer a great deal of that."

"And what of Mrs. Collins?" Enara asked us. "What sort of lady is she?"

"She is full of a great deal of sense," I answered. "Though, accepting Mr. Collins does not show her sense to advantage. Or maybe it shows that she has too much of it, for she got her good luck when she did. That's why I like not being wholly sensible."

"You don't?" Enara asked.

"No, I do not. In fact, I praise it, because for some reason, being wholly sensible seems to always lead to someone being an absolute idiot."

"Kitty, really?" Georgiana said, amused. "Now that is going too far."

"Perhaps it is, but I cannot help but see what I see."

"I have to disagree with that mentality, but go on and explain to me why you say that? For I am curious."

"Ah, I am being interesting?" I grinned. "The joys of being clever, I suppose."

And thus, the maxim we were talking of was proven. Perfection does not make a good story or an interesting speaker.

But an image of pure imperfection...now that is how you captivate an audience. How perversely sad!

"Well," I continued, "I speak as I find. And as I have seen. When I speak, I criticize conceit, but not expertise. We need experts and people of skill. But many an intelligent person of sense who is boasted of seeing everything clearly can't see past their own noses. They are too busy being logical, that they don't wholly achieve logic, or they suffer from the Oedipal impediment: their insufferable pride. That's why I pride myself on not being the sharpest mind in the world—say what you will of me, but I see everything clearly. The first step to wisdom, is to acknowledge that you are, initially, quite stupid."

Arthur and Enara laughed, looking out the window and admiring the scenery unfolding around them.

Georgiana, however, could not let my words lie where they were. On the contrary, she was eager to converse more on the matter.

"Kitty," she said, giving me a 'superior' look.

"I know, I know, I know. You revolt against my maxims."

"Oh, it's not that," she responded. "I know, deep down, that there is some truth to that statement. Those who often preach of superior thoughts, and claim that they know everything, do tend to have inferior minds, due to their hubris. Wisdom comes from humility. But I don't want the world to think you are evil, when I know that you are not. Such talk will lead to them thinking that about you."

Her advice humbled me a little. Perhaps she was trying to help me.

"You think so?" I asked.

"Oh, I know so. You have been around your own family for so long that your free-spirited tones have gone unheeded because it didn't need to be censored. We understand that your wicked tones are spoken by a moral person. But the average looker-on will not determine such. They will not understand that you jest or speak indirect truths. I don't want my aunt to have anything worth despising you for."

I sighed.

"You are asking me to not be myself, aren't you?"

"I hate to do that, but I must. Wicked speeches only work when the person is the kindest and most considerate person underneath. You are. But my aunt and Anne de Bourgh do not know that. I do not want them to say anything unkind to you. Because I know that it will hurt your feelings."

"And that I will make my family look vulgar."

Georgiana was quiet. She didn't need to give any response, and perhaps it was better that way. What I said was true. How painful it is to not be allowed to be oneself at all.

Welcome back to society and all the confinement that came along with it.

"Oh, look!" Georgiana said. "Here we are."

We looked out the window and up ahead, we saw Rosings Park.

It was a lovely house, large, and very well-situated. It was on rising ground, which was all for its favor.

And yet, despite all its grandeur, I found something imposing about the house. Or rather, I found something awkward and unfeeling about it.

How different when I compared it to Pemberley. Pemberley was a place that always seemed to exude hope, beauty, elegance, and grace.

Netherfield Park projected ease and comfort.

This house just felt...imposing. It was as if it clashed against the natural terrain that surrounded it.

Or perhaps I was projecting my own feelings toward the house itself.

I didn't want to like those who inhabited it, therefore, it seemed natural to not like the house at all.

Oh well, at least I knew this about myself, and that surely must count for something.

Also, I think I was angry. And I felt that, since Rosings Park was not Pemberley, it was not where I wished to be. Everything about my present circumstance felt constrictive, and as if I would spend the entire Christmas holiday most uncomfortable.

I wished we had never come.

And, upon greater reflection, I think I understood why I was so provocative and out of sorts.

But I knew not to project it on anyone else but my most intimate of acquaintances.

There was only one solution to my present circumstance: I had to spend much of my time not speaking at all. That was the only way that I could survive this Christmas holiday without polluting the halls of Rosings Park.

We rode up to the house and, the closer that we got, the more we were able to admire the great house of her ladyship.

As the servants exited the house to see to us, Arthur helped Enara, Georgiana and me out of the carriage.

From the other carriage, Mr. Darcy and Mr. Bingley helped Lizzy and Jane down. Since both were now with child and were fully beginning to show, they had to be very meticulous about their movements.

Now that we stood there, in front of the great house, we could marvel at it in full.

Going up to Jane and Elizabeth, I stood in between them as the servants began to transport our luggage into the house.

"Well," I said, "did you see Charlotte and Mr. Collins through the parsonage windows?"

"Yes," Eliza said, "we did. Now I must step lightly. Because, to encounter a little bit of folly this festive time of year is one thing, but to be bombarded with it every day might be too much for me. But I will be happy to see Charlotte again."

"And I confess that I am curious to see the parsonage," Jane said. "Also, with more friends to be met, it shall make our holiday into a truly festive time of the year."

"You would find the joys of this all," I put in.

"Yes, I will. And Kitty and Lizzy, you must promise me that you both will be very agreeable?"

"You shall get no incivility from me," Elizabeth said,

"unless I am met with it first. Then that is not offensive, but defensive. And Kitty?"

"I know," I said, groaning, "I am your chief worry. But I can assure you that I will do everything not to disgrace this family." Out of the side of my eye, I looked at Georgiana. "I have been humbled enough."

Georgiana looked at me, after saying something to Enara. Seeing her look at me with such apprehension, I knew that it would be better to reassure her that I was not offended by her advising me.

And it ought to be done now, before we entered the house and had to meet Lady Catherine.

Walking up to Georgiana, I took her arm.

"Never fear for me, Georgie. I know what I am about. I bear you no ill will for telling me to mind myself. Even though it's hard, I will listen. I know that you are trying to protect me."

"I am," she said, smiling. "I am happy that you see it that way. I just don't want you to suffer under my aunt's ill judgments. That's all."

She gave me a keen look.

"You wish that we never came, don't you?" she questioned. "You wish that we still were at Pemberley."

What a question to ask. I did not wonder of it because of its randomness. But only because it was a very shrewd observation.

"Yes," I answered, "how did you know?"

"Because I know why you are out of sorts and are speaking so wickedly."

I blinked.

"You knew that as well?"

"The answer is simple. I know it...because I know you, Kitty."

I smiled at her sadly, and perhaps my eyes also appeared wistful.

"No," she whispered, "none of that for now. I didn't mean for you to be sad." She tapped my hand, affectionately. "We will talk of this later, after dinner."

"Yes. Thank you. For now, I must appear happy."

"You will. I have faith in you."

"Well," Mr. Darcy said to us all, "let us go in. My aunt would be waiting for us."

"And her ladyship does not like to be kept waiting," Elizabeth said as Mr. Darcy wrapped her arm in his. They each exchanged a look, and their looks spoke volumes.

"No, my aunt does not."

In my mind, Christmas bells were ringing.

Somewhere else.

But not here.

Chapter Two

MOTHER & DAUGHTER

We all proceeded into the house and entered Rosings' atrium. The floor was marble and was very well-polished. The rooms were large and spacious, and I offered all the compliments that seemed proper, but I still felt like I wanted to immediately rush to my guestroom and not have to meet anyone.

Fortunately, I got my wish.

We had been met by Mrs. Preston, who was the housekeeper. She received us very civilly—and very coldly.

The only kind thing she had to say was to Mr. Darcy and Georgiana. But as for the rest of us, she used her words economically. That meant that she spoke only as much as was needed. This stiff manner among the housekeeper gave me no choice but to wonder if it hinted at the tone of the house in a general sense. Fortunately, Lucy, Sarah, and Betsy were with us, and could spare us from the grave aura that the house was exuding.

In fact, their fussiness was heard as they arranged for the servants to carry our luggage to our rooms. Hearing

Betsy and Sarah bicker felt so complete that it wouldn't be Christmas without them.

"Since you all have been traveling since this morning," Mrs. Preston said, "her ladyship has the foresight to assume that you all need to retire to your rooms to change your clothes and refresh yourselves. And since Mrs. Darcy and Mrs. Bingley are with child, both need a little time to rest."

"Tell my aunt that I thank her," Mr. Darcy said, "for it spared me from having to ask her to give our ladies some proper time to themselves."

I sighed, happy to hear this. I just wanted to be alone for a minute. A minute was all that I needed to collect myself. Inwardly, I had to thank Lady Catherine, for she did do right by us, in that regard.

Eagerly, we were shown to our rooms, where mine was next to Enara's and Arthur's.

As my things were brought into my room, I collapsed on the bed as Lucy began to unpack my luggage.

"You look happy to find a bed," Lucy observed as she hung up my gowns.

"And I will be even happier when I get to have a bath drawn." Rolling over, I looked at her. "Do you ever feel like, when you take a bath, you are born again?"

"Oh, yes! I am even stranger than you, pray."

"How so?"

"If I were a woman of leisure, I would bathe twice a day. In the morning and then in the evening. I feel like I would be wholly new if I did. As if I was being reborn every day."

She looked at me.

"You don't want to be here, do you?" she asked.

Raising myself up, I removed my shoes.

"How do you know that? Am I that easy to read?"

"Yes, you are. And it is not necessarily a bad thing, I tell you."

"I just wish that I was around closer family than what is going to happen. To be at Pemberley and invite the Gardiners, or to see the Philips' again... even mother and father. Mary and Mr. Atkins."

"There will be other Christmases."

"Yes, there will be."

Lucy laid out a gown for me.

"But it's more than that, isn't it?"

"Yes, it is."

Rolling my eyes, I realized how stupid I sounded.

"And here I am, complaining about my life to a servant —as if I am the one who is scarcely worse off."

Lucy chuckled.

"Finally, someone realizes that complaining to servants about your privileged problems is not what we revel in."

"I know, I know, I know. I am an ungratefully horrid creature."

"Don't worry. I like that you confide in me, and I can suffer your complaining a right-side better than anyone else."

She sat down on the bed next to me.

"I can't say that you have no reason to worry about this holiday," she coaxed, "because I would be lying. All I can say is this. You are not the one that Lady Catherine is angry with."

"I know. But Elizabeth is my sister. I will not like her being dictated over, criticized, or me being guilty by association."

Lucy tapped my hand.

"This is a miserable business, isn't it?" Lucy asked.

"Yes, it is."

We laughed.

"Thank you for letting me speak of my frustrations, even though my problems must sound so trivial."

"I like you, Miss Bennet. Therefore, your complaints are a pressure that I can bear."

Lucy stood up.

"Now, step lightly. The sooner that you dress, the sooner that you can meet the ogre."

"Lady Catherine is ogre-like?"

"Oh, yes. Didn't you know this?"

"Yes, I knew it!" I felt so triumphant.

Outside, we heard bickering.

Sighing, Lucy went to the door, opened it, and it was Sarah and Betsy arguing with each other.

"Unbelievable!" Lucy hissed. "No matter how the scenery around us changes, you both will never change with it."

"What is the joy in changing?" Betsy asked. "Well, I am right to never change. Sarah, on the other hand, could do with a whole character alteration."

"Thus speaks the woman whose personality is like that of a toad," Sarah groaned.

"Toads don't have personalities."

"Precisely."

I grinned.

Without them making things difficult, Christmas could be done boringly.

After we changed and were rested a little, Mrs. Preston informed us all that Lady Catherine was ready to receive us.

Nay, what joy is mine?

Dressed in my pink gown, I left my room, to find Georgiana waiting for me outside of my room.

"You were worried that I would get lost if I walked downstairs myself, didn't you?" I asked her, graciously.

"Perhaps I might have been."

"Thank you. Now, come. The Philipses will need you to save them as well."

"Will they? Yes, perhaps they might."

We retrieved Arthur and Enara, and together, the rest of our company met us along the landing.

With Mr. Darcy and Elizabeth in front, we all followed them downstairs, and through the halls.

As we walked, I saw more of the house, and each room seemed to mold into the next. It was all rich and expensive furnishings, and slowly I began to understand something.

But it did not do to dwell on just now. When alone with Elizabeth and Mr. Darcy, I would ask them about it later. They had the strength to stomach such talk without being affected.

Mrs. Preston escorted us into an antechamber in the house. Upon entrance, there was much in the room to admire.

Until I saw three figures sitting down, on the other side of the room.

We were ushered forward, and the figures came into full view.

There were three women presented before us.

One was a young woman, who was thin and a little frail in appearance. She was not grotesque at all, but there was nothing remarkable about her look. I was left to presume that this woman was Miss Anne de Bourgh.

To her left, was another woman. She was elderly, dressed simply, had a humble look about her, and she seemed to tend to Miss de Bourgh. Quickly, I knew that this was not her ladyship. It was Mrs. Jenkinson, who tended to the daughter.

Especially since, when looking at the third person, it was undeniable.

There was no mistaking it.

From her tall person, to her stiff and erect posture.

Finally, I was standing in the presence of Lady Catherine de Bourgh.

~

There she was.

At long last, I would re-meet the woman who did everything to sever all ties between Darcy and Elizabeth. I knew not to expect any act of contrition.

When seeing her, I had to remind myself that I heard nothing of Lady Catherine that spoke her awful from any extraordinary talents or miraculous virtue, and the mere stateliness of money or rank, I thought I could witness without trepidation. In the brief time that I saw her at Longbourn, it was not enough to make an impression. At most, I heard that she was a lady who was angry that her plans had been ruined. When facing her, I had to tell myself that she could have gotten over it tolerably well and was looking forward to her family increasing.

But I had been wrong before. She could be horrid. And her appearance did her no favors. When seeing us, she stood and, with great condescension, rose to receive us. By doing so, I could see her height in full. She was actually somewhat tall—a little taller than Lydia. Her hair had tinges of gray that ran through it and was done up in a respectable style that did not suit her face very well.

She had wrinkles on her forehead, but her face still clung to the handsomeness that she must have acquired when she was younger. Moving with the air of a great lady, no movement she made felt like it was anything else other than deliberate. Unlike her daughter, her features were strong and defined, as if nature knew that it gave birth to a woman who would one day inherit a great house and title.

This was a woman who knew what she was about. Even if she didn't know what everyone else truly was.

"Aunt," Mr. Darcy said when he entered. "Dear aunt, it is a delight to see you once more."

Darcy's tone did not strike any sort of eager nephew attitude. He was gentle in how he spoke, but there was no exertion on his part. He did not rush to eagerly embrace his aunt or be congenial. And I understood why. His aunt had offended Elizabeth, greatly, and took way too long to embrace her. This led to Mr. Darcy looking on his aunt with a cold civility and thus placing the decision to be obliging entirely on her side. Lady Catherine would have to set the tone of how this interaction would go.

Would it lead to the family getting along charmingly, or for Mr. Darcy to order us to leave as soon as we came, was entirely dependent on how Lady Catherine received us.

"Darcy," Lady Catherine declared, "nephew, I am glad to see that you arrived at a very good time. Everything that is punctual. After all, you know that I despise when someone writes that they shall arrive at a certain time, and they do not do so."

"We are happy to oblige you, aunt," Mr. Darcy said, "but when so much of one's travels depends on uncertain circumstances, such as a broken wheel, animals along the road, or a carriage accident, sometimes lateness is not the fault of the traveler."

"All of those things can still be laid at the feet of the traveler," Lady Catherine overrode him, "for the first, one should check the stability of a wheel before one departs. For the second, animals can be removed from the road if one demands the herder to be quicker at removing them. And thirdly, a carriage accident can occur out of negligence. I am right, to be sure."

Mr. Darcy said nothing to this and instead thought it best just to introduce us.

"Aunt, allow me the honor of finally introducing an old acquaintance of yours as my new bride. You remember Miss Elizabeth, and now she is Mrs. Darcy."

Elizabeth stepped forward and curtsied.

"Lady Catherine," Elizabeth said, "I trust you are in good health at this festive time of year."

"Yes, I am, thank you. For my health is never indifferent, but always robust."

"I suspected as much, your ladyship. I am glad that you are well."

Lady Catherine looked at Elizabeth's belly.

"You have been fruitful in your married state. I suppose I might boast of being a great-aunt very soon."

"We sincerely hope so, your ladyship."

"And speaking of another lady who is blessed in our family," Mr. Darcy said, "this is Mrs. Jane Bingley, my wife's eldest sister." Then he gestured to me. "Miss Kitty Bennet, the fourth of the Bennet sisters, and Mr. and Mrs. Philips, their cousins."

Lady Catherine analyzed everyone else with intense scrutiny, except myself. Rather, her eyes studied me very briefly, and then it seemed as if she dismissed me quickly before she turned to Arthur and Enara.

"Cousins?" she asked them.

"I am the son of Mr. and Mrs. Philips," Arthur explained. "My mother is Mrs. Bennet's sister. My wife has become a cousin through marriage."

"Oh," Lady Catherine said, turning to Enara, "well, you have?"

"Indeed, yes, your ladyship," Enara replied.

"Who are your family, child?"

"The Rileys of New South Wales."

When hearing this, Lady Catherine leaned forward, interested.

"Australia?"

"Yes, indeed, your ladyship. My family are the Rileys from Sydney."

Lady Catherine raised an eyebrow.

"Sydney?"

"Yes, your ladyship."

"Sydney is the capital of New South Wales," Arthur said, sensing a little offense that might occur. "And is overseen by the same governor who resides over Brisbane."

"Who would that be, pray tell? Is the man of any note?"

Enara opened her mouth to answer it, but Lady Catherine cut her off, answering it herself. Enara didn't think to say anything to confirm this, because she suspected that the great lady didn't want her to speak at the moment.

"Well," Lady Catherine continued, "you seem to be a prettyish sort of woman. Mr. Philips, you are to be commended."

"I thank you, your ladyship," Arthur responded, "but I cannot take credit for my wife's beauty. Rather, I think the sole credit must be given to Mrs. Philips's mother, who she looks a great deal like."

"Oh, your mother is handsome?" Lady Catherine asked Enara.

"Yes," Enara answered, "I may speak from daughter-like praise, but I believe my mother is one of the handsomest women in Australia."

"There is no wrong with taking pride in one's mother." She approved of Enara. That much was certain. "Yes, you shall do very nicely here."

Next, Lady Catherine turned to Georgiana.

"My dear Georgiana, it is a delight in seeing you."

"It is a joy to see you again, Aunt Catherine," she said, kissing Lady Catherine's cheek. "It has been too long since we have seen each other."

"Indeed, it has. It was merely due to circumstances arising that were not as I predicted. Yet, your presence here is most appreciated, for at this time of year, your superior playing is welcome. I daresay there is no one in this company who is your equal."

"Oh, I cannot boast of such praise. My sister, Mrs. Elizabeth Darcy, plays and sings very well."

"You flatter me, Georgiana," Elizabeth responded, "though, I acknowledge that I will never be your equal."

"I heard Mrs. Darcy play when she visited Rosings Park," Lady Catherine said, "and I pray that you subscribed to my recommendations, Mrs. Darcy. Do you not recall that I declared that you would never play very well unless you were to practice more?"

"Yes, I do recall, your ladyship."

"And have you listened?"

"Whether she has done so or not," Mr. Darcy administered, "does not diminish that I take great pleasure in listening to her whenever she sits down to the instrument."

"Thank you, Mr. Darcy," Elizabeth responded. "You are the most unprejudiced listener that I have ever encountered. Yet, I confess that I have been quite neglectful of my studies," and here, she pressed her stomach, "for now, I have more cares to consider."

"Yes, indeed you do," Lady Catherine said, "of which, I am glad that you have taken your holiday here. The greatest care must be taken to secure the health of the future Mr. or Miss Darcy that you shall bear. As well as Mrs. Bingley."

"I have heard that you have many proscriptions on how to successfully tend to infants and raise a child."

"I do, indeed," she said, turning to her daughter. Anne de Bourgh sat there, next to Mrs. Jenkinson, and her face was so very blank, her color was sallow, and her mannerism always appeared to be in a perpetual state of shrinking. The poor creature was sickly, and that must have made her into such a miserable sort of person. "As you all can see, my daughter has a natural grace and elegance, which is worthy of her rank."

My eyes widened at this comment. How easily parents blind ourselves to the truth about our children. Then again, our mother and father were also proof of that. Anne de Bourgh and I had not said one word to each other, and I was quite convinced that she was not born easily and given the best chances of nature. As a result, her beauty was diminished and almost destroyed by her delicate health. If she was 'the very model of aristocratic perfection' then we were all doomed.

"Do sit down," Lady Catherine announced to all of us at last. Finally, we were seated, as she arranged for tea to be brought—and we would see what we would see.

~

The first thing to do was to thank Lady Catherine for inviting us.

This was done, without any help on my part. But, I declare that it was not done out of any desire to be disagreeable, but because there seemed to be no opening for me to speak. The great lady felt her position in life most keenly and would often speak more like that of sermons than conversation. She spoke but seldom required responses to things.

The second thing to do was compliment her on the beauties of her home.

This job was done by the Bingleys. Mr. Bingley would never lose his ability to please and be pleased by everything. Jane echoed his sentiments in a quieter way, but that was to her ladyship's pleasure.

"Mr. Bingley," Lady Catherine said, "I also must compliment you on your choice of wife, for she has a natural grace and proper female elegance to her nature."

Mr. Bingley nodded.

"I thank you, your ladyship," Jane responded.

"You, on the whole, are quite different than your sisters."

"Indeed, I am, and for their part, I find that to be a benefit for all five of us."

"A benefit?"

"Yes. It is a matter of individuality."

"Individuality? What does that have to do with attributes?"

"Oh, my sister is wise, for she is correct," I voiced. My sudden interruption lent Lady Catherine to raise her eyebrows and look at me.

Her gaze was not only direct and was filled with scrutiny, but, unless I was mistaken, it was filled with a subtle wrath. One is told to never base anything by first impressions, but I could not help it. Lady Catherine didn't like me. And she had resolved herself to not do so.

"Are you about to speak your opinion very decidedly?" she asked me.

I looked between my family, and they all were a little unnerved, except Elizabeth. She did not look surprised but gave all the implication that she had sensed that something like this would happen.

I cannot say that I was not a little unnerved by Lady Catherine's eye on me. As much as I wished that I could be brave all the time, there were some things that still scared me. Lady Catherine was one of those things that did alarm me a little. And that's what made the situation all the worse.

"Well, I do not see," I said slowly, trying to gather what little courage that I had, "how one can give their opinion without having a sense of decidedness about it."

"Pray, what is your age?"

"I am eighteen years old, your ladyship."

"At such an age, how can one determine what is the proper way of being?"

"Right and wrong do not always discriminate on a determined age," Elizabeth added. "Age does present wisdom, of course, but sometimes, even youth can present a fresh and proper viewpoint."

"Oh, I am not surprised that you think so, Mrs. Darcy," Lady Catherine said. "I am familiar with your tendencies toward independent thought. That does not come upon me as a surprise in any way." Then she looked at me again, and her glare intensified. "But, of your younger sister here, I did not expect for such decision on one's views. But since she is determined to speak, let us see what she meant all the while."

As I sat there, I felt Georgiana take my hand, which was placed on my lap. That simple touch was enough to help fortify me. I figured that I was already not favored. As such, 'in for a penny, in for a pound'.

"I merely wished to clarify," I said, "that Jane does have a valid point when it comes to the dangers of character conformity."

"Conformity? You mistake the pleasures, and correctness, I daresay, of there being a '*right*' way to behave and a '*wrong*' way. That is the proper proscription for a most moral lady and proper character."

Inwardly, I wanted to scream out. For whom was she to

adhere to a maxim placed upon us ladies about a singular way of being when she did not submit to that herself? Whatever she declared as what was the proper conduct of a 'lady', was not how she behaved. On the contrary, it could be set down that she was the opposite of all that, especially since her manners were very direct, sometimes impertinent, and a little insolent. For a second, I wished that our Uncle Philips were there to give her a piece of his mind.

"When it comes to morality," I added, "of course, there is a right way and wrong way to treat others, and to treat oneself. But it is characteristics, tone, beliefs, perspectives, and attitude that we refer to. When Jane said that it was to our benefit that we were not all like her, she was both being kind as well as logical. If every woman in the world were to adhere to one way of being, of one form of conduct, then life would be decidedly dull, wouldn't it? Is not individuality the very joys of life? If my sisters and I were to be similar, and less like ourselves, I do not think it would be to our benefit, but to our discredit. For none of us would have the courage to be our own person. The idea...would frighten me."

When I finished, Lady Catherine leaned back.

"You are very young in the ways of the world," was all that she said, before she turned and began to speak with Elizabeth and Jane, administering all her advice on how to rest, eat and behave in a way that would suit the child's health better.

For the rest of our first day there, Lady Catherine did not speak to me again. I confess that I did not regret this, because I knew that there was nothing for it now.

Lady Catherine, perhaps, probably regarded me as the least worthy person in the company, and marveled at my very presence there.

I was upset with myself, but not because I lost her good

opinion. It's hard to regret losing something when you never had it to begin with. No, it was for another reason entirely.

At some point, her attention was diverted back to Georgiana, and her skill in music.

Lady Catherine expressed a desire to hear her play. When this occurred and some music sheets were brought forth, it gave me the chance to accidentally draw near Miss de Bourgh.

Out of the side of my eye, I took notice of her blonde hair being done up well, but the hair that came down was not done in a style that flattered her features. Actually, the golden aspect of her curls only made her skin look even more unhealthy, because her skin clashed against them. She was around my height, but since her shoulders were a little hunched over, it gave off the impression that she was shorter.

"Are you looking forward to the Christmas festivities, Miss de Bourgh?" I asked her.

"Yes," she answered, simply and quietly.

"I do not deny that I always find great pleasure on being able to open presents when the day actually arrived."

"I get similar things each year," she said. "Nothing different."

"Oh, nothing?"

"No, nothing different. But I suppose that we must honor the birthday of our savior and lord."

"Oh, then you grow excited over the service that shall be performed at church?"

"We are expected to."

"Expected to, well, yes. But do you prefer it?"

She looked at me, confused.

"We are expected to like it, so we do. Of course."

"Yes," I said, sighing inwardly, "yes, we are expected to."

That was the last thing that she said to me because I had quite given up trying to converse with her.

When someone does not help me on when I attempt to converse with them, I cease to try. After all, if they do not think me worth the effort, then I shall reciprocate their feelings.

As Georgiana played masterfully, I could not help but observe where I could. I watched Anne de Bourgh most acutely, and then I also watched Mr. Darcy. In all that time, neither of them really looked on each other. Not once.

Now, I knew. Lady Catherine would have had it that her daughter and nephew were intended to marry.

But reality would have it to be the reverse because it was. Both Darcy and Anne did not seem to care about the other's existence. And it had nothing to do with them ignoring each other because their love was burned. But rather, it was because both easily were never in love with the other. They were two people who didn't know how to talk. When it comes to those sorts, the spouses they seek need to have a comfortably voluble nature.

Mr. Darcy found Lizzy.

Anne needed to find someone similar. If she would ever speak up and find someone at all.

But what was certain was that, perhaps, Anne de Bourgh did not care for me either. However, unlike her mother, it was not hatred. It was more like indifference.

Was it better than hatred, or worse?

A person who was better than I, would have to decide for themselves.

After Georgiana performed perfectly, we all clapped, and soon it was time for us to go into dinner.

Afterwards, we sat around for a game of cards being made, and then eventually supper was called upon. As we stood up for the final meal, I was near Anne de Bourgh as she rose. Her foot got caught in the hem of her gown. She stumbled, and Mrs. Jenkinson held her arms to stabilize her.

Thank goodness she did not fall. Not for the humiliation of it—for most of us, a fall usually leads to nothing but a tumble. For Miss de Bourgh, I worried that she might hurt herself.

Why was I worried? I could not fathom why.

Chapter Three

REGRESSION

At long last, I was able to enjoy the comforts of being alone. How interesting it was to consider the woman that I was from almost two years ago. Before then, I preferred not to be alone, to the point where I almost never forgave Mary for neglecting me. And now, I sought it. Is this what it meant to grow older? If so, I do not know if I preferred it or if I didn't.

But one thing that remained constant, a consistent companion of mine, was my journal.

Since I had filled up my previous diary, I had purchased a new one at Lambton before we came here.

Opening a fresh diary for the first time, to see that empty page, is like entering a fresh new world, where you feel as if you have begun something beautiful.

Writing the date at the top, I began to write down the events of the day. Finally, I could unleash my feelings on an unsuspecting page, which had no idea that its owner was a temperamental and inferior sort of creature.

I was upset, and I could not control it. When I reached

the point in my entry that focused on when Lady Catherine addressed me, I could now sort out why I was so upset with myself at the time...

I thought that I had grown so very much and discovered my own sort of courage. So much so, that I felt as if no one could overwhelm me or unsettle me. And yet, there I was, inwardly shaking like a leaf before the great LADY CATHERINE herself. She is important in the world, and she knows it.

Easily could I see that she would have driven all that way to order my sister to not marry Mr. Darcy. Everything about her behavior gives off the indication of a woman who controls so much of her own life, that she must govern everyone else.

And I was scared of her? Yes, sadly, I was. I was very intimidated by her presence, to the point where I almost halted from giving my opinions. What has happened to me?

All that I learned when living at Pemberley, all that I overcame when I left Longbourn, and I found myself to still be that same young and impressionable girl that I once was.

What a blow to one's pride. I'll speak of this to Georgiana, and maybe to Enara, but it would be foolish to talk about this to Elizabeth and Jane. For both have their own problems, at the moment, for they are beginning to suffer more from morning sickness and the setbacks that occur when a woman is with child. And as for Elizabeth, she has to face the subtle rude remarks that her ladyship does her best to conceal, but the contempt is still present. No matter how hidden it appears to be.

Poor Lizzy. But then again, who am I to say so? After all, I think that now I might be the one that Lady Catherine likes the least. I wonder why.

Tomorrow, I will write a letter to my uncle and aunt Philips, as well as to my parents, to tell them of the events that occur here. But I will write a special letter to the Philipses only, because they might help give me the best advice on how I am feeling. They understand me best and saw me as I grew.

It's a blow to one's life that one cannot go to one's parents for such advice, but despite it all, my father and mother never fully saw me correctly. As such, neither of them would give me the best advice that one is needed in this case.

Father would make some caustic remark.

And Mama might still just recommend that I focus on getting married off as soon as possible. Perhaps I am being unkind, for she has made great progress since the time I unleashed my anger at them both. However, it is her nature to still think the cure to anything in my life is to marry me off.

As well as something more.

I don't think I can listen to any advice that they might give... because I do not want to, I suppose. I would feel oppressed under anything that they would advise. It sounds perverse, I know. And yet, it is the truth.

Aunt and Uncle Philips would understand. The sooner that I can receive their reply, the better.

I jumped when there was a knock on my door. Instinctively, I wrapped my shawl over my nightgown and used my powers of deduction.

"Georgiana?"

"Who do you think?" Georgiana called from the other side of the door.

I smiled and told her to come in.

When she entered, her hair was done up in curling paper.

"I had a feeling that you would still be awake at this time," she noted, "and when I saw the light under the door, my assumptions came true."

"And mine were incorrect. I thought you would be in

bed. You seemed so tired after supper, that I thought you wouldn't want me to visit you."

I closed my journal, tucked it away, and sat on the bed, opposite Georgiana.

"I knew that you needed to talk," Georgiana said.

"You are about to tell me that I behaved badly."

"No, I'm not."

My eyes widened in surprise.

"You are not?"

"No, I won't."

I sighed, relieved.

"I don't know why, but I cannot help but sound paranoid now and profess that, when I walked into the room, I felt like Lady Catherine despised the very sight of me. And that's where it all began when it came to me being out of sorts."

"You are not paranoid. She does not like you."

When saying it, she realized that it might have hurt my feelings to hear it put so simply.

"Never fear," I said dismissively, swiping the air with my hand, "I am not afraid of the truth on two counts. First, I am happy to know that I was not overreacting. I thought that maybe it was her general way to be like that. And second, my self-worth is not tied to gaining Lady Catherine's opinions."

"Yes," Georgiana chuckled, "I saw that."

"But you saw that she does not like me either."

"Yes, I did. And I don't understand it. I knew, when coming, that there might be a strained sort of civility toward Elizabeth. What I did not know was that it would extend towards yourself."

"You think that's all it is? That I am responsible because I am Elizabeth's sister—and I'm also Lydia's sister."

"Oh, yes! That's right. Lady Catherine is aware that you are close in age to Mrs. Wickham. But still, I do not think that is the problem either."

"You don't?" I was eager to hear anything that Georgiana had to say. After all, she knew her aunt better than I did. "Then what else could there be?"

"I don't know, but there's something else. There has to be another reason for why she has taken a decided dislike toward you."

"I wish I knew what it was."

"So do I. Depend upon it. We shall discover it soon enough. My aunt cannot hold someone in contempt and conceal the reason for too long. She wants her opinion to be known and will unveil it eventually."

"What are the chances that she will do it sooner than later? That is the question. To be critical, or not to be critical...yes, the question indeed."

"Words, words, words."

"And perhaps not a reasonable one in between them."

The clock reached the top of the hour, and Georgiana and I had exhausted every avenue of what was in Lady Catherine's mind. When we had reached every theory we had, I thought I would have made Georgiana tired, but she had something else to say.

"Well," I furthered, "I shall need your stability throughout this visit. I feel like I might fall to the wayside of decorum."

"It shall not be too difficult, for my part," she responded, "because I know the source of it. You are still angry, aren't you?"

I looked at her, perplexed.

"How did you know?"

"And you don't know where it's coming from, do you? You just feel restless and resentful."

"Yes, I do. I feel perverse. But it's like I cannot stop myself. It just seems like I am on a runaway cart and cannot get off."

"It's the chaos that occurs the day after. Or the week or month after."

"The week or month after what?"

"After taking leave of someone you love."

Closing my eyes, I rubbed my face.

"Colonel Fitzwilliam and Lieutenant Finlay."

"Yes. You are parted from them both, after having not been parted from them for so long. Much of your happiness has been dependent on their presence in your life. And now, you are separate from them. And you feel the void that's in your heart."

I stood and walked over to the wall, leaned against it, melted to the floor, pressed my knees against my chest and held them there. This sudden action didn't surprise Georgiana. I daresay that nothing I did ever surprised her anymore. She must have grown so accustomed to my nature that she was used to my impulsive manner.

"This is humiliating."

"What is?"

"That, when all things are considered, perhaps you are right. They are gone from my life, and I am not accustomed to that, for their presence became a constant for long enough. Their lives were tied to mine."

"Then why are you humiliated?"

"Because it is pathetic. Do you know why I was optimistic about coming here, despite that I knew I was walking into the unknown? I did it to give Finlay time away from me. With Colonel Fitzwilliam, he was already set to leave, so I didn't have to worry about him. This would give them the ability to move on, because the fact is, that they need to. What I didn't see was the workings of my own heart. I was so determined that they move on from me, that I didn't see that I am unable to move on from them. Georgie, when did this happen?"

"When did what happened?"

"You know what. Even when I was in love, my spirit and happiness was my own, and not dependent on either of them. If they were there, I was happy. If they were not there, I was still happy. Now my happiness is tied to them both. And I feel that there is something shallow about it all."

"You feel that you are not correct because your happiness is dependent on a man that you care for."

"Yes. I don't know why. But, with this mentality, I don't feel whole."

Georgiana stood up, walked over to me, sat down next to me, and tapped my hand.

"Kitty, I am saying this out of pure affection."

"Yes."

"Shut up."

⌇

When Georgiana offered that instruction, I didn't know how to react. First, I was shocked. Then I was amused. Then I was offended. And then I understood why she said that.

"Everyone falls away from humanity sometimes," Georgiana said, "and that is fine. It's even good to establish yourself, independently, all over again. But there is nothing wrong with coming back to humanity. It's inevitable. Passion is not an evil word."

"That's the odd thing. I knew that once. Then I forgot it. I feel as if I am regressing. Why is that?"

"I don't know. But whatever you are feeling, you simply

34

have to let the feeling continue until it ends. Then you will receive clarity again."

"Ah, the 'sense of clarity'."

"Let me tell you the sad fact about life," Georgiana continued. "Sometimes, this is a phase that you have no choice but to experience. You are not deficient for feeling such an intense bond with the other sex, nor are you small-minded for it. The fact is that we are built this way. Women are drawn to men. Just like they are drawn to us. There is no weakness about this. Hard as the world tries to make it seem like otherwise, there is something to be said for deep affection between both men and women. Even from a friendship standpoint, each sex offers a perspective that the other one does not have. And never can."

"So, the problem is not what I am feeling, but that I simply need to govern it."

"Precisely. There is no real evil to sensibility, as long as sense governs it afterwards. But the truth is that you are suffering under the after-effects of being separated from a great passion. Your soul will need time to find its way back to a proper balance again. And it doesn't help that this is not the best place to do it in. Or maybe it is, for one reason."

"What reason would that be?"

"One thing can be said for my Aunt Catherine; she is very good at being diverting."

"Yes, she is, isn't she? She will distract me a lot. And maybe I need distraction, for better or for worse."

"Feel better?"

"Yes, I do. Thank you!"

~

When it grew very late, Georgiana bid me goodnight. As she went to the door, I called out to her.

"What?" she said, turning around.

This discussion had led me to being more introspective than usual. It gave me the time to ask the question that perhaps I should have asked before.

"Why are you friends with me? After all, what am I but a rising and shrinking sort of banshee, who is being torn between logic and irrationality half the time?"

"You forget, don't you?" She pointed to herself. "The one who was willing to elope with Mr. Wickham and still has not fully recovered from that. Also, the one who almost married Mr. Atwell."

"Oh," I groaned, rolling my eyes, "that dandy!"

"Yes, that dandy!"

"He was entirely too pretty."

"I know. What was I thinking?"

"You were in love. That was excuse enough."

"See? And when I did that, I experienced the chaotic whirlwind that was love, the intense ties that you feel toward that person, and the agony of when you are separated from them. Weeks after Wickham showed his true nature, I still longed for him. I thought of him every moment and felt the loss of his company. I regressed. Then I woke up, and one day it hurt less, and less and less. Therefore, this is just another bridge you must cross."

"I am about to confess to something terrible."

"What?"

"A part of me is happy that those marriages didn't work out. I need you to be as human as me in some way."

"Never fear. I understand why. Misery does love company, no matter how logical we try to be."

"Forgive me for that?"

"Yes, I do."

"Thank you. Sleep well, Georgie."

"And you do the same. Tomorrow is another day."

She closed the door behind her.

That night, I went to bed, feeling lighter. When one's mind is a little perverse in nature, nothing helps it better than having a friend who understands.

Chapter Four

THE COLLINS' CAME BACK INTO OUR LIVES

The next day, brought us a fresh encounter on our hands.

The Collins' were coming to dine with us at Rosings Park, and then there would be a little display of musical talents afterwards, followed by discussion.

"I suspected that you would wish to see your friend and cousin," Lady Catherine said to us, as we sat down to breakfast. "But, due to your condition," Lady Catherine said to Jane and Elizabeth, "I deemed it unwise for you to be traveling more than one is required."

"Thank you, your ladyship," Elizabeth said, "for, I acknowledge, that I was curious as to visit them at Hunsford Parsonage."

"I pride myself on sometimes foreseeing what one thinks. I am often praised for my powers of deduction."

"Indeed, madam."

"Yes."

Food was placed on Elizabeth's plate.

"Now," Lady Catherine declared, "I suggest that you have two helpings for breakfast. You are eating for two now, and the infant needs as much nourishment as possible. But you must still be wary of your figure. In my time, our corsets were exquisite at helping us return to our traditional body size, for a pregnancy does greatly alter a woman's figure. But now, with your present attire, as well as the cut of your stays, your clothing does not always assist you all in the manner that it did in our era."

"I confess to liking our manner of dress," I announced, "it offers us a freedom, a physical liberty of such."

Lady Catherine gave me a quick look, looked away from me and continued speaking as if I had said nothing.

"When you do eat," Lady Catherine said, "eggs, ham and toast are the best for a breakfast meal. During supper, it is best to order a leg of lamb or healthy side of beef, along with a salad, and potatoes. However, for supper, bread and cheese are the best options."

She then went forth to explain all the things that it would be best for the soon-to-be mothers to drink.

Eventually, it came time for the Collinses to arrive at Rosings Park, and we awaited them very eagerly.

When the hour was close, I stood by the window, next to Elizabeth.

"Mr. Collins is going to walk from their parsonage, along with Charlotte," Elizabeth explained. "They will come from this direction."

"What is this like for you?" I asked her.

"I am certain that I do not know what you mean."

"No need to play coy with me. We are about to meet Mr. Collins again, and Charlotte, after so long. What is that like for you?" I asked. "Or will you conceal that from me as well?"

Elizabeth rolled her eyes.

"Are you trying to persuade me to tell you my thoughts, out of guilt."

"Oh, you know me so well. By the by, is it working?"

"No. But since I am not ashamed, I shall tell you anyway."

"Thank you for stooping to care about what I think."

"What else am I to do? Things always go awry when I leave you in the dark. Therefore, I will always be happy to see Charlotte. But the fact is that we can never be the same that we once were to each other. Marriage changes friendships. Especially a marriage that causes distance between two people, and where the husband proposed to both friends."

"Yes, in that regard, there was no chance of you and Charlotte maintaining the same bond that you always had."

"There was a time where I did not know if I ever fully knew her."

"Was it after Mr. Collins proposed to her and she accepted?"

"Yes. I felt like the more I saw of the world, the more I was dissatisfied with it. And with her. Then I realized something."

"What?"

"That Charlotte never deceived me. She did precisely as she always said that she would do, all along. I deceived myself about her nature. That should have been the warning sign that I did not always see matters clearly. But instead, it took a little more time."

"It always does. It was the same with Lydia. She was what she was. It took me a little time to see it."

"Do you ever miss her?"

"I do, in the sense that she is our sister, and I still do have fond memories of her. But since I have Georgie, the sting never lasts more than a few minutes. Besides, as with you and Charlotte, when one's eyes are opened, they are opened. Lydia and I can never go back to being the way that we once were. Try as one might, we cannot go back."

"That's true." Elizabeth looked at me. "Kitty, do me a favor."

"What?"

"No matter what Lady Catherine says to you, try to maintain your composure. She is not worth you becoming upset."

"I am trying."

"I know. Just uphold your self-importance, and her words will not affect you. And please do this for me. I need to establish a peace between Pemberley and Rosings Park." Here, she pressed her hand on her belly. "When you have a child, your perspective changes. You begin to want domestic tranquility all around, and to have no rifts in the family. You want the child to grow up in a household where all love him or her. I want this for my child, Kitty. Please, try to remember your self-assurance, and that you do not need to mind what Lady Catherine says."

"I will try, Lizzy, but I just—I am at a strange point in my life."

"And what point is that?"

"I am angry. I know why I am angry, and that counts for something. But I am not fully balanced. I'll try to hold my tongue. Hopefully that will help."

"You will. I have faith in you."

When hearing her say this, I felt elated.

"You do?"

"Yes."

"Well, it's about time."

"Kitty..." she groaned.

"Sorry. Thank you."

"You're welcome."

We parted with me being happy that I was able to

speak to her about what had been on my mind, for quite some time.

~

At last, the Collins' arrived, and we all gathered to meet them. When they entered, Mr. Collins was both grave but also overflowing with obsequious energy.

And then there was Charlotte. Her attitude was calm, confident, and she was as she always was. Her dress was fancy but still clung to the simplicity that Charlotte possessed.

After taking her face and gown into consideration, only then did I notice her belly.

Charlotte was also with child!

Despite her calm manner, friendship will always be friendship. When seeing us all again, especially Elizabeth, Charlotte's face lit up and she glowed a little.

"Elizabeth!" she professed.

"Charlotte!"

Both women reached out to each other, and they embraced. Their joy of seeing each other again was very refreshing, and I wondered if Lydia and I would ever embrace like that if we were to meet again.

Then again, I knew the truth. We would not. For I could never feel for her the way that I used to.

My eyes shifted over to Mr. Collins, who looked a little ashamed by his wife's behavior, and he shifted his gaze to Lady Catherine. In his eyes was an apology.

That was all the indication that I needed. Mr. Collins had not changed at all.

When they released each other, Elizabeth looked at Charlotte's belly.

"You kept secrets from me," Elizabeth said.

"Not a secret. But a surprise."

Elizabeth turned to Mr. Collins.

"Good day, Mr. Collins."

"Good day, Mrs. Darcy. I never had the good fortune to congratulate you on your happy union, and I am proud to call you cousin."

"Thank you, sir."

"As you can imagine, when I first heard of your good fortune, naturally, I approved of the match."

Liar! What a liar. He did not approve of it. Rather, he wrote to father, advising Elizabeth not to engage herself to Mr. Darcy. How quickly the world takes to ignoring its past mistakes.

For a second, I assumed that Elizabeth would let him indulge this nontruth, but she made me proud.

"I recall matters a little differently, sir," Elizabeth said. When she said this, Mr. Collins looked a little uncertain. "In fact, I believe that you once wrote a letter, stating the reverse of what you declare now. But no matter. In the future, I hope that we shall always be of one mind."

"Yes, I believe so, Mrs. Darcy," Mr. Collins declared. "I believe so."

At last, he turned to Lady Catherine.

"Lady Catherine, I humbly apologize for my wife's and cousin's incorrect appealing to each other before greeting you. But it felt proper to let them give way to their sensibilities. But now, we shall give you all the credit that is due. Won't we, my dear Mrs. Collins?"

"Yes," Charlotte agreed, diplomatically, "as you know, your ladyship, we always are honored whenever you condescend to invite us to your dinner parties. We thank you for our share of the favor."

"Mr. and Mrs. Collins," Lady Catherine said, "I understand that you are well-acquainted with most of the members of our company, excepting the Philips'."

She introduced Arthur and Enara.

"The Philips'?" Mr. Collins said. "You are Mr. and Mrs. Philips's son and daughter-in-law."

"We are, indeed, Mr. Collins."

"Might I compliment you on your excellent parents," Mr. Collins said, "your aunt was so gracious that she was willing to invite me most readily to all her dinner engagements when I was in Hertfordshire. And I do hope that you have followed your father's line of work: being an attorney is a modest, but respectable calling."

"I found that the halls of justice did not appeal to me," Arthur responded. "And since my father has forgiven me for my spirited nature, I have discovered that there is no need to excuse my wandering ways. I was a sailor, a midshipman for his majesty's navy, for the longest time."

"While we celebrate your contribution to keeping our shores safe, of course," Lady Catherine said, "I confess that I do protest at the effects that the sea has on a man's features. It can ruin a man's complexion and shorten his youth. And, between the harsh conditions, and the baseness of the way that sailors live and speak, it can easily lead to disorderly conduct and drunkenness through bad influence."

"The naval profession is not something you prefer, your ladyship?" Enara asked.

"No, it is not. But since it is necessary for protecting our freedom and prosperity, then I choose to excuse and overlook the negative attributes for the common man. And that, I declare, is a great deal of flattery and good sense coming from me."

"Yes, it is, your ladyship," Mr. Collins said, "such good

sense and perfect logic. Very few can seldom boast of being filled with the keenest intellect."

Lady Catherine smiled at his praises. Secretly, I felt disgusted. Such flattery was so intensely bestowed that I was certain it could not be felt so keenly by the recipient. It's always nice to receive compliments and be puffed up by pretty words, but the flattery has to be delivered in a way that does not bend itself to overreaction. And the compliment has to be earned. Nothing Lady Catherine said was worth any praise. It was only worth her pride.

But I kept my mouth shut. I did it for Elizabeth and Mr. Darcy. They so much wanted this visit to go well, and now I had the bitter lesson to learn: sometimes, the best thing you can do is not speak your mind at every turn. Sometimes freedom of speech means remaining quiet. However little you don't wish to adhere to it.

No lesson is always easy to learn. And I was in agony now. This would easily be one of the most difficult Christmases that I would ever have.

Sitting there, listening to Lady Catherine speak, while the rest of us barely did, reminded me of a tradition that would be lost to me, and remain at Longbourn. No more would we be allowed to run to each other's room and sing a Christmas carol through the halls. No more would we dance.

The halls of Rosings Park were too solemn, too lifeless, too strict, and stiff to allow such a liberty. I was too afraid of the great lady to ask.

In that moment, I felt the pain of a tradition dying.

Even worse, Lady Catherine and I shared the same first name. It is a little mortifying to share such an intimate thing, such as a label, to a person that you know that you are averse to. It creates a link that both parties do not prefer to be there.

~

As we sat down to dinner, Lady Catherine continued to speak a great deal. If she had not set the tone for our mutual discord with each other, I might have found her amusing.

She was filled with such an inflamed self-importance that I could write about her, in my journal, for days, and no page would do her justice.

This also led to a strange irony about her. While there was much to object to and lament over, she was like many antagonists to one's life. She was striking to be near, and it was hard to look away from her.

Even when she said such absurd things like...

"Never accept anything from the butcher but young flesh, and the fat white," she had been instructing Mr. and Mrs. Collins about, when it came to ordering from the butcher. The subject had not been introduced by the reverend or Charlotte, but for some reason, Lady Catherine brought it up entirely on her own. And her comment didn't end there but continued to speak about the preferences on how to order meat and not be cheated, "If yellow, the beast has been fed on corn cake. Do not leave the servants to deal with the butcher. They are a cunning race."

"Mrs. Collins and I do promise," Mr. Collins assured his patroness, "that we shall always adhere to such advice, so readily given with superior intellect."

"Indeed, madam," Charlotte said, "my mother also offered me such advice when I tended to the kitchens. Therefore, I will always preserve such maxims."

"Well, what your mother did forget is something that I also must stress. When you are dining with just the two of you, sometimes, you have been known to order a whole leg of lamb for one day. That will not do. You and your servants do not require so much for one day, especially at such a time when you will often be dining here at Rosings Park."

"Thank you, your ladyship."

Charlotte's reaction was calm, cool, and collected, but Mr. Collins almost choked when hearing about the superfluity of the invitations.

"To be invited to Rosings so very often for the Christmas season!" Mr. Collins cried. "What a joy, what a delight. This is such a great compliment to us. Isn't it, my dear Charlotte?"

"Yes, it is. We thank you, your ladyship. This is a much looked-for event." She looked at us. Elizabeth, in particular. "When there are such friends to see again, it cannot help but lift the spirits."

"It is strange, to be so far removed from each other's society," Elizabeth inferred.

"Yes, it is. To go from being neighbors to being so wholly separated by counties. That is the one great alarm about marriage."

"It does have a tendency to alter a social circle. Mind you, it is a welcome interruption, but what is fact, is fact."

"And fact must bow down, whether it be good or ugly."

"When I married Sir Lewis de Bourgh," Lady Catherine said, "there seemed to be not enough time in the day. But I did not regret the change, for it gave me a chief delight in my daughter." She looked at Anne. Anne smiled weakly but did not exert herself any further than that. "Mrs. Darcy, Mrs. Bingley, and Mrs. Collins, when you have your children, you will not consider any of the loss from your social circle as being wanting. Your children will be treasures enough."

"We believe so, your ladyship," Jane answered.

"It is merely that we comment on the distance that married life does present," Elizabeth said, "no more and no less. There is something to be said for when you have the good fortune to marry so near one's family. And then there is the negative aspects of marrying *too* near one's family."

"It all depends upon if one likes one's family," Charlotte said.

"And not all can say that they do."

Charlotte and Elizabeth laughed, and we all did so, even Anne de Bourgh.

"You both are engaged in merry battle of wits," Lady Catherine said, "I must advise against that. Wit never becomes a wife."

"But why not?" I asked. This led to Lady Catherine looking at me sharply. Once more, I grew afraid of her. Swallowing, I braced myself and thought that the only thing that I could do was continue. "After all, not all men are the same. Therefore, different husbands prefer different things."

"True words," Elizabeth supported. "One man's dislike of a woman for particular traits can guarantee the likes of another man to the same woman. Thus, it does present an opening for wit to some men, who find amusement with a play on certain words and phrases."

"I am a very different sort of man than Mr. Bingley," Mr. Darcy said, "just as Mr. Bingley is a very different sort of man than Mr. Philips. Three of us different men do require three different brides. That leads to seeking three different sorts of women. And we found them, and for my part, wit is vital to my happiness."

"And Mrs. Darcy has a great deal of that wit to her, I am sure," Lady Catherine said, then she looked at me, "however, when it comes to a single woman, who has not already found her good fortune, wit is **not** one's friend. Rather, it can be the means through which men might flee from her company. It would be better to adhere to the grace and elegance of smiling a great deal and speaking as little as possible. One gains much virtue, by sitting around and doing nothing."

This comment not only hurt my pride, but it also hurt every natural inclination to my own instincts.

I was offended, and it hurt me. Imagine the inner resentment that swells within a person when you are either too scared to say anything, out of your own defense, or you are unable to. I was suffering under both of those restrictions.

However, I had the good fortune to invoke the sympathy from the rest of the company, because Elizabeth did her best to change the subject.

"Lady Catherine," Elizabeth said, "before we came here, our reverend and his wife had paid us a visit at Pemberley. And they told us that they were plagued with red ants. We offered them some advice on how they could rid themselves of the infestation, but I was wondering what your advice was on the matter."

The play on Lady Catherine's vanity did just the trick. She abandoned her pointed remarks against me and now returned to her authoritative advice-giving.

"Green sage in every closet will make them disappear," she said. "Purchase them in the village or pick them yourself. Either one is suitable to do. But if you are to gather them yourself, then make sure to inspect their properties before you proceed."

As she continued to speak about this, Enara leaned forward to me and whispered:

"That woman does not like you, Kitty."

"No, she doesn't," I whispered back.

"Why?"

"Only Lady Catherine knows. And I doubt that she will ever tell me. Which is tragic because I am dying to know."

~

When we sat down to eat, Mr. Collins complimented Lady Catherine on the food and dish presentation. Lady Catherine, once more, fed off the praises.

"Do you see?" I whispered to Arthur Philips, who sat down next me, "that whenever Mr. Collins gets too profuse in his compliments, he starts to sweat a little?"

Arthur chuckled.

"Yes, I did. The poor man. He must be careful. If Lady Catherine were to be exceptionally kind one day and offer him to dine here at Rosings every evening, his compliments might lead to an apoplectic fit and he will die before even seeing his child come into the world."

I giggled but then had to stifle it before it got too loud. Unfortunately, I did so at a time when no one was speaking, and my mirth was overheard by the whole table.

"What are you both speaking of?" Lady Catherine declared. "Tell us all, for I must have my share in the conversation. For truly, anything that I say can be nothing less but an addition. And Anne," Anne, turned to her, apprehensive. "This will be very good for you to learn how to immerse yourself into a conversation."

Immediately, I turned to Anne, whose fair skin turned an even greater shade of pale, while her cheeks turned a deep shade of red. The poor woman was embarrassed by the last remark. Her mother did not know what humiliation that she had inflicted on her own child. Then again, often our parents are never aware when they do humiliate us in that sort of way, because they wish to help so very much. But they result in accidentally doing the reverse.

"Well," Lady Catherine said, "what were you speaking of?"

Arthur and I looked at each other, alarmed. After all, he and I were speaking about something that should not be publicly shared.

Luckily, Lady Catherine did not despise Arthur, therefore, he readily gave some excuse. The truth was not sufficient for the moment, and a lie was much better.

"We were talking of a time where we both ate dinner at other houses," Arthur said, "and the dishes that were served were not fit to be eaten. Unlike now, which is the opposite."

"Oh, you have touched on a very important matter! Too often I have visited another home, and the meals were not fit for a pauper to eat. Those people must have cooks that come from very provincial areas. I made it a habit to only get cooks that were recommended from the very highest circles. My cook uses rosemary in a lot of his seasonings and does as much baking as boiling."

She went on to speak a lengthy while about the best way to prepare meals.

During the whole time, I watched Elizabeth and Charlotte exchange glances at each other across the table.

The former had made the ultimate match.

The latter had made the practical one.

And both knew to measure the size of each of their lives. But within their faces was something I expected to see in Lizzy's face, but not Charlotte's.

Neither one of them had any regrets.

Chapter Five

HUNSFORD PARSONAGE

When the Collins' departed, Charlotte expressly requested if we would like to visit Hunsford Parsonage the next day. The invitation was readily accepted, and the Collinses left for home.

The rest of the evening left nothing remarkable to comment on, so we retired at the reasonable time that Lady Catherine recommended.

As we ladies went to bed, I saw Anne de Bourgh out of the corner of my eye. Mrs. Jenkinson was on her left and was speaking with Georgiana.

When taking a look at Anne, something stirred in me. I analyzed her features, countenance, and something about it struck me as being familiar. The defeated feeling, while also being boosted up through one's wealth.

That was it. Now I saw it all clearly.

She reminded me of Mary King! Though they didn't look precisely alike at all, there was a link, a familiarity to how they both held themselves. Anne was a little prettier than Mary King, but because they lacked any sense of attraction, their features rested in comfortable complacency.

But Mary King developed countenance at the very end. She found her voice.

Anne still had none. And when I recalled how she said nothing at dinner, I couldn't help but wonder if her quietness was not due to a natural character quality, but a result of emotional insecurity.

I think that she was afraid of life.

Without thinking, I approached her as we walked up the steps and touched her arm.

The sudden touch of another person alarmed her. She did not jump back, but her face was merely surprised.

"Sorry, did I disturb you?" I asked.

"Oh!" she blurted out, horror-stricken. "No, you did not. I assure you. It is merely that I was too busy falling into the recesses of my mind."

"We have a word for that in Hertfordshire. Daydreaming."

"Oh. Well...of course one ought to think of serious things. But I... well, I..."

"There is no shame in that, I assure you. I do it often throughout the day. Just make sure to never do it upon the steps. It leads to bad footing."

"Quite."

"I just—well, I thought that maybe I ought to apologize to you."

"To me? What have you done to me at all?"

"Not a particular apology, but a general one. I realized that my conversation with Mr. Philips led to you being quite put on the spot. It was not what we meant, nor intended."

"Oh. Well, that was not your fault at all. You have nothing to apologize for."

I nodded, then I grew pensive.

"Did that situation cause you pain?"

"Pain?"

"Yes. Did that whole encounter cause you pain?"

"No."

I knew that she was lying. But I did not think to press the matter, because it would only make the situation worse.

"Oh, well that is good. Then goodnight, I suppose."

"Yes," she said, her face still filled with alarm as well as desperation, "good night, Miss Bennet. I—"

She cut herself off, and I thought that maybe she needed some encouragement.

"Yes?"

She opened her mouth and closed it again.

Then she opened her mouth and closed it again. With great difficulty, she finally was able to form words.

"Good night, Miss Bennet."

"Good night, Miss de Bourgh."

She went to her room.

As I walked to mine, I knew very well that she had wanted to say more, however, she thought better of it, and changed her mind at the last minute, reverting to safe topics.

The next day, our entire company returned the visit to Hunsford Parsonage.

Upon receiving us, Mr. Collins was at his full element. Mr. Collins and Charlotte appeared at the door, and our carriages stopped at the small gate, which led by a short gravel walk to the house, amidst the smiles and nods of the whole party. In a moment we were all out of the chaises, rejoicing at the sight of each other. Despite that Mr.

Collins was ridiculous, his manners did give us all something to talk about. Imperfect people have a right to always exist: they are the only ones who give stories, give us neighbors something to make sport of, and lead to lessons being taught.

"Friends!" Mr. Collins said as he stepped towards us, with Charlotte behind him. "Welcome to my humble abode. Cousin Elizabeth, you have seen our simple but quaint domicile, but your sisters and cousins are whole new to the scene."

"Yes, they are," Lizzy responded, as Mr. Darcy helped her up the steps. "They shall marvel at the structure, as I had, I daresay."

Mr. Collins turned to our group.

"You see," Mr. Collins said, "that since ever I moved in here, everything is perfectly suitable for a clergyman of my station. Take note of this entranceway. See how no space is wasted, no structure is either too plain or too ostentatious. A perfect sort of architecture to receive visitors, is it not?"

We all looked at each other, confused. After all, unless we were walking into the Notre Dame, Buckingham Palace, the Vatican, the Blue Mosque in Istanbul, or Christ Church in Pennsylvania, an entranceway was an entranceway.

Mr. Bingley, however, was there to save us all.

"It's as serviceable an entranceway as I have ever seen, sir," he noted.

"Yes, it is." Mr. Collins breathed in, smugly, "yes, it is."

"I think," Charlotte said, "that due to the cold, our guests would like to come in, my dear."

"Yes, come in. Come in."

We all entered, shaking ourselves from the cold that was without.

When I entered, I looked out of a nearby window, and up at the clouds above.

"I wonder if it will snow," I observed. "Georgie, what do you think?"

Georgiana came behind me and looked as well.

"When coming, I didn't take the clouds into consideration," Georgiana noted. "But maybe it will."

"No," Mr. Collins said, "I do not think it will. The wind is full west today, and as such, I do believe these clouds threaten but will not fully provoke us. You all may come to my parsonage and not suffer the dangers from some damp bit of snow."

"Never fear, Mr. Collins," Elizabeth said, "my husband's horses are very fine, and we have the strength to brave a little bit of snow on the ground."

"Snow can be so very disagreeable," Mr. Collins said, sniffing the air. "I do not understand why it even has to occur."

"Snow is like a cough, I imagine," I said, "it is inevitable, and we ought not to question nature for being nature."

Enara and Arthur laughed.

"My sister still has her phantom cough," Jane explained to Mr. and Mrs. Collins.

"Still?" Charlotte said. "That cough still haunts you every now and again?"

"Yes, it does."

"I had hoped it would free you from its shackles."

"So did I," I said, chuckling. "But here we are, and—"

"Let us all have some refreshment," Mr. Collins said. "My dear Charlotte, call for the tea."

"Yes, Mr. Collins."

Mr. Collins turned to us and introduced us to his house, for a second time, with ostentatious formality.

"And all the furniture," Mr. Collins said to Mr. Darcy in particular, "has been analyzed, chosen and catalogued expressly under the superior eye of Lady Catherine. A better patroness I could never imagine. Take this sofa here, is it not a remarkable design?"

Mr. Darcy did not respond, therefore, Georgiana took up the difficulty of having to talk to Mr. Collins.

"Yes, it is. I see our aunt's influence in the choice of cloth."

"Yes, I am certain that you do, Miss Darcy. You surely have a superior eye yourself in noticing it. And what do you think of this sideboard and fender? It also is heavily inspired by your aunt's recommendations."

Since Georgiana was the second most esteemed person in his eyes, due to her being Lady Catherine's niece, Mr. Collins appealed to her most particularly now.

After Mr. Collins finished giving us every detail about the parlor, he also told us about how often he traveled to Rosings Park, and how Lady Catherine often read his sermons and even made some recommendations and revisions on his work.

On Sunday, we would attend Mr. Collins's service and then all would be revealed.

"What are the chances," I whispered to Georgiana and Enara, "that when we attend service, much of what he says will not be his own words?"

"I am counting 40% of his speech will be his," Georgiana said.

"I am counting 30%," Enara said.

"I count twenty," I said, "I wonder if we should bet on this."

"I am game enough for it."

"We'll bet later," Georgiana whispered back. "But I recommend that we go no further than one shilling."

"Agreed," I said.

When we turned back to the party, the topic of discussion had changed to a lighter subject that held more interest than discussions of furniture.

We had three pregnant women, who all were old friends. Therefore, discussion about children would be the inevitable topic. In this case, we all were attached to the discussion, because it went in the direction of children's names.

"Mr. Collins and I are quite torn," Charlotte explained, "if it were to be a girl, we both agreed on the name of Ruth. It is a classic name but is not too often used. It will offer individuality to her."

"I chose it from the holy bible," Mr. Collins said, "from the Book of Ruth. It is an often-overlooked section of the good book and tells the tale of a most devout and moral woman. And with such parents any daughter of ours has, it is no doubt that she will grow to be a fine and moral woman."

"Yet, if we have a son," Charlotte said, "that is where our minds shift."

"But it is a small difference of opinion," Mr. Collins overrode her, "in any other subject, we are always of one heart and one mind with each other."

"That is very good to be," Jane said, holding Mr. Bingley's hand. Mr. Bingley returned her gesture with an affectionate expression of his own.

This emotional display caused a chain reaction.

Mr. Darcy and Elizabeth looked on each other, with passion in their eyes.

Arthur and Enara also exchanged pretty glances.

This led to Georgiana and I exchanging a 'yes, here we

are' look. After all, she and I were the only single ladies in the room. All were married and most were soon expecting a growth in their household number.

Only Georgiana could understand me. Being single is no disease, no matter how the world tells us the reverse. Mind you, things have changed greatly since the times of Queen Elizabeth I and Mary, Queen of Scots (poor Queen Mary!). Back then, a single woman was considered a great nuisance and as if she lacked any place on this earth. Although, nowadays, a woman of either respectable wealth, or surrounded by family who will always include and provide for her, can find herself charming or considered agreeable.

Only poverty would condemn her, because it is often considered to be one of the worst sins, and you become the sport of jokes. To the worldly eye, poverty only works on the young, who are given a chance to find their fortune somewhere.

If I were to be an older woman, and poor, then I still think I would be merry. I abandoned being generally out of spirits long ago and saw no common sense in it.

Without my family, I am poor. But I have a plan. Yet, if I fail, and if poverty finds me in old age, I must prepare myself for the crude remarks that would come my way. Yet, this is Christmastime, and good will toward all men and women will prevail for now. Therefore, I will not give in to such gloomy thoughts. After all, bells are ringing, presents are being placed in hiding places, pine trees are being brought into homes and there is the occasional decoration that is done to indicate the season.

And carols are coming forth, along with the possibility of scary ghost stories being told by the fire.

It truly is the most wonderful time of the year. And I

had family. Therefore, I do believe that I was worth something, even if not much.

"And what choices have you made for boy's names?" Arthur asked. "I long to know which name you both prefer?"

"Well," Charlotte said, "Mr. Collins prefers the name George. I am not averse to the name at all and would gladly accept the name if we were to have a second son. However, for our first one, I always preferred the name Briar."

"Briar?" I remarked, "well, that's a lovely name."

"Lovely, but too different," Mr. Collins said, dismissively toward me, "such an uncommonly used name can incite prejudice."

"Prejudice?" I asked. "Why so, when it has never been a name associated with anything of the negative and—"

"It is incorrect," Mr. Collins overrode me again, "and I trust that I am right in this case."

"My sister-in-law is correct," Mr. Darcy *overrode* Mr. Collins. "I have never heard anything negative attributed to the name of Briar. It is a known name, and if you worry of anything said about it, think of it as a journey that all names must take. Every name had to start somewhere, and might have been criticized initially, until it became as common as anything else."

"Oh," Mr. Collins said, turning both grave as well as eager, "I had never considered it from that perspective. Since you have phrased it with such intelligence and logic, I am now converted. Briar is a name worthy of consideration. I stake my life on it."

Turning to Mr. Darcy, I offered him a smile of gratitude. He returned it with a nod and a gentle expression.

Who would have thought, when he and Mr. Bingley first rode into Hertfordshire, that we would grow to respect each other? Neither Mr. Darcy nor I could have ever predicted it.

After showing my gratitude for his standing by me, I turned to Charlotte Collins.

She also offered me a sympathetic look, and in that moment, I wondered if she ever regretted losing the name Charlotte Lucas and taking the name Collins in its place.

However, that look was soon replaced by complacency. The more that Mr. Collins spoke in a way that would make her ashamed, Charlotte blushed, but afterwards, she acted like she didn't hear what he had said. That, perhaps, is the only means through which a woman can stay attached to our cousin without being driven out of her mind.

~

While our party had separated around the room, I stood by a window, looking out of it.

I noted the landscape, which was very fine, but it did not capture my thoughts. I needed time away from the group to collect myself and suppress my rage. I was getting angry again. Truly, I could not bear to look on Mr. Collins right now. He and Lady Catherine seemed to be in league with each other in disliking me, and I did not want to play their game. But I did not want to submit to being intimidated by them. All was left to do now was to take time away from them, so that I could maintain my self-control.

At some point, Charlotte had come up to me and stood with me, by the window.

"Do you notice our poor garden?" Charlotte asked me.

"Garden?" I repeated.

"The winter has quite taken it away from us now. I wish you could see it in the summer. Mr. Collins works in it almost every day. It is one of his most respectable pleasures."

"Indeed." It was the only thing that I could think to say back, since it held so little interest to me. A garden can be commented on when it's there, but not when it's gone. "Well, I am certain that it is lovely in the summer."

"It is. As I said, Mr. Collins spends a great portion of each summer and spring day in the garden. It is not without my recommendation. I confess that I encourage him to be *as much* in his garden as he can. Then he walks to Rosings almost every day."

"So often?"

"Yes. I encourage him *in that* as well. And then he has to also visit with his parishioners, often, especially the elderly and the sickly. I encourage him in that as well, or I encourage myself, and attend to them. Yet, when I call on them, it is usually at the same time that Mr. Collins visits Lady Catherine."

Now I understood. Charlotte was not just speaking idly for the sake of saying something. Oh no, she had a purpose, and it was to be kind toward me. She gave me a shrewd look, which I appreciated.

"Therefore, between his separate activities and my own, a whole day can pass and him and I have spent no more than an hour or two in each other's company."

I smiled.

"Ah, now I see."

"Yes, you do. That is my definition of domestic felicity, don't you think?"

"Yes, I do. Rather, I think you have achieved the perfect scheme for your marriage."

"I had a feeling you would agree."

I looked out of the window. It had begun to snow.

~

Soon, it came time to end our visit at the parsonage. As we prepared to leave, Charlotte handed me my gloves and pelisse.

"I neglected to mention," she informed me, "Maria has written to me. She wanted me to give you her regards, and to say that she misses you."

"She does?"

"Of course, she does."

"I miss her as well. Tell her that I have not forgotten her, and that I think of her often."

"She wonders if you will ever return to Longbourn."

I sighed.

"Charlotte, I do miss her as well as Diana, the Philips', and my parents, of course. But sometimes, it takes a great deal of walking away from something before you are ready to walk back to it."

"I understand."

"Will she?"

"Yes, she will. Maria is more intelligent than people give her credit for. She understands humanity."

"She always understood me. That was a great testament to her abilities to empathize."

"It wasn't. You and she were very much alike. I think she felt like the one who was obliged."

They saw us off to the carriage, and Mr. Collins was as profuse in his farewells as he was in his introductions.

Like it was with Lady Catherine, he barely took much notice of me, but he was kinder than he had been when I first arrived.

That change of character only confirmed what I had suspected in him soon after I had arrived at Hunsford Parsonage.

We journeyed back to Rosings Park. I was in the carriage with Mr. Darcy and Lizzy. As I watched the parsonage disappear behind some trees, I turned to Elizabeth.

"And that was the man who Mama wanted you to marry," I professed.

"Yes," Elizabeth responded, "it was."

"Did she ever apologize to you for her being so thoroughly wrong?"

"No, she never did. But I take pride in one thing."

"What is that?"

"She never took credit for bringing Mr. Darcy and I together either. Only the Gardiners can take credit for that."

I turned to Mr. Darcy, and my tone was gentle.

"Thank you," I uttered.

He understood.

"You're welcome."

Chapter Six

HOW EASY IT IS TO CAUSE A SCANDAL

When we returned to Rosings Park, we were expected to sit in the main parlor and Lady Catherine was our chief entertainment. I noted some Christmas decorations did adorn the place, however, it was not nearly as quaint as what we had done at Longbourn.

As soon as we removed our outerwear, I had the impulse to compose a letter to Colonel Fitzwilliam. Therefore, I was given permission to sit down at a desk that was across the room and overheard the Lady speaking as I wrote.

"I rise early," I overheard Lady Catherine over my shoulder as I wrote, "and never sit up late, and it is best to never read a book while in bed. Never eat a hearty supper, drink water often, and make sure to bathe regularly. None of this whole 'bathing once a day is too harsh for the skin'. It all has to do with administering the proper soaps. Much advancement has been made since lye soap has become the fashion. Avoid it at all costs and only have your laundresses use it sparingly. If one can afford super fine crown soap, always use that instead..."

Soon, I was able to focus harder and write to the Colonel.

...well, this has proven to be a very interesting holiday. We have arrived safely at Rosings Park and have been here for no more than two days.

I know that I should write with only good news, but I would be lying. First, I must acknowledge that whatever problems that I write, shall be trivial in the eyes of a man who must lead other officers to battle.

But I am no soldier. Only the painfully misunderstood Joan of Arc can boast of having that title.

I am merely a young lady in a drawing room, and so what else is my world but limited? Therefore, cousin, allow me to complain about the mundane and the little aspects of life that plague and torment us when confined to a room full of individuals who have no choice but to provoke each other.

Soon after I arrived, I came upon a painful revelation.

Your aunt hates me. Even before I opened my mouth to say anything, she seemed to take an immense dislike towards my character. Even without knowing my character.

I see you now, Cousin Richard, and you are shaking your head. Is Kitty exaggerating again?

Well, this time, I can prove it. Georgie is witness to it all, as my close confidante, and she has confirmed my suspicions. She does not hold me as being extreme in my findings. No, she assures me that her ladyship does not prefer me to be a part of the company. I wonder why? If the lady had reason to hate me, then I would understand. I have made mistakes in my past, that cannot be denied.

However, since this is the first time that she has met me, she has no cause for alarm.

And that is not the end of it. Hate is like love: it is the most contagious and infectious emotion to feel. Human nature seems to perpetually swing between the pendulum of extremes. We either love something or hate it immensely. Black and white are how we view things, and not as shades of gray, as life truly is.

It has to do with her reverend, Mr. Collins. He already went from respecting our family, to disregarding them after Lydia's plight, then to advise my sister not to marry Mr. Darcy, and now he returns to esteeming us.

Excepting me.

I suspect that he is in league with Lady Catherine, in some way. She despises me, and he is always so careful about doing as she wishes. Since she detests me, he feels compelled to do the same. Or rather, he is eager to do the same.

The only chief consolation that I have is family who try to shield me from such offenses. Mr. Darcy defended me against Mr. Collins's dismissive tone. That speaks for itself.

And as for you, Colonel, how do you do? Was the officer you retrieved truly a deserter, or was there some sort of misunderstanding?

It is hard that you cannot be with your family at this special time of the year. This is the one time that it ought to be so. But I suppose there is always some foe that our country must fight. How strange it is, have you ever learned, that the chief way a man can earn a living for his family is if he is constantly risking his life? When money is more important than life itself!

Yet, I do admire patriotism. So, I appreciate your efforts, and the efforts of your officers as well.

But I do miss you. I may be impolitic for saying it because it puts me in a very direct position, but you know how we are. You have become so vital to my life, that you being removed from our society is difficult.

There is nothing cemented between us, but I flatter myself that you will understand that I must say it.

I miss you, cousin.

I just needed you to know that. Oh, I lie! I am being vain. The truth is that I needed to say it to make myself happier. But I believe that you know how that feels.

How wicked we both are.

May God bless you, Cousin Richard, and that you survive this Christmas season, and can at least celebrate the new year with gaiety.

Stay safe, Colonel.

KB

"Miss Bennet!" Lady Catherine called from the other side of the room.

Her sudden cry made me accidentally break my pen and splash a little bit of ink on the table.

"Yes, your ladyship?" I said as I began to clean up the ink spots.

"What do you do so singularly?"

"I am writing a letter."

"To whom, pray tell?"

"I am writing a letter to our cousin, and your nephew, madam. To Colonel Fitzwilliam."

"What?" she asked sharply.

As I began to fix my pen, I looked at her. Once more, her eyes were filled with a subtle disdain.

"You write to the Colonel?" she questioned.

"Indeed, I do, madam."

"You will not send that letter, I declare."

I looked on her, shocked.

"Why not, madam?"

"You are a young lady. You cannot possibly write to a gentleman. That is outrageous and scandalous." She turned to Mr. Darcy. "Darcy, I am astonished with you. What goes on at Pemberley that you allow such brazen acts in your ladies?"

Since Mr. Darcy had defended me earlier that day at Hunsford Parsonage, I felt compelled to return the favor.

"Mr. Darcy is not to be criticized for my actions," I said, "no one is responsible for them but me. I shall bear responsibility for what I do. Darcy and Elizabeth have followed decorum in every way. If it will please your ladyship, I also can easily give an explanation that will satisfy you."

"What explanation could you give that would be satisfying? Heaven and earth, nothing you say will change my judgment."

"But when has there ever been error in writing to family? Through marriage, the Colonel is my cousin. And I promised him, most ardently, that I would write to him about the events that take place."

"Darcy can do it for you."

"But that will not make Colonel Fitzwilliam happy," Georgiana said, "for he was desirous for us all to write to him, from our separate perspectives. This will help him at this time of the year. He wanted to be here, but his duties took him away from the most festive season. Our letters will bring him cheer. He demanded that Kitty write to him as well, to help him feel like he is still amongst us."

"You treasure Richard, Aunt," Mr. Darcy confirmed. "He must be granted this one gift, mustn't he? I know you would wish to make him happy."

"I do wish to," Lady Catherine said, "but it is extremely vexing."

"You need not worry about anything being written that was without propriety. Kitty gives me the letters, I peruse them, and if they are proper, I have them sent."

"Oh," Lady Catherine relented, "if that be the case,

then I am willing to accept. But mind you, Darcy, I will still keep a discerning eye on everything that is around me."

She looked at me again.

"Yes, I will."

I finished my letter, but did not close it, so that Darcy could read it at his early convenience.

To write to a gentleman who you are related to through marriage... I might as well have run through the halls of Rosings Park in my undergarments.

Chapter Seven

A WALK TO CONSIDER

Since the snow had melted the next day, Georgiana and I were taking a walk about the grounds, alongside Arthur and Enara.

"Three women pregnant at the same time," Arthur said, referencing Elizabeth, Jane, and Charlotte Collins. "I cannot help but wonder if pregnancy is contagious at this time of year. My love, do not get any ideas."

"I have not the inclination, Mr. Philips," Enara said, "however, one cannot control these things."

"You don't wish to have children at present, Mr. Philips?" Georgiana asked.

"I should imagine not," he answered. "I have recently gotten married, and I am enjoying the pleasure of my wife, more than anything. To have a child would mean that I would have to share her attention with the infant. I prefer to be so selfish right now. Next year, I will be selfless and then I would consider it."

"How trying that nature does not agree with you so well," Enara commented, amused. "We can try to prevent being parents soon into our match, but fate might have other plans in store for us. Never fear, my love. I will help you through your selfishness, since it is well-meaning."

"Selfishness must always be forgiven," I quoted, "because there is no hope of a cure."

"That is very clever, Kitty," Arthur said.

"Thank you for my share of the compliment," I said as I pulled a small branch from a tree and began to twirl it in my fingers, "but those words were not mine. I was quoting something I once overheard Mary Crawford to have said."

"She said that?" Georgiana asked.

"Yes, she did. And do you know what I find very frightening?"

"What?"

"That she is correct. As long as it is executed moderately, and being selfish causes no one physical or mental harm, I cannot help but think about myself every now and again."

"We are born to be that way," Georgiana encouraged, "it's a part of our nature. The second that one accepts that, the moment that they are in control of their selfishness. Flaws are like invisible beasts: feed the beast, or it feeds on you."

"And I know what you think of," Arthur said to me, with a wicked look in his eye.

I saw what he meant, and I rolled my eyes.

"I am an easy mark, Arthur. There's no sport in teasing me because it is so easy."

"But I cannot help it. Your selfishness tends toward the wishes for many yesterdays. You selfishly wish to be returned to Pemberley, and in the company of one or two men."

"Arthur!" Enara gasped. "You really are forcing her onto the spot."

"Kitty is not afraid of being forced, in that manner, are you Kitty?"

I sighed, but in a light-hearted and amused manner.

"Thank you, Enara, but Arthur is correct. I do not take offense because we are among friends. I like speaking freely among us." I gave Arthur a face. "You are content to torment me, aren't you?"

"Well, as you can see, what else do we have to do?"

"True. These careless and lifeless days of ours will not do. Go on then, stick pins at me and see if I will squirm. We need some diversion, and I might as well be the subject."

"Do you miss both men?" Arthur asked. "No chiding me. You said that all was fair, in love and regimentals."

"One thing that can be said is that I chose neither man for his uniform," I vowed, still with a light tone. "Arthur, you don't believe that I was hopeless in that way, do you?"

"I judge no one."

"Very well. I truly must see that I am among friends. Well, yes, if you must know. I do miss both gentlemen."

"It's natural to feel the loss of such men," Enara said, "they were diverting characters. Sometimes, they even brought the flare for the dramatics in their wake. There is something to be said for characters who make life interesting." Enara looked at me, shrewdly, "Have you any knowledge on if there is one man that you would prefer more?"

"No," I lied, "I am still as provocatively divided as I have ever been. It's strange, I know."

"Not so much. Both men have something to recommend them. Being tossed in love, and then torn away from that as often as you are, would lead to confusing feelings. I am not jealous of your fate."

"I daresay that no one ever is, or ought to be." When looking at Georgiana, I saw that she looked at the ground, complacent. Suddenly, it occurred to me to realize that maybe something about this conversation was trying to her. Ergo, I thought it best to simply change the subject.

"Are you looking forward to returning to New South Wales?" I asked. "Enara, you must miss your family."

"Oh, I do, to be sure," Enara said, "I mean no offense to you all, I can assure you, but nothing is more comfortable than being among family now."

"I quite agree," I said, "that's why being here is not the easiest for me. I miss it just being us, and the rest of my family."

"I can see why," Arthur said, "my plans might not make it convenient for me to return to Hertfordshire before we leave for Australia, but I'm hoping that I will."

A sudden thought occurred to me. Despite that the plans were not entirely fixed, I thought it best to make the request.

"If you do choose to return to Hertfordshire before you book passage across the ocean, can I come with you? I think I need to return, for one reason or the other. If you worry about travelling plans, then you don't need to worry. When you go to London to board The Lilia, you can deliver me to Cheapside."

"Oh, the Gardiners," Arthur said. "Yes, it would be nice to see them as well before setting sail. What a happy thought."

"Yes, it's been too long since we saw them. If we arrange everything properly, we achieve this all, while you still make your ship in time."

"Oh, it can easily be done," Arthur remarked, overjoyed. He turned to Enara. "What do you say, Enara? I should really like to see my parents again, and I would like you to meet my uncle and aunt Gardiner before I leave."

"I am not averse to the idea. Will they like me, I wonder?"

Arthur smirked.

"No, not in the slightest."

She slapped his arm.

Chapter Eight

INSECURITY

As we returned to the house, I asked Georgiana if she could come to my room and help me choose my gown for dinner.

She did so, and as I pulled out my white muslin, I looked on her keenly.

"Well," I said, "do you suspect that I actually did not need your advice?"

Georgiana looked at me.

"I sensed it, but I didn't know for certain. You have something else on your mind that you wish to speak of?"

"No, but you do, evidently. And we don't have much time. Don't be afraid. Whatever you are feeling, let it spill out for me to hear. You'll boil over if you don't."

I hung up my white gown and began to remove my shoes and stockings.

"I noticed that there was something wrong when Arthur mentioned Finlay and Colonel Fitzwilliam."

Once again, her face looked a little flushed as she looked down, uncomfortable. Silence would not do, and I would not let it defeat her.

"And there is that look again?" I noted. I removed my gown and undid my hair. "Georgie, reveal all or forever hold your peace."

When Georgiana raised her head again, embarrassment rushed over her expression. In the next instance, she tried to hide it, but I saw all.

"Why are you afraid? Georgie, I have never given you reason to be so."

"I know. I suppose that I am more afraid of myself. Or rather, I hate myself."

"Why should you do that? I'd call you irrational for thinking that way about yourself, but sometimes a little self-loathing can be cathartic. Explain why, and then I'll decide if it is well deserved."

"I feel foolish about thinking something."

"Welcome to the life that is *me*," I responded, very colloquially, about how her feelings are not something that is foreign to how I often am. "Nothing you say, emotionally, can rival my lunacy."

"Try not to judge me."

"This room shall not confine you toward cold prudential judgment." I untied my muslin gown, and Georgiana helped me put it on. "Now, are you finally ready?"

"Yes."

She didn't speak as she tied up my gown from the back, but I was not alarmed. I knew, when she was ready, that she would unveil all. Like the rest of us, she merely needed time to face a bitter reality that she was ashamed for feeling.

When she finished clipping my gown closed and tying the sash under it, I looked into the mirror to see how I looked.

"Sometimes I wish that we could walk around with our

hair down," I said, "but I suppose that it would ruin the aesthetic."

"Yes, it would."

I looked at her image in the mirror, and she looked so forlorn.

"No one loves me," she said at last.

When hearing her say that, I didn't move. I don't know why, but I didn't go to her. Perhaps it was because I knew, deep within, that she didn't want someone to embrace her, or to be profuse in their caresses. She needed to stand alone. Never could I fathom why that was my impulse, yet it was.

"Georgie," I asked, "why do you say that?"

"Because it's true."

"I would say that you are wrong because you are. But at the same time, I have been in your predicament, where you felt that the whole world did not care for you. With myself, there were moments where I felt that no one cared. No matter how untrue it is, it is something that all of us feel, and share. But with you, I am glad to profess that you cannot be more wrong. We all love you terribly, and we Bennets think that we could not have been fortunate to have a better sister-in-law."

"Oh, forgive me," Georgiana clarified, "when I mention love, I do not mean by the way of familial love. I am aware that I am very blessed with all that I have received. When I mention love, I mean..."

I saw where her mind was going. Very rarely in life could I say that I precipitated when someone felt such a thing, but it made all the sense in the world. First, Arthur and Enara mentioned the three couples who would soon have their first child. Second, they commented on their own domestic joy. Thirdly, Arthur inquired about Colonel Fitzwilliam, Lieutenant Finlay, and my torn heart. That all, augmented with me complaining about why I felt forlorn by no longer being in those men's company, would inevitably lead to this circumstance.

For so long, I had considered Georgiana and I as partners in every way, never once taking into consideration that there was a difference. But there was. We were both single, but our paths parted in two ways:

She was a handsome young woman, of perfect manners, and wealth. As such, the worst sort of men were drawn to her, but it was not love.

I was a not-as-handsome woman, of human manners, and had little wealth. As such, the best sorts of men were drawn to me, because they had time to fall in love, and time to get to know me better. But they could not choose me, due to my lack of a dowry.

And then there was Mr. Dixon, who had proposed, even when I did not have a dowry and would have made a poor catch for him.

Poverty can create true love between two individuals.

Wealth can create true love, occasionally.

But more often than not, wealth can create alliances being made. Don't believe me? Ask any royal monarch who was dragged into an arranged marriage. It's rarely ever a pleasant experience.

"Romantic love," I finished Georgiana's statement. "You mean romantic love."

"Yes," Georgiana uttered, her voice gentle, indicating a sense of heartache. "Yes, I do."

Turning to her, I sat down on the bed. Sitting very still, I looked at her.

"I could tell you much advice," I began, "and assure you of your self-worth. I could give you line after line about morality, confidence, and of higher mental views. But I am not. Because I sense that it is not what you need at this moment. I think you need to let your feelings pour forth and just be allowed to feel what you feel."

With sad hope, she looked at me.

"You saw this about me?"

"Yes, I did. Therefore, go forward, with all your beliefs, and I will listen."

Her lips quivered, feeling the desperation of her point of view.

"Mr. Dixon proposed to you," she uttered. "He didn't care that you had no money. Lieutenant Finlay can hardly abandon you and only wants to find his fortune to choose you. My cousin, the Colonel, was so in love with you that he had to run away from you, to ease his pain, but then he comes back, to ease his pain once more. And even when they know that you love both of them, that you cannot choose, they still feel for you. Who feels for me?!" she cried.

Her exclamation, with such a raised voice, made me blink. Yet, I give my firm assurance that it was a small reaction that hinted of larger sensations that rested in my spirit. Georgiana had screamed. If resonance was something she was used to projecting, then it would not have frightened me. But since she was not the sort of person who was known to give way to spiritedness, this was shocking. I froze again, and remained ever so still, but I was alarmed to my inner core.

However, it must not be considered that I was upset with her or felt that she was wrong to react in such a manner. On the contrary, I felt that this was the best thing for her.

"What about me," she uttered, her tone still a little loud, "is so repulsive? So horrid, so unworthy of being made love to?"

"Georgie," I argued, "that's not what is happening."

"Don't lie to me to spare my feelings," Georgiana cried, "everyone has that someone in their lives. My brother has Lizzy. Bingley has Jane. Mr. Philips has Enara. Mary has Mr. Atkins. Even Charlotte can find life tolerable with Mr. Collins. And you have two men! Two men, Kitty! And neither man despises you for the other one of them being in your heart. Two men. And none for me! Do I make myself so disagreeable?"

"Georgie, you know the truth. You are handsomer than me and more genteel."

"Then why? If I am, as you say, handsomer—which I am not. You merely just don't see yourself properly—and more proper, then why don't men love me? I hate it. I hate that no one chooses me." Backing away from me, her body began to shake. Violently. "No one chooses Georgiana. And no one ever will."

Now, I could move. Her erratic movements, her fragile state of mind, now reached a point where she needed someone to hold her.

Going to her, I grabbed her arms and held her as she collapsed into me. With her head resting on my shoulder, she wept into my hair.

"I'm tired," she wept. "I'm tired of no man thinking that I am worth loving. I feel so worthless."

"You are not," I said, soothingly, "you are everything to us."

"I am a sister, I am a cousin, but I am not what men want. I feel useless."

"There, there now..." I said, rocking her like a baby. For a while, I let her rest there for a time, letting her have her cry out.

After a while, I thought that I could dare to speak.

"Please, Georgie, give me the chance to coax you into a better way. I am going to tell you some advice. I know, due to your circumstances, that you will not want to hear any kind words. It is because, when in such a state, we don't always want to be soothed but give way to our grief. It's natural. But you must let me try to cheer you, to help you see that you are loved. Please, hear me. Will you?"

Georgiana didn't respond, so I took that as encouragement.

"First, you have to understand who you are. You are a kind, generous, lovely, and worthy woman."

"But I don't feel such."

"You don't feel it because you connect your self-worth with the concept of 'being loved' as opposed to 'loving'. That is where your mistake lies. That's the misstep that Henry Crawford took. And secondly, I understand this, because I have the good fortune to have been where you are now."

Her stifled cries subsided when she heard this. She didn't move her head from my shoulder, but her body stopped shaking.

"You have?" she asked.

"Yes," I said, happy that I could be kindred with her again. There really is nothing wrong with misery loving company. "Many times. Georgie, you know me now as a woman who is tied between the beauties of two worthy men. However, you forget that I am Jane, Lizzy, and Lydia's sister. Jane and Lizzy had long been considered the belles of the county. Not me. And Jane was always the one that men admired the most. She was the first one to incite a man's affections when she stayed in London with the Gardiners. That man wrote her poetry and called on her. Mama assumes that he never proposed because Jane was probably too young at the time. She also would boast that we were nothing compared to Jane."

"That was very wrong of her."

"It was. Never did she see the harm that she had done. Now she does, but it doesn't change the pain that it once spawned. And soon into coming, Bingley fell in love with Jane and wholly ignored me. Darcy fell in love with Elizabeth and barely cared for my existence for a while. And often, the reason why the officers preferred my company was because they liked Lydia. They were fond of me, due to association. I have been where you are, Georgie. I just had the benefit of experiencing this all first, and now you are undergoing it."

"But Mr. Dixon proposed to you."

"He did so because he knew me for years. Also, he probably thought, due to me being one of the least loved Bennet girls, that I was attainable. And that brings me to the third matter. Everything about my situation makes me attainable, and that is a fine quality in a woman when a man considers her. You are Miss Darcy of Pemberley. Your Uncle is the Earl of Matlock, and your aunt is Lady Catherine de Bourgh. For most men, you are unattainable. That makes a slew of men, who could love you, but since you are an impossible dream, they will not choose to consider it. Even if they are modestly wealthy, they still might feel as if they are beneath you. That is the way our society functions. Too many are told of their lack of self-worth, while others are puffed up, due to their rank and station in the ton."

"You really think so?"

"Oh, I know it, believe me. Also, due to your wealth, you will always be under the supervision of chaperones. Especially since, every time that you are not, fortune hunters seek you out like the savages that they are. Finlay was like Dixon; my parents left me to be liberal in my time with the officers. I had time to speak with him, to become better acquainted, and gain an intimacy that cannot be achieved under supervision. Even with Colonel Fitzwilliam, I had the freedom to gain an intimacy with him. Through marriage, we had become cousins, and therefore, were both above and below suspicion. Each time, I was given the freedom to get to know each man who felt for me, whereas you were never given that time."

"And when I was given that time," she said, sighing, "Wickham and Mr. Atwell found me."

"Yes, they did. My poverty makes me a terrible choice for a wife, but it also makes me available for men to gather a true acquaintance with me. Your wealth, personality, face, and figure make you a perfect choice for a wife. But it also makes you a primary target for mercenary men."

"Then, I might never find love, because when men look at me, all they see is my purse."

"Yes. Wealth is considered a definite virtue, and in some ways, it is. In other ways, it is not. But the fact is that, until men see your person before your purse, they will come to you for all the wrong reasons."

"And come to you for the right ones."

"Yes. But not choose me. Does this help you?" I asked.

"Yes, it does."

"Good. Well now that I found you in a happier way, can I finally give my advice?"

"I thought that was your advice."

"It was the buildup to the advice."

"Oh. Very well. I am in a more sensible way. Proceed."

I began. "It is natural to feel as if one is worthless when no one is in love with you. I have shared your sentiments and your situation before. It is a natural trap to fall into that way of thinking. Especially when we are surrounded by so many happy couples. One can feel so inadequate when in their presence."

"They never know about the harm that they cause by

being happy in their domestic felicity. I sound wicked in saying that."

"It's good to speak wickedly, every now and again. That way, you can expel the demon that is within you. Wickedness is an immortal state of mind. It's best to exorcise it, rather than let it fester within. Our relatives have made excellent matches. They understand each other so very well. Even when they argue, they are perfectly matched. Images of perfection are to be admired, and we should aspire to it, but every now and again, they are antagonizing. In fact, it can be unbearable to even look at such images, because it's almost as if that perfection mocks us."

"Precisely," Georgie agreed. "It provokes me to get so very angry, for no good reason at all."

"It's natural. And that leads to me telling you this: as you once told me that I was not a foolish creature for feeling lost without Finlay and Fitzwilliam's company, I tell you this now. No one is ever worthless for being single. There is no shame in it, nor does it indicate one is unworthy of being loved. It is a state of being. I know that marriage is a lesson that is engrained in us. But when our emotions boil over, we burn in them, and then the smoke clears away, we realize that our explosion was all for nothing. There was never anything wrong with our single state.

"Also", I continued, "as there are benefits to married life, so there are to single ones. Personally, as single women, don't you ever notice all the pleasures that we have? We are free to experience more because we have less cares to care over. We can fall in and out of love. We can see plays, take more solitary walks, have dreams, etc. It's the 1800s, for heaven's sake. Single women are no longer regarded as a nuisance, the way we used to be. As long as we are respectful, charming, not a burden, and engaging, there will always be someone who wants our company. And there are those who will always want you in their life. Especially this imperfect little imp," I said, pointing to myself.

"Oh, Kitty. I think I do feel better now."

I actually gave good advice? Now I can say that I can raise the number of my good advice-giving to the number '5'.

There was a knock on the door, and Sarah entered before we even said she could come in. She had been so used to doing that at Longbourn that she never learned how to adjust.

Since she had done so before Georgiana was prepared to be seen, Sarah came in upon us scuffling around, trying to look calm. Instead, Sarah saw Georgiana rubbing her eyes and trying to hide her sadness.

When witnessing that she had done wrong, Sarah naturally became unsettled and shifted in her stance.

"Forgive me, I must learn to wait to be called in. I am sorry, missuses."

"No, never mind that," Georgiana said.

"I came to help you dress for dinner, Miss Bennet. But I can see that I am forestalled. Well, that gives me the chance to assist you, Miss Darcy. Betsy will do it terribly."

"Sarah, really?" I asked, trying to detract attention from Georgiana's fretful state as much as I could. "You do this now? Wait till you and Betsy are in the same room. Or else your slights will count for nothing. Put simply, if a tree falls in the woods, and no one is there to hear it, does it make a sound? It's the same way with you and Betsy."

I had done my best to speak until Georgiana could make herself presentable, but I had nothing more to say.

"Yes," Sarah said, "I must remember that." Seeing that there was nothing for it, Sarah had no choice but to confront Georgiana's melancholic state. "Well, my dear, you look like you are not in the merriest of way." She reached out her hand, to have Georgiana take it. "Come my dear. Nothing helps a bout of sadness like looking lovely in a new gown."

Giving in, Georgiana took her hand and let Sarah lead her out of the room.

"And when you see the way that I arrange your hair, you will want for nothing. I do it better than Betsy, I daresay. Much better. And when you see her again, you can tell her that."

I was left alone in my room, and I rolled my eyes. I got the sense that Sarah had amused Georgiana more than I had, and perhaps even had reached her in some way.

Even when I think I won at something, someone always comes along and brings the laughter in.

Oh spite! Oh hell!

Chapter Nine

THE DREAM THAT BECAME A NIGHTMARE

When we sat down to dinner, Arthur Philips mentioned the plan that we had of returning to Hertfordshire, to see his parents and my parents before they disembarked across many oceans. I mentioned my desire to go with them, and that I would not be getting in their way at all if I wrote to the Gardiners and asked to stay with them until I could be fetched to return to Pemberley, or when the Darcys would go to London to stay in town.

As such, Enara had to apologize for us having to leave a whole two days early, so that we could reach Meryton at the perfect time.

Lady Catherine was naturally upset with this because she had taken a liking to the Philips'. After all, Arthur was charming and a good listener, and Enara was striking and was elegant company. However, she wished them well, and expressed that if they were to break their journey at Bromley inn, that if they mentioned her name, the waiters would attend them.

They thanked her very much for her kindness, and Mr.

Collins went on to boast very much about his patroness's goodwill.

Unfortunately, this led to a tidal wave of plans that vexed Lady Catherine greatly.

"It seems correct that we should visit our family, before returning to Derbyshire and Godfrey Park, is it not?" Jane asked Mr. Bingley. "Maybe it would be proper to..."

"Join the party?" Mr. Bingley said, then he turned to Arthur, "what do you say, Arthur? Would you prefer some company when going into Hertfordshire?"

"We would be delighted, Bingley."

"No, you will do no such thing, sir," Lady Catherine ordered. "To lose the Philips' makes sense, for they do right by seeing their parents again before leaving for another world. And naturally, Miss Bennet's mother shall want her home, for she is a great deal needed there more than anything else. After all, a young single lady ought to be home, until she may find suitable prospects for herself."

Biting my lip, I suppressed my sense of feeling offended and took a sip of my soup. Sitting next to me, Georgiana touched my hand, to offer me solace.

"Thank you," I whispered, "I hope to see you soon after I arrive in London."

"Maybe I can come with you," Georgiana said.

"You don't have to. I pressure you too much into being my constant companion. I'm very bad at that."

"On the contrary, I am not certain that I want to return home just yet. I think I should like to join you very much."

Her company brought me instant relief, and I spoke without thinking.

"Our number will increase to four, Arthur and Enara. That is, if it is permitted. Georgie has expressed a desire to join us and go into Hertfordshire."

"You wish to join us, Miss Darcy?" Enara said, flattered.

"Oh, that is delightful. If you both are to stay in Gracechurch Street, then that means you can see us off when we set sail on The Lilia."

"That's precisely what I wanted to do!" I exclaimed.

"There is no need to talk so loudly, Miss Bennet," Lady Catherine chided me.

"Forgive me, your ladyship. I was merely excited."

"Well," Mr. Darcy said, "this scheme is not something that is so sudden to hear as you might think."

"Mr. Darcy and I had been doing a little thinking," Elizabeth added, "and we realized that we ought to visit our family in Hertfordshire. Mama and papa, and the Philipses ought to receive our notice."

"Does that mean that you would join us in coming too?" Enara asked. "I should like that."

"Well, since the rest of the party is already of the same mind, it can easily be done."

"Heaven and earth," Lady Catherine hissed, "have you all lost your minds, by forgetting what is owed to myself as your host? You are being most offensive by not considering my feelings on the matter and not owing to your promise. I will only release the Philipses and Miss Bennet. But as for the rest of you, no, I will not be imposed upon. You formed an engagement here, and you will honor it."

"Aunt," Mr. Darcy said, "you shall never feel offended, because we will not have you feel as if you have been neglected. I speak of another plan." He turned to Arthur and Enara. "You both were to remain in a London inn for three days before setting sail on The Lilia, am I to understand?"

"Yes, that is the plan."

"Well, I ask if you are willing to forego that part of your plan? Can those three days be spared, and transferred to Hertfordshire?"

"Of course," Enara said for them both. "Seeing my parents and Mr. and Mrs. Bennet is infinitely superior to trying to see London's diversions in three days' time."

"Then that settles the matter," Elizabeth said. "Aunt Catherine, we can still have our full visit here and then leave for Hertfordshire afterwards."

"Then, when we go to London to escort the Philipses on their journey," Mr. Bingley said, "we can stay at Darcy's and my townhouse until we have relaxed, refreshed ourselves and returned to Derbyshire. That is, if you all wish it."

We all settled on the plan, readily, and Lady Catherine had nothing to reproach us for, except that, perhaps, she was upset that this was a plan she could not schedule herself. The Collins' asked us to make sure that we sent the Lucases their regard when we returned there, and to inquire after Maria.

As such, altogether, we were now going back to Hertfordshire after the New Year.

This was more than I could hope for. When going back home, I was happy to not be alone when it came to us Bennet women. Mama would be happier to see Jane, and Papa would be happier to see Elizabeth. They would be kind in seeing me, but my sisters' company would enhance the experience. Their presence kept me safe.

I needed to feel safe right now.

~

After dinner, the Collins' returned to Hunsford Parsonage, and we all sat down, in each other's company.

I requested a servant to pull a book from the library, so that I could research the War of the Roses in a history book. When sitting down, I opened the book and did my best to sit through the tedious distribution of facts.

How could such an interesting historical moment be written so horribly? Even when our facts are interesting, we love to be boring. What tedious fellows created the rules that run our society? When did they believe that 'pleasure' was an ugly word? There seems to be a direct correlation between scholars and tediously dull texts that they produce.

However, the heavy words and distribution of facts were enough to make my eyes grow weary. When the hour grew late, I confessed to being exhausted and was allowed to retire.

Falling into my bed was all that I wanted to do. When pressing my head against the pillow, I covered myself in the blankets and treated the cloth like a cocoon that was protecting me, until the coming day.

My eyes closed. With all the historical facts swirling in my brain, my thoughts grew heavy.

And heavier.

And heavier.

Sleep found me.

～

"Ah!" I cried, waking up with a start.

Darkness.

It scared me for a moment, because I felt as if I had awoken in a dark void of existence.

It only took me a few seconds to feel the familiarity of the bedsheets around me, of the bedding, and that I was safely in Rosings Park.

Beads of sweat trickled down my cheek as I breathed in deeply, trying to calm my nerves.

Swiping the sweat from my brow, I removed the blankets from my legs, stood up and moved around the room. The darkness was not provocative, but it helped me feel so much more comfortable, because I needed to be alone now.

Crossing my arms around my person, I paced back and forth around the room, trying to remember the dream that I had.

Or rather, the nightmare...

It had been a lovely summer's day, and once more I had fallen back into the world that my subconscious made for myself.

The perfect world that my mind had created for itself to take refuge in. Gone were the harsh English winter days in December. Instead, I had fallen into the way of a different world, wholly unlike my own.

There was something about the land that felt so familiar to me, so correct to my character, that I began to run along it, once more.

Despite that I was alone, I did not feel loneliness at all. Instead, I felt complete.

Then I stopped suddenly.

I stood still.

I sensed two figures who were behind me, moving along the trees.

For some reason, I grew afraid of them both. Even though my instincts told me that neither of them was dangerous, I still felt that fear.

I could not turn around and face them.

There was only one thing to do.

Run, Kitty, run.

Looking below me so that I did not trip on any root that had come up from the ground, I ran.

Through the trees, I dashed, and along underbrush.

What was even more frightening was that I felt the footsteps of the men as they chased after me.

Each step they took pounded in my chest, as if I was connected to both men inwardly.

I knew who they were.

I knew my connection to them both.

And yet, I still ran anyway. The trees grew denser, yet I knew where I was going. It was as if the path was guiding me, telling me where to go.

It was Nature.

I knew that I could trust it, because it had never let me down before, and was not likely to do so again.

The trees, dirt, leaves, rock, and stone told me where to run and each time, I knew where to turn, what path to make to evade my pursuers.

For a moment, I felt as if an arm was nearby, outstretched, trying to pull me back. When I turned to face the captor, his features were dark and concealed from me.

But I knew who it was.

Why did I see Colonel Fitzwilliam's expression in the darkness?

Then, to my left, I heard Lieutenant Finlay grow closer from the left.

Why was I scared? Never were they villains in my life, but for some reason, I felt as if they were here to draw me away.

And sure enough, I saw why.

In the background, far behind them, the nature that I had invented, the world that I had created, was falling away. In its place was the British countryside, and the industry of London.

Like spiderwebs, the image was clawing away at the world that I had imagined for myself. The world that I knew was behind me, overshadowing Fitzwilliam's and Finlay's faces.

In their eyes was defeat. Intense defeat.

I recalled that it wasn't evil they were dragging me into, nor were they the villains. They were pulling me back toward something—rather than pushing me forward.

They were pulling me back, because something was pulling them back as well, yanking them toward an oppressive yesteryear, rather than allowing them to tread forward to a more liberal tomorrow.

They did not want to be alone. They wanted company. And they knew that they needed me as much as I needed them.

Yet still... I ran.

'Onward,' the soil cried from below me. 'Onward you must go."

The magic of the voices that rose from the earth beneath lent speed to my step.

I outraced Colonel Fitzwilliam's hand, as well as Finlay's gaining on me.

Yet they did not relent but only increased their pursuit. Winding along the pathways, I sped, with the branches and trees opening before me. Between the bracingness of the air that whipped across my face, to the courageous spirits that rolled beneath the rock and stone that offered me sanctuary—

Sanctuary!

That was it. I felt a deep and long sense of sanctum sanctorum, and that I could not abandon it in the same manner that it no longer could abandon me. We were linked, and the bond cried out to me, giving me the strength to journey onward, even when my limbs cried out from the exertion.

Light was ahead, and like a starving woman, I ran toward it, seeking liberty in the open air. Yet, the light proved to be the danger. When I rushed out to it, I came upon a rocky precipice, and a cliff was ahead that led to a sharp decline, with a gushing waterfall down below.

Managing to catch myself before leaping over the edge, I immediately regretted not remaining under the dark cover of the forest.

Turning around, I aimed to find where I could turn to. Sadly, there was nothing for it since Colonel Fitzwilliam and Lieutenant Finlay had caught up with me.

Through the wood's edge, they emerged from the two different directions.

When seeing me trapped where I was, they slowed down and calmly walked forward, encircling me like I were the ultimate prey.

Behind them, I saw the British countryside, the London industrialization, as well as the factories in Northern England, widen, and increase clawing its way over the beautiful trees and animals. The scene overrode my sanctuary, as Colonel Fitzwilliam and Finlay came closer to me.

"What do you want?" I asked them.

"To come home," Colonel Fitzwilliam said. "To come home."

"Kitty," Lieutenant Finlay said, reaching out his hand to me, "it is time."

I looked between them, as the factories, homes, and English landscape grew ever larger in the background.

I could not get on at all.

Within both of these men were the strongest connection to myself, the binding tie, and the most incredible link.

There was compassion.

Camaraderie.

Wantonness.

Rapture.

And love.

But as England rose behind them, I felt threatened. It seemed as if it was rising to devour them. And by association, they would take me with them.

"Now that I'm here," I managed to utter, "I do not think that I want to. I love you," I said to them both, "but I cannot follow you."

They both looked at me, so heartbroken.

"You will fall if you don't," Lieutenant Finlay said.

"Or you will drown," Colonel Fitzwilliam said, "and we cannot bear the idea of it."

"I cannot help but look away," I said.

Then, as is the way with dreams, the memories of it began to slip away. I had recalled saying something back to them both.

Then, as they reached forward to take me once more, I stepped too far, wavered along the brink, and fell over the edge.

Crying out, I turned midair and saw myself falling toward the water pit down below.

Closer and closer, I fell, horrified as I cried out. When getting to the surface, I closed my eyes, avoiding my fate...

And that was when I woke up.

∾

Wiping the last bit of sweat from my face, I looked out of the window and saw that the sky was now a deep blue.

It was the precise color that the sky had just before dawn approached. There was no falling back asleep now, for my mind was too awake, too active, and too bent on clinging to the nightmare that had befallen me.

I was baffled as well as alarmed.

Dreams are afterthoughts that our brains recycle and display into a collection of perverse and disjointed images.

They don't mean anything.

But how many always believe that? Not when so much of literature and even our holy book stresses the importance of dreams.

When the biblical character Joseph was given the gift of translating dreams that others had, we don't ignore that tale. It's quite as much a part of our religious education as any other story.

And then, there is the prominence of dreams in Shakespeare and other forms of literature.

But to have the same dream repeatedly, and each time, the dream gets further and further along, displaying another section to my experience.

Could it count for nothing?

And it was even more provocative than ever.

For how could my mind translate Colonel Fitzwilliam and Lieutenant Finlay's images into depictions of confinement and oppression?

So often, they were the means for me to seek out liberty, sweet liberty, and rise above the tedium of commonality and the singularity that haunts us women, that nips at our very heels like hellhounds.

They willed me to go forward, or they listened to me when it was them that needed to learn a lesson. The freedom to agree and disagree liberally is the very epitome of bliss.

I experienced both with them.

Then why would my brain translate their images into catalysts that weighed me down?

It made no sense at all.

Determined not to diminish their importance in my eyes, or to not belittle their self-worth in my judgment, I was resolved.

These dreams perhaps meant something, or it meant nothing.

What can be sure was that, when it came to my reflections, perhaps my dreams did hint at the rocks beneath.

But as for the two men that I loved, no, I would not view them as the means through which brought me down and made me low.

Soon, it was time to begin my day.

CHRISTMAS EVE

Christmas Eve was upon us!

When getting dressed, I was greatly looking forward to a day of goodwill and gaiety.

The next day, letters were sent to Longbourn, Meryton, and to Bingley's and Darcy's townhouse, so that all could be arranged properly.

We spent the day visiting another family and staying there for dinner. The family's name was Fairfax. They were an amusing set of individuals, and we spent a great deal of time speaking about many Christmases that were long past for both our families.

When Jane talked about our tradition of waking up and singing a Christmas carol in the hallways at Longbourn, the Fairfax family took delight in that notion.

Lady Catherine found it to be a little absurd, because it disrupted the household on Christmas Day. After all, be it church service, or the opening of presents, that is the tradition that a person should first be met with.

None of us Bennets responded to her criticism, but that did not mean that we agreed at all. Sometimes, in silence, a disagreement is keenly felt because one offers no encouragement.

The Fairfaxes were a family with four children. Two daughters and two sons. Neither of them was particularly handsome men at all, but they were very agreeable and good-humored. They both were a few years older than Georgiana and me and were at the time in their lives where they wanted to say all the right things but didn't know how to always say them.

Seeing that we were disposed to find them worthy company, in the general sense, they clung to Georgiana and me. The whole visit that we spent there, they remained close to us. Their parents arranged it so that they led us into dinner and had us seated next to each other.

This easily could have been another situation like that of Mr. Osmund Granville or Mr. Atwell and Mr. Wright, where we were being pursued by men who sought either wealth or connections. Yet, I was determined not to think that way.

In the average teachings of life when it comes to both sexes, it's very easy for one's mind to jump from conversation to thoughts of matrimony in the blink of an eye.

However, I had to tell myself that it was not often the case. Some people just preferred to be charming for the sake of enjoying their fellow man and fellow woman.

Not all ladies are kind or flirtatious toward men for the sake of being a siren and drawing them in.

Not all men are rattles toward ladies for the sake of breaking their hearts and leaving ruined women in their wake.

Such bad characters exist, but they are not waiting around every corner, seeking to jump out at anyone who crosses their path.

No. Sometimes people are just agreeable, and there can

be no harm in liking an agreeable person. The Fairfax brothers were animated and enjoyed talking to women near their age.

With Georgiana and I being the perfect set, and being connected to Lady Catherine de Bourgh and the Darcys, we were in a fair way to be the perfect sort of contemporary companions for them.

When it came to Georgiana and Mr. Roger Fairfax, who was the eldest son, his parents looked at them, with a pleasing expression.

If our visit was not so short, and our time in Kent not so brief, I am certain that Mrs. Fairfax would have let her mind work toward establishing a union between them both.

Regarding myself, Mr. Walter Fairfax, the second son, was very attentive. But I was not the ideal match, so his mother only was casual in her respect towards me. But Mr. Fairfax, the father, was different.

"Walter likes a pretty face," Mr. Fairfax whispered to me as he led me to the fire. "He's like his dear old father, in that way. And your face is a picture. Being the younger son, he naturally must have a profession. But he has great hopes for a fellowship at the University at Cambridge."

"Oh," I remarked, "Mr. Walter wishes to go into education? That is admirable."

"It is indeed. Initially, he was intended for the church. But he proved very strong-willed in a spirited way and needed more diversity to his life. I do not insult my boy, rather I am proud of him. You see, he is like me, in that way. And I have done right by my sons, Miss Bennet."

"I am certain that you have, sir."

"What I refer to is that I also have sorted out my estate in that all my children receive a share of inheritance. Roger gets the lion-share, since he is the eldest, but none of my children will be paupers. What I mean is that, while we encourage Walter to marry with some consideration for his wife's dowry, he is more at liberty, since his profession can give him a steady income. I encourage all my children to marry someone that they can respect and feel a deep affection for—mark my words." Out of the side of his eye, he looked at Georgiana as she was laughing at something that Roger Fairfax had said. "It's best to love whoever one marries, to be sure. I would never encourage Roger to marry a woman simply for her dowry, Miss Bennet. I wish for you to be aware of that."

I smiled at him.

"You are very good, and I believe you."

Whether I meant that last sentence or not, I shall never fully know.

"However," he said, returning to Walter Fairfax, regarding myself, "when it comes to Walter, he's a good and steady lad. He's also very exciting and is not averse to a bride who comes with little income. He's most accomplished when it comes to economizing his household."

I smiled but did not want to show any more encouragement than that.

"He strikes me as the sort who is," I said, "and that is to your son's credit. However, I suspect that it is not only a part of his nature, but also due to the lessons that you and Mrs. Fairfax instilled in all your children."

Mr. Fairfax felt the compliment most ardently, as I hoped he would. By flattering him, I was able to divert the conversation away from myself and more toward him. This worked as he began to regale me with stories of the days that each of his children were born. His stories didn't last long because Mr. Walter Fairfax approached us.

"Father," Walter interrupted, "I am quite out of my depth. I understand why you speak with the pleasing Miss

Bennet, but you are severing me from Miss Bennet's company. Can you be kind to your son, and hand her company over to me?"

"Of course, my boy. The young ought to enjoy the company of the young."

Mr. Fairfax left me alone with his son and went over to speak with Lady Catherine, Bingley, and Jane.

"I must sound like a greedy coxcomb," Walter Fairfax said to me as he sat down next to me, "for shooing my father away."

"He was not offended," I responded, "but if you feel as if you have done wrong by him, you can apologize as soon as we leave."

"It is just that I am so eager for company, especially those of young ladies."

"It is no different than when ladies enjoy the company of men. Especially when it comes to country estates. The country is pleasant, and one can enjoy the beauties of nature every day, but the society is confined and unvarying. Sometimes, if the weather is disagreeable, one can go for days or weeks and not see another living soul outside of one's family."

"Precisely. At our stage in life, we want to see others. And, as vain as this sounds, we sometimes want to be *seen* by others."

"Vanity is one of those vices that must always be forgiven, because it is something that we all have no choice but to feel, every now and again."

Walter Fairfax smiled.

"You understand me, perfectly." We heard his brother, Roger, laugh. Turning, we saw that Georgiana had said something funny, and Roger found it amusing.

"Miss Darcy makes my brother laugh," Walter said,

"that is very good of her. My brother loves to laugh. Don't they make a handsome couple?"

I see why he said that, but it was not right to agree.

"Mr. Walter, you know that I cannot agree to that, because I would be presumptuous for placing Georgie in a coupling that she has not agreed to. No, let us let those two decide what they are to each other."

"Do you think they could become anything, though?" he asked, unable to resist his curiosity.

"Anything is possible in this mad, mad, mad world. We can only govern the fate of our own hearts—unless you are royalty and you are often thrown into an arranged match—but as for others, no, we must leave them to their fate."

"Yes," he said, looking at me fondly, "yes, we must determine our own hearts for ourselves."

The poor man! With any luck, he was merely flirting in a casual sense.

But if he felt anything true, he could never know that I could never come to feel for him. My heart was taken, and that was all there was to it.

Once more, I found my solution: diverting attention away from myself.

"But I will say this," I offered, "when we leave, thank your brother for giving Georgie company. There is nothing wrong with enjoying the company of an agreeable person who makes us comfortable. She looks happy right now. Sometimes, that is all that we humans can give to each other."

"Yes. That is what I find to be so beautiful about the country. Not only does the fresh air prepare oneself to receive the beauties of our holy redeemer, but it also gives us humans time to fully become each other's chief pleasure. Town is fast, busy, diverting, and it supplies us with immersing ourselves into the world. And country brings contemplation."

While I personally believed that one could still think and philosophize in a city, I still understood what he meant.

As I was about to acknowledge this, I noticed that we were not being unobserved.

To our left, Lady Catherine's gaze was fixed on us. Or rather, on me, to be particular. Her eyes were narrowed, and it was an expression of intense disapproval and dislike.

Even in company, she despised the very sight of me. Although, what was I presently doing that caused her to be enraged?

In fact, I thought that I was giving a good first impression to a family that she wanted to like us.

Oh well, it didn't do to dwell on what she thought. All I could do was enjoy my Christmas Eve as I would.

After dinner, Roger Fairfax stood up and asked if any of us would care to dance.

"Since we rarely have so many in number, I could not resist taking the opportunity. Is there anyone else who is willing to seize upon a reel?"

Jane and Elizabeth were unable, due to their pregnant state.

However, that left Darcy and Bingley to dance with the Fairfax sisters, the Philips to dance with each other, and the Fairfax sons to dance with Georgiana and me.

As I saw Walter Fairfax approach me, I noticed that Anne de Bourgh was sitting by the fire, alongside Mrs. Jenkinson. When she saw the younger people all congregating to dance, her eyes looked so forlorn that I assumed that she felt slighted for not standing up with us.

Despite that she didn't care for my company, I felt an

immense pity for her. No one ever wants to be pitied, but we also do want it, all at the same time.

Before Walter could ask me to dance, I stood up and whispered to him.

"I think that Miss de Bourgh might want to dance, but no one ever thinks to ask her. If she wishes, would you be so kind as to stand up with her."

Walter immediately looked less enthused, but he agreed to it.

Walking up to Anne, I appealed to her.

"Miss de Bourgh," I said, "we are all gathering to dance. I was wondering if you would like to join us?"

When hearing my request, she showed more animation than she had since I met her. At first, she looked surprised, and it brought color to her cheek. Next, she stuttered a little, expressing surprise to being appealed to. Then she agreed that the activity would interest her, and was preparing to stand up, when her mother called out to me.

"My daughter is too ill to dance," Lady Catherine declared, "and if she does, she would naturally offer the respect that is owing to me and ask me who she ought to dance with. Miss Bennet, I would entreat you not to recommend Anne to overexert herself and, by extension, send her into an early grave. Anne, sit down."

I didn't look at anyone else, but Anne de Bourgh. I sensed that everyone in the room felt sorry for me, since I had been set down.

However, I realized that the chief humiliation went to Anne herself. First, it was evident that she wanted to dance. It was merely her illness and her mother's demands that kept her from doing so. When being told that she must sit back down, she felt like a schoolchild who was forced to return to the nursery, and not be allowed to take part in the gaieties that everyone else could experience.

She felt mortified.

But that did not stop her from gathering her strength, looking up to me, smiling gently, and thanking me for considering her.

"You're welcome," I said, then I turned to Walter Fairfax. His eyes were filled with intense empathy for Anne and me. "Well, Mr. Walter, do you still wish to dance a reel?"

"Very much so," Walter answered, offering me his arm, "and I shall be glad of the partner that I have."

Placing my arm in his, we walked to the dance floor where us five couples stood up and the dance began as Mrs. Fairfax played for us.

Later, when it was time to depart, the Fairfaxes eagerly invited us to dine with them if we ever were to return to Kent.

Lady Catherine was not entirely without grace when it came to sensing when an invitation was owing. She invited the Fairfax family to dine with us on New Years' Day.

This invitation was precisely what the Fairfax family had hoped for, and they readily accepted.

With Roger Fairfax giving Georgiana every assurance that he hoped to dance with her again when they would visit Rosings, our party left the Fairfax residents with nothing but good feelings toward them.

On the journey back to Rosings Park, Georgiana sat near me in the chaise. Her face was alive and animated. When she saw me smiling at her, she chuckled.

"What is that look for?" she asked me. "What?"

"You are feeling better," I observed. "Don't pretend like you are not."

"Now I am the one who is feeling the shallowness of finding importance in being noticed by the opposite sex."

"Really?"

"Yes. All your grand speeches about valuing my self-worth, that was obviously meant to help me into a better way, and I didn't feel better until Mr. Roger Fairfax paid particular attention to me."

"Well, as you said, men feel flattered, and their characters feel more complete when we take notice of them. It is the same with women. There is something very uplifting about it, and there can be no harm in a man being agreeable to us. Mr. Roger Fairfax likes you, you know."

"I think he is merely lonely. He doesn't meet many new women in his society. There is something to be said for novelty."

"Indeed, there is. While he either wishes to tread slowly, or he just wants your company, his parents think differently. His mother wants him to marry you, and his father wants Walter to marry me."

Georgiana's eyes widened.

"Truly?"

"Oh yes. You can believe me. Mr. Fairfax didn't say it directly, but he did hint strongly at it. He finds your person entirely agreeable. As he said, your income is just another charm to you, but mercenary people have been known to say such things. He could be sincere or deceptive. I do not know."

"And he doesn't want a wealthy wife for Mr. Walter?"

"Mr. Walter Fairfax is to become a professor at Cambridge. The fellowship he will receive will set him up nicely, and all he needs is a pretty-enough wife who will do credit to him and bring in good connections. I provide that. We are the Fairfaxes ideal hope."

"Should we tread lightly and be careful?"

"Somewhat. But I believe we should only worry when there is something to worry over. Until then, let's just enjoy their company."

"Yes, that is precisely what I think. There is no point in

planning for a doomy tomorrow, when there are no signs of catastrophe."

"You hit the nail right on the proverbial head. I forgot to ask, by the way, what do you really think of Mr. Roger Fairfax?"

"He is charming, agreeable, and appears steady. I cannot know, for certain, if he is truly like that, or if it's a façade. Wickham and Mr. Atwell have forced me to always consider deception. But what I can honestly say is that, while I like Mr. Roger Fairfax, I could never fall in love with him."

"You cannot?"

"No. I need some sort of spark to be between the man that I choose and myself."

"That is natural. Where there is no spark, it is bound to be a cold match. Then again, when my parents married, there was much spark."

"There was?"

"Yes. And it turned cold eventually. And yet, my aunt and uncle Philips also had much spark when they married. And they still have the spark."

"I suppose, in the end, it is all a matter of luck."

"Yes. And compiled with the fact that the man you choose comes to the match as he really is, and not with many facades to him. When it comes to marriage, there is a great deal of one being taken in. Just look at Mary, Queen of Scots, when she married Lord Darnley. That was the biggest disaster that easily helped undo her."

"But until then... yes, I confess that his attentions to me have helped my confidence rally. Oh, dear. Now I am the one who is validating myself through being admired by someone. I feel foolish."

I grinned.

"And that makes me happy, because now I can say something that I have long wanted to say to you."

"What?"

"Georgie, shut up."

Chapter Eleven

TO BE ON THE WRONG SIDE OF A LADY'S WRATH

When we returned to Rosings Park, Lady Catherine arranged for us all to go to our rooms, baths to be drawn, and us to rest before we would go down to supper.

As I waited for my bath to be prepared, I wrote a letter to Mrs. Forster. After all, it was the only way that I could communicate with Finlay.

Between her eagerness to maintain connections with the Darcys, as well as feeling obliged to help me due to the guilt she felt in not taking Lydia's interest in Wickham seriously, I knew that she would pass on any message that I wished.

Ergo, after telling her about our intended plans to return to Hertfordshire for the new year, I asked her to remember me to Finlay. Though not writing much, I wrote only a few things that were not scandalous to tell him:

Mrs. Forster, please inform Lieutenant Finlay that I wish him a happy new year, that I consider his happiness from time to time, wish him to be in good health, and that his safety is in my prayers.

I shall return to Hertfordshire in the new year, and I find something romantic about returning to the place where I first met him.

While it is inadmissible to tell a gentleman that we ladies will miss them, I can say, without bordering on impropriety, that he still remains as one of the most agreeable men in my acquaintance. Almost no men are his equal.

Thank you, Mrs. Forster.

When I finished the letter, I sealed it, just as Lucy entered and informed me that my bath was ready.

Overjoyed, I raised my fist in the air and cried out merrily.

"Oh, come on, you little imp," Lucy said, laughing as I handed her the letter and danced out of the room.

"Yes, I am an imp. I am, I am, I am."

When sitting in the water, I bathed with energy. I just felt as if I was very merry and was feeling the joys of the holiday.

I raised up my hand and let the droplets from my fingertips fall back into the water.

For some reason, that small action mesmerized me. I continued the action and wondered why it amazed me.

Then again, what is an ocean but billions upon billions of those same droplets that bathed me? That was how Arthur and Enara would be transported to Australia. Such a powerful force water was. It could save, purge, transport, and it could hurt. But for now, it made me feel anew.

Lucy came in, gave me a towel, and handed me my robe as I dried off, and returned to my room.

When sitting in front of my mirror, I dried off, and Lucy helped me into my dark green gown. I told her to never mind my hair, because I knew how to put it up myself, and that she could enjoy having time to herself.

Happy to be relieved of her duties, Lucy left me to my solitude.

Before I tended to my hair, I thought it would be nice to write in my journal for a time, to list the events.

Soon into writing my next entry, there was a knock on my door.

"Come in," I said, assuming that it was Georgiana, Enara or one of my sisters. The knock was unfamiliar, so I was at a loss.

The door opened and I put down my pen, turning to receive my visitor.

I froze.

Lady Catherine de Bourgh had come to see me.

Of all the people to come to my room, it had to be her.

The woman who showed no interest in my existence.

And there she was, as plain as day. Her face had traces of the lines that were on a woman's face when they were being perfectly serious about something. It could be argued that her ladyship was serious about me, but not in a congenial sort of manner.

"Lady Catherine," I said, standing up. "Is there something wrong?"

"That remains to be seen, Miss Bennet."

She closed the door behind her. That action seemed to

be like some sort of morbid foreshadow that I dreaded. Sometimes, one's instincts are correct.

She sat down on the other side of the room. When she looked at me, her nose sniffed the air, disapprovingly.

She pointed to my hair, which hung about my shoulders loosely.

"You look improper, Miss Bennet."

I touched the strands of my hair.

"Oh, yes. I hadn't had time to do my hair."

"Where is your servant? She ought to have done it when she dressed you."

"Since I have experience at doing my own hair, I sent her away, so that she could enjoy more of her Christmas Eve. Servants are not given enough time to themselves during this festive season."

"She can have tomorrow to enjoy herself, but for now, you are quite incorrect to be so independent."

I didn't respond to that because I knew that it was of no use. Uncomfortable, I thought it was best to get to the heart of the matter.

"Have you come to visit me to tell me something, madam?" I asked.

"It is not proper to order a lady, of three times your rank, to speak when you will it, Miss Bennet."

"I meant no offense."

"I suppose that I shouldn't be surprised. Experience with your family has taught me to have base expectations."

Now that was an offense that had gone too far. My parents were my parents. It was my right to criticize them. But it was not hers.

"I believe my family to be respectable people, madam. My father is a gentleman. My uncles are respectable men of the law or industry, and their wives are worthy women."

"You think that, but what connections are they, but

tradesmen and your younger sister—oh yes, I know her story all too well. And from what I hear, you were very much her bosom friend and constant companion."

"She is my sister. There is no harm in liking one's siblings. I daresay that loyalty to family is quite the common and correct thing."

"You agree with her shameful elopement?"

"No. I merely forgive it."

Her eyes flared and I knew that was not what she wanted to hear. Then I made a deduction.

"Wait," I said, "is that why you dislike me so? And have me suffer so much criticism, by your means, because you associate Lydia with myself?"

"That is part of it. Reports have often reached me about how she and you were always seen together, and the shameful acts you got away with."

"What shameful acts? I have never hurt anyone."

"You were known for running amok, like madwomen, flocking to the officers like lemmings. It must have appeared as vulgar."

I was beside myself. For the first time in so long, I no longer felt fear. Rather, I felt anger. If the situation were not so provocative, I would raise my hand in the air, in triumph. Finally, I had got my courage back and was no longer governed by cowardice.

"There is no harm in spending time with the men who defend our country and our freedom. Also, what your lady-ship was not informed of was that I spent a great deal of time with the officers' wives. They were good company, and it is always pleasant to meet new people. What is wrong with liking humanity? Being cold and distant to them hardly encourages compassion to one's fellow man."

"Not when you do it as a relentless and determined flirt!"

Ah, now it all came down to it!

All the reports of my past had come back to haunt me, as I knew it one day would. But I was not in the mood to feel guilt over it.

"If you are trying to make me feel ashamed of myself, your ladyship, then I am happy to disoblige you. After all, what pain did my past bring to anyone? What harm have I caused? Nothing at all. Ask your niece and nephew. I have been a respectful companion and a good sister-in-law. If my company is good enough for them, then I will not hold myself in contempt over the matter."

"But it is not only that which makes your behavior despicable," she said, standing up, "because other alarming reports have reached my ears."

"And what reports are those?"

"I know, Miss Bennet, how you have done everything to attach yourself to my other nephew, Colonel Fitzwilliam."

I sighed. How did she know?

"Your ladyship," I said, "if you are wondering about my involvement, then I can assure you that the Colonel is free."

"And is that true, or is that a façade that you have put on? Secret engagements have happened many times before."

"You think that we are secretly engaged?"

"Stranger and more unnatural things have been known to happen. Therefore, I insist upon knowing it. Are you, at all, engaged to him?"

"While I do not think his matters are the business of anyone, I have no pains in telling you all. No, I am not engaged to him. As I said before, the Colonel is free. But even if we were engaged, I do not believe that there would be anything unnatural about it."

When hearing this, she looked relieved.

"And will you promise me," she said, "that you will never enter into any engagement with him."

"I will do nothing of the sort."

She glared at me.

"Your sister was the same way," she hissed. "So unwilling to oblige me and ignore all the dignities of honor and gratitude."

"Gratitude toward what? You? You have insulted me, madam, in ways that I do not deserve. And who are you to decide Colonel Fitzwilliam's heart? Only he governs himself."

"No, it is not so. I have every right to make my sentiments known, because of your trifling manners of flirtation."

"What?"

"The Colonel needs an heiress. You are as poor as a church mouse."

"Whatever the Colonel chooses to do with his heart, should have no concern of yours. In fact, I daresay that it only concerns himself. Who he chooses to fall in love with is his own affair. Also, my behavior has never been reprehensible towards himself. If there were any true impropriety of my behavior, I think I would be sensible of it."

"That is an erroneous view upon your own conduct. I saw you, while you spoke with Mr. Walter Fairfax, and your behavior left much to be criticized."

"How so?"

"You addressed him with warmth."

I was fuming inside. "He spoke with me, therefore, I believed it proper to speak back. I cannot help it if people ask me questions, and I am not afraid to give an answer. There is nothing base, nor wrong with a lady engaging in conversation."

"A true lady ought to be silent and hold her tongue."

"You don't."

Lady Catherine blinked, and I think that I was the first person to ever point that out. Being caught out in her own hypocrisy, however, was not long-lasting. Soon, she rallied and grew defensive.

"That is different. I am an elderly lady, of noble family, and I am your host."

"My respect for you as a host extends towards that, but *only* that. It does not mean that I have to be treated thus just because you're the mistress of this house. And is not the role of host and guest intertwined? Don't both require respect of each other?"

"I came here to make my sentiments known, and I will be heard," she pressed. "You will cease any attentions you make to the Colonel."

"How will that refrain from the Colonel paying particular attentions to me? He is a free man."

"I am certain that, once he is removed from your company long enough, he will remember what he is about."

"And by that," I sniffed, angrily, "you mean that I am the one who drew him in."

"Through your paltry acts. I don't know what your mother has taught you ladies."

"Oh!" I remarked, for now I saw her mind. Truly, I began to see everything clearly. "I see how it is. I am aware of your desire to separate my sister from your nephew, in favor of him choosing your daughter. Yes, Lady Catherine, I know it all. Just as I know that you, in your heart, never recovered from that disappointment. You still cannot fully forgive that event, can you?"

"The wrong arrangement was made," she stated, "but that is in the past, and I have grown to accept."

"Begging your pardon, your ladyship, but that is nonsense. You are projecting your history with my sister onto me. First, do not think me ignorant of this. You failed to prevent a marriage that you found unsuitable to your taste. And now, this is your last chance to have your way. This is you choosing to write history as you see fit. But these circumstances are quite out of your hands, as they are out of mine. And secondly, I will have no ill words spoken about my sisters. My parents raised us, to the best of their ability, and I am content that most of us have grown up proper and true."

"And what of your younger sister," she spat. "The foolishness of that creature!"

"Whatever my sister has done, it is not reflective on the actions of the other four. No one is responsible for the actions of another when those individuals are so different and separate from one another. If my sisters and I had encouraged Lydia to elope, then we would be partially responsible. However, since none of us encouraged it, and were very surprised when it occurred, no one has any right to place the blame upon us."

"A family with a lady like that is no family."

Driven to my bitter end, I staked my claim like a woman of spirit.

"We *are* family. I daresay that we are true as any other family in the world. As true as yours."

She turned on me with a venomous expression.

"You dare to compare your family to mine. Unfeeling, ignorant, and idiotic child! We are of noble blood, and of superior upbringing."

"Ask your daughter. You might find that she doesn't look down on us."

"You have no right to speak for my child."

"I don't speak for her, but rather, I ask that she be permitted to speak for herself. Maybe she respects us."

"You will no longer deter me from my direct point. I

came here to make my sentiments known, and therefore I have the right to know all. Let me know once and for all. Do you and Colonel Fitzwilliam have a secret engagement?"

For a moment, it hurt to have to say it. I accepted the inconstancy, the unknown aspects of my life, and loves, long ago. However, now, to be difficult, I wished that there was some certainty to it all.

"We have not," I uttered at last.

When hearing this, Lady Catherine closed her eyes, relieved. She had got what she wanted. In that respect, at least. It angered me that I made her so happy. Truly, that was the last thing that I wished to do.

"Colonel Fitzwilliam is unfettered," I continued, unwillingly, "unshackled, and not tied down by me. He is his own man."

"He probably knows that you are not right to marry," she said, "yes, the Colonel knows that."

"Whether my wealth is what stops him, or his preferences," I continued, "it does not change the fact that he does not belittle my worth, as you do. You don't know the half of my experiences with him. But you only know what you have been told. I do not know who informed you of my past with your nephew, but it is not romance that links my life to the Colonel."

"Whatever you call it, it still is a wickedness of drawing a man in through arts and allurements. Let us speak plainly."

I took a deep breath. "I will speak plainer. There is more to the relationship between men and women than just marital options. There is friendship. I am the Colonel's friend. And he is mine. And, if someone were to come along and taint that idea, because their notion of female delicacy is ignoring others, fearing being under other people's suspicions, and not being afraid to bestow one's powers of pleasing, then I will most certainly not adhere to such strict maxims."

"I have never been spoken to in such a manner, excepting you Bennet girls. You lot are like a growth that is detrimental to my family's limbs."

"When last I checked, there were weeds sprouting in your society already."

"And what does that mean?"

I refused to answer her.

"You have spoken what you wish. Is your ladyship quite finished offending me and my family in every method?"

"Authority is not given to you to tell me when and where not to go, in my own house."

"I do not order you to go, your ladyship. I just presumed that you no longer wished to be in my company."

"I do not, but not so hasty, if you please! I still have one more point to carry through."

"One more? I have told you what you wanted, and it was the truth."

"Yes, it was. But now, you must swear to me that, if that you will abandon even friendship with the Colonel, and hardly ever speak to him again."

My eyes widened at this woman's presumption!

"What?" I scoffed.

"If the Colonel tries to rekindle any sort of bond with you, that you will do right and relinquish any friendship at all."

"I will not promise that."

"You will not?"

"No, I will not, and I certainly never shall. I do not know what is in store for me, but if our hearts do find our way to each other, then I will not resist him. I am working to become a practical sort of creature, and I am improving in my own way."

"That is not good enough for him."

"Let him decide what is good for him and leave me to it."

She stood up.

"I could have you removed from this house, immediately."

"That is a choice that your ladyship must make," I said, "but you will find, that I am by no means friendless or helpless. Throw me out, and I will land somewhere. That I promise."

With that, her ladyship left me alone.

Oh spite! Oh hell!

Now that I was alone, I could unleash all my anger and frustrations.

I paced back and forth, back and forth, I felt my insides fuming.

Eventually, I had no choice but to begin talking to myself, as we humans are wont to do when we feel something deeply—or when we are alone and need to unleash something or other.

If anyone were to overhear me, at present, they would think that I was a madwoman.

Unable to control my wrath, I must have been ranting and raving.

How dare she address me in such a way?

First, she had cornered me, pushing her irrational intentions at my feet.

Next, she dared to act as if she had a right to speak for Colonel Fitzwilliam, as if he did not have a mind and will of his own.

Afterwards, she berated my family, unveiling all its insignificance on the world.

I didn't care how wealthy, prestigious, or entitled she regarded herself as.

What was her title to us?

What good did it bring? Ultimately, none of her plans came to fruition, her daughter was intimidated by her, and afraid of having any sort of conversation, for fear of not knowing what to say.

To the outside eye, it could be construed that she was even sickly and cross, when perhaps it was something deeper. Anne de Bourgh was a woman who was never given the chance to chase down any sort of liberty. Her illness limited her but want of spirit also is affected by an inability to voice one's inner sentiments, philosophies, findings, discoveries, and woes.

Was this a home for the girl, or a mausoleum in waiting?

Either way, I was so angry that there was nothing else for me to do. I had to tell someone, and I knew who the first person it was owing to explain myself to.

Chapter Twelve

SIBLING AFFECTION

"She said that!" Elizabeth exclaimed.

Soon after I knew that Lady Catherine was no longer haunting the hallway anywhere near my room (I had Lucy discover where Lady Catherine was, and she reported back to me so that I knew where *not* to walk), I sought out Lizzy and Darcy.

When I heard that they were in the music room, and Darcy was listening to Elizabeth practice, I went to them and immediately told them all that unfolded. To say that Elizabeth was angry, was expected.

What I did not expect was that Mr. Darcy would be equally as bitter.

"I had no notion she was even aware of Richard's feelings for you," Darcy said, frowning. Then he turned to me, concerned. "I want you to believe that I never informed anyone at Rosings of such matters."

"I believe you," I said. "But the fact is that maybe the Colonel and I haven't been so secretive as I expected."

"No," Elizabeth said, "it's not on your part. The fact is

that Colonel Fitzwilliam still feels for you, and his entire family is aware of it."

"You think that those in Matlock told Lady Catherine?"

"It's very possible. After all, Lord Fitzwilliam is Lady Catherine's brother. It would be instinctive for him, or someone else in the family to say something about it."

"Naturally," Mr. Darcy added, "they probably thought it to be something that Lady Catherine would have no opinion over. It's always proper to tell family of one's business. However, I doubt anyone at Matlock would have expected my aunt to take it so abominably."

Elizabeth turned to Mr. Darcy.

"You don't think..."

Mr. Darcy squinted as he looked at her.

"What, Lizzy?"

"I cannot help but wonder. After all, you were your aunt's intended choice for her daughter. Now that we are married, that option is gone. Since Anne's first husband never came to be, there is the possibility that Lady Catherine is now on the hunt for another husband."

Mr. Darcy looked at Lizzy, then me, and he understood the logic of it.

"We won't know for sure," Mr. Darcy continued, "but that is very logical. To swing from one nephew to the other is not all too outrageous."

"And Lady Catherine did stress to me that the Colonel needs a woman with a dowry," I pointed out.

"And Anne de Bourgh has the right sort of one," Elizabeth uttered.

"Yes," Darcy confirmed, "she does."

"That would make sense," Elizabeth furthered, "and now she is replaying the very same scene that she played with me."

"And I am on the receiving end," I said. "Well, this is just delightful."

I plopped into a chair and rubbed my forehead. "And tomorrow is Christmas. So much for goodwill toward one's fellow man. Mr. Darcy?"

"Hm?"

"I'm sorry to put you in this predicament, but how soon can you have the carriage drawn for me? It is terrible that I ought to leave on Christmas Eve, but the Bromley inn is close enough. I can look after myself, I believe. I can spend a Christmas alone."

"Kitty," Elizabeth said, "that is preposterous."

"Preposterous?" I echoed. "I have no choice. Lady Catherine said it herself. She is willing to turn me out of the house as soon as may be. We have to prepare for the fact that soon, I will not be welcome in this house. I'd rather be prepared."

Mr. Darcy looked at me stoically.

"Kitty, you are not going anywhere."

I stopped rubbing my forehead, preparing for the headache that was forming, and I straightened my posture.

"I'm not?" I asked. "But your aunt—"

"Will not dare turn out a guest in so unceremonious a fashion. Especially on a day such as this. Christmastime is a time for family. She will do well to remember that. I will see to it myself."

"Yes," Lizzy said, sitting down next to me and putting her arm around my shoulder. "Darcy shall speak to his aunt, and everything will be put to rights. That, I promise you."

"How can I apologize for such terrible behavior?"

"It's not your fault, Mr. Darcy," I said. "It's your aunt's, and your aunt's alone."

"I'll speak to her after I have sent a letter," Mr. Darcy said, standing up to leave.

"A letter?" Elizabeth asked him.

"I need to write to the Colonel. He needs to know what our aunt said to Kitty. When he does, he can write to her himself. He will convince Aunt Catherine that she is being foolish. If he can be spared from his duties, I will not even be certain if he would ride up to Rosings Park himself, to voice his contempt at how you have been treated."

Mr. Darcy turned to me, directly.

"I will send the letter by express. He needs to know, Kitty."

"Yes," I whispered. "He does. Thank you."

Mr. Darcy went to Elizabeth, took her hand, and kissed it.

"I'll return soon."

"I know that you will," she stared back at him. Both exchanged a look of passion before he left us alone.

Elizabeth watched him as he departed, and I could tell that she was feeling his absence already.

"You really are deeply in love with him, aren't you?" I asked.

Elizabeth smiled.

"You know that I am. He is the best man that I have ever known."

"Not all women fall in love with men for their virtue."

"The same can be said for men. When Darcy fell in love with me, he didn't know any actual good of me. Usually no one does think of that when they fall in love."

"But you did?"

"Yes, I suppose that I did. I did not see that about him for very long, but he needed time. Like I did."

"You married a superior man."

"I am glad that you noticed."

I sighed, stood up and walked to the window.

"Eliza," I began, "I am sorry that I broke my peace and

that I ruined things here. But I need you to know that I couldn't help myself anymore. I could not suppress it—truly, I will never know how to play that game. I've never known how to play *that sort* of game."

"I know. I am not angry with you. I am angry with myself."

This surprised me. Truly, of all things that I expected to hear when she spoke to me, I didn't know that it would be that.

"You're angry with yourself?" I repeated.

"Yes, I am. From the very first day of your coming here, I knew that she was bullying you. She was being subtle in her cruelty, but it was present. And rather than confront her about mistreating my little sister, I did something terrible myself. I told you to try and ignore it. To take her insolence and exchange it with silence on your part."

I nodded. "I understood why you did what you did. It was for the sake of the children that you and Jane are going to have. You wanted peace. And usually, that would be proper. After all, not all battles have to be fought. Sometimes it is best to walk away."

"But when peace is brought at the hands of weakness, it is not properly achieved. I told you to roll over and allow yourself to get abused. I did it for selfish reasons. I did it because I wanted that peace, without thinking about how it affected you. I said to myself, 'soon we shall be gone, and Kitty will be free of it'. I trusted your ability to be self-reliant, but I suppose that is what I have always been doing. Standing by when you get chided for things that are out of your control. I do that a great deal, don't I?"

I didn't answer her, for fear of hurting her feelings. She was a woman who was with child. Of course, she had to think of the baby that was soon to be. I saw where her mind had ended. And sometimes, it is best to not fight back. Some battles are meant to be walked away from. But yes, she was right about chastising herself. When she acknowledged her own fault, I could not deny its existence. And my silence said enough. Words weren't needed. She knew what I felt.

"Kitty," she said, taking my hand, "I promise, I will stop doing that. I am tired often, and right now, I don't have the energy that I usually have. But I won't allow you to suffer under the cruelty of others. I will try and improve. Can you forgive me?"

I smiled.

"Lizzy?"

"Yes?"

"Merry Christmas Eve."

Chapter Thirteen

THE FALL THAT SAVED US ALL

S oon Elizabeth was feeling a little sick, and I could tell that it was due to her delicate state. Ergo, I helped her back to her bedroom, where both Sarah and Betsy tended to her.

Pregnancy seemed to be like a charm that was cast over them, because they didn't bicker the entire time that they assisted her. Since she was in capable hands, I informed them all that I was going to go to Mr. Darcy to tell him where Lizzy was.

On my way there, I had to go down the stairs, to the library where he had gone to.

When I returned from delivering my message, I thought it best to take refuge in Georgiana's room. She had been feeling tired, therefore, she had gone to rest. If I found her asleep, I would not disturb her but quietly go to my room and seek solitude there.

As I began to walk up the steps, I heard a sound coming from the landing. For fear that it was Lady Catherine, I started to flee down the steps again.

I took only a few steps before I realized that it couldn't

be her. The footfalls were too light, and there was more than one person. When I looked up, my nerves immediately quieted down when I saw that it was Mrs. Jenkinson and Anne de Bourgh.

Breathing a sigh of relief, I continued to walk up the steps.

"Good afternoon," I uttered to them both.

"Good afternoon, Miss Bennet," Mrs. Jenkinson said to me, pleasantly. Her cheery reception gave the immediate implication that neither she nor her charge were aware of my disastrous meeting with Lady Catherine.

Then I turned to Anne de Bourgh. While she still had all the meekness of appearance that I grew accustomed to, her eyes were kind, and she looked calmer.

While the mother despised my very existence, the daughter was accepting.

But in life, there are all the little things.

All the moments that you cannot wonder why you are curious about noting certain details.

Perhaps it was because I was happy to see that neither of them hated me.

That led to me analyzing them both.

It also led to me noticing that Anne de Bourgh was wearing the precise same dress that she did when she once tripped on the hem of her gown.

And that led to me noticing that Anne was not being wholly attentive to how she stepped.

Then that led to her foot catching in the cloth.

After which, it all felt as if it was happening to someone else.

But I was there.

It happened to her.

And it also happened to me.

We both were hurled into the predicament that would cause a great stir on Christmas Eve.

Without even knowing it, Anne tripped.

Mrs. Jenkinson was caught completely unawares as her charge fell forward and was about to meet a horrible fate.

I cannot recall how, nor did I even feel as if I was thinking as I rushed up, reached out, and caught Anne de Bourgh in my grasp as my other arm grabbed onto the railing.

She shouted as her body fell into mine, my knees buckled. Anne's body swung around, and we nearly toppled down the stairs that were below us.

But I held firm. I didn't know what I was about. Every single action of mine felt as if it had been controlled by another force as I clung to her on one side, and the banister on the other.

I felt Anne's arms cling to mine as I kept her in my embrace.

"Oh my god!" Mrs. Jenkinson cried out, frozen from the horror of her charge almost dying.

"I..." Anne cried in my arms, as she looked down at the remaining steps. She clung so desperately to me, her nails digging in my arm, that I wondered if I would draw blood from it. When it hurt, I welcomed it. For some reason, the pain had brought me back to life, and out of my instincts.

"I almost," Anne whispered, clinging to me more, "I almost..."

"But you didn't, Anne," I said, forgetting to use her last name. "But you didn't. You are here. You are here."

The cries drew other servants, and soon, many other visitors in the house.

Mrs. Jenkinson finally found the ability to move. She came down the remaining stairs and helped me stand Anne up. Miss de Bourgh was not hurt but merely suffering under shock.

"We must get her to her room," I instructed Mrs. Jenkinson as we helped Anne up the steps.

"She will need some wine," Mrs. Jenkinson said, "and smelling salts. She might swoon. Never fear, Miss de Bourgh, you will be put to rights soon."

"What goes on here!"

That familiar bellow could only belong to one voice.

Closing my eyes, I felt her presence could not have come at a worse time.

Looking over my shoulder, I saw that it was Lady Catherine de Bourgh who had entered, followed by Mr. Bingley and Jane.

When seeing her face, I knew what she was thinking. As she looked up at us, she took this scene out of context.

All she saw was that I, her chief bane, was holding her daughter. Her most prized possession.

And since everyone around us wouldn't know the context to our relationship, they would not know why she might react the way that she did.

My eyes locked with the formidable patroness.

Her eyes locked with mine.

For a second, we were lost in each other's resentment.

The spell was broken when Anne whimpered and asked to be brought to her room.

"Miss Bennet and I will accompany you, my dear," Mrs. Jenkinson said, moving forward. Then she called down to Lady Catherine. "Your ladyship, you must come. Miss de Bourgh has suffered a great shock, and she needs you beside her now."

"Miss Bennet," Lady Catherine bellowed, "remove your hands from my daughter."

She rushed up the steps and pushed me off Anne's arm. This sudden act alarmed everyone. Gasps were heard from all around.

"Kitty!" Jane cried, rushing up the steps to see to me.

"Madam," Mr. Bingley cried, walking up the first step, "Miss Bennet was merely trying to help your daughter, I am sure."

"She was, Mama," Anne de Bourgh said, shocked at her mother's behavior. "Miss Bennet saved my life."

When hearing this, Lady Catherine's eyes enlarged, and then became overwhelmed.

"What could you mean?" Lady Catherine asked.

"It's true, madam," Mrs. Jenkinson said. "Dear Anne nearly fell down the stairs, and Miss Bennet caught her before it grew calamitous. Miss Bennet saved Miss de Bourgh from injury and most likely death itself."

Turning back down to the ground floor, I saw that Mr. Darcy had emerged. Along the landing, Georgiana had come from her room to see what the fuss was all about.

For some reason, I had no inclination to look at Lady Catherine de Bourgh as she heard this news.

I didn't know why, but I got the sense that she would be angrier.

I had done the most unforgivable thing in the world. I had saved the most important thing to her.

After she had forsaken me.

I saw her fail. I saw her make one of the biggest mistakes of her life. She would never forgive me for it.

"Come Anne," Lady Catherine de Bourgh said, "You need rest and some time by the fire. Mrs. Jenkinson, help me."

"Yes ma'am," Mrs. Jenkinson said as I moved aside and stood against the wall.

Imagine my surprise when I felt a hand grab my arm.

Looking up, I saw that it was Anne de Bourgh. She had managed to untangle her arm from her mother's strong embrace.

She opened her mouth to say thank you. But for some reason, the words didn't come to her. But her eyes said it.

"I know," I said for her, "you're welcome."

She placed her hand into mine, shook it, and then allowed herself to be taken away.

When I walked down the steps toward Jane, she reached out to me. I fell into her arms and let her embrace me.

"I think..." I began.

"What?"

"That I am scared. I don't know why I am scared, but I am."

"I know. I know. I'll take you upstairs."

I saw Mr. Darcy, standing down below.

"I will go in one minute. I just need to do something."

Walking down to Mr. Darcy, I leaned up on my tiptoes.

"Have you finished the letter to the Colonel?"

"Not yet."

"Thank goodness. While I would rather you sent the letter, you may also tell him that the matter is resolved. Lady Catherine might never look kindly on me, but she cannot cast me out now."

"She is in your debt."

"Yes, and I suspect that I still might suffer for that as well."

"Yes, you just might."

"Thank you, Mr. Darcy."

I nodded to Mr. Bingley, touched Jane's arm, sympathetic, and then I walked up the stairs.

"Kitty?" Georgiana asked as she met me. "Come into my room."

"You have a headache. I don't want to be bothersome to you."

"Nonsense. Come in."

Going into her room, I allowed myself to be guided by her.

"Sit down," she said, "and—"

Suddenly, I grabbed her arm, to steady myself. For the life of me, I couldn't fathom why, but I had lost my bearings. My eyesight had grown a little hazy, my stomach felt as if I might purge my dinner at any moment, and my knees felt as if they were buckling.

"Georgie, help me," I cried as I began to collapse into her.

"Come, sit down to steady yourself," she said, leading me to the bed to sit down on it.

When she saw that I wouldn't topple over, she wrung the bell.

No more than a few seconds later, Lucy entered.

"Yes, Miss Darcy," she said, then she turned to me, "Miss Bennet, you need something."

"That's what I rung you for," Georgiana said, "Lucy, can you bring Kitty a glass of red wine."

"Yes, I can, Miss Darcy. That'll put you to rights, Miss Bennet. That's flat."

Lucy left as soon as she had come.

"I cannot help but wonder if she was waiting on the other side of the door," Georgiana said, by way of explanation for Lucy's swift entrance.

"Yes," I said slowly, "I believe so."

Georgiana pulled up a chair and sat down opposite me.

"Kitty, what happened?"

Poor Georgiana! I must have looked so broken to her. And no wonder for it. Because I felt it. Every second made my soul feel as if it was cracking up.

"Georgie," I said, "I'm sorry that I am not being so forthcoming. It's strange. A few moments ago, my emotions were not there. And now—it is as if they are coming back with a swiftness, and I don't know why I can't bring words to it."

"Whatever it was, you clearly suffered a big shock. From what I understand, sometimes the body freezes over, preparing itself for whatever it was enduring. Then, afterwards, all the madness, the frenzy, and life returns to them. And they understood what they almost lost."

"That is why I am scared?"

"Perhaps it is. But Kitty, please tell me what it is."

I told her what had happened and when I finished, she praised me.

"Oh, Kitty, you are a hero. Lady Catherine should be thankful for you. And at this time of the year."

"I do not think Lady Catherine will care for me. She will care for the act, but not for me."

"How can you speak so?"

"Because I know so. Georgie, you remember how she treated me when she saw me holding Anne."

"Oh, that was just surprise. But once she accepts the truth of the matter, she will feel as if she owes you a great deal. And you do. You have given her back her child and her future. She will appreciate it, for the rest of her life."

"There is something that you do not know."

"What?"

"I know why Lady Catherine has always been so disagreeable to me. She told me so."

"She did?"

"Yes."

Now it was time for me to tell her what Lady Catherine had said earlier that day. When I finished narrating that part, Georgiana had many things to say about it.

Since most of it was an echo of what Mr. Darcy and Elizabeth said, what I focused more on was her belief that my fortune would change.

"Well," Georgiana said, "all of that is now quite over. Lady Catherine cannot hold down to older prejudices now. She will remember everything about you. And she will be proud of you."

"I do not think so."

"Why not?"

"With some people, when you do a kind thing for them, they don't always believe in gratitude. Rather, she might take it as a reason to be harder on me. Or she cannot bear to see me because I remind her of how she was wrong about something. That will lead to her being silent around me. I am not sure. Only time will tell."

"I cannot believe that. But you are right; only time will tell. And—"

I burst into tears. She stopped talking when she saw that I was breaking up.

"Oh, Kitty," she coaxed, now sitting down next to me. "There, there."

"I was not frightened," I began, "when I saw her foot get caught. No, I was not scared. I was not scared when I saw Anne fall so intensely. No, I was not scared. I was not scared when I knew that, by the way she fell, she would die. Not scared again as I wrapped my arm around her waist and steadied her. I knew, very well, that I could die if I did not hold onto the banister properly. I just knew. My arms, legs and strength just knew. And when Lady Catherine pushed me off her, I was still not scared. But now, all those fears are rushing back. They are all descending upon me, and I don't know why I can't stop weeping. I can't explain it."

"Shock, Kitty. Shock. This is good."

"Why?"

"At this time of year, it's good to know that one's heart is still working."

Lucy returned with the glass of red wine for me.

$\sim$

The next hour led to everyone coming to visit me in Georgiana's room. They wished to inquire after me, and to hear the story from my own point of view.

By the time that I told the story for the fifth time, I felt like I could not tell it again.

Eventually, it came time for supper. Despite all that had occurred, we all sat down, as usual. After all, it is natural for our lives to believe in that one notion: always carry on.

The only one absent was Anne de Bourgh and Mrs. Jenkinson. The Collinses had been invited as well, and Mr. Collins was as verbose as ever when it came to praising the meal. And Lady Catherine talked as if nothing had really happened. When the Collinses joined our party, she was equally willing to distribute the demanding advice that she gave the world.

"Mr. Collins," she said, "you are looking very pecky. You are often leaving too much on your plate."

"Oh, pray, do forgive me, Lady Catherine. With this next dish, I will consume everything that is on my plate. Wonderful meals such as these ought not go to waste."

Lady Catherine turned to Charlotte.

"And are you keeping active, but restful, Mrs. Collins?"

"I am, indeed, your ladyship."

"Now that you are with child, I should tell you what

herbs one ought to eat in abundance, and which ones to avoid. We want that child to come out healthy and whole. After all, a child's life becomes the most important thing in the world to a mother."

"It does, indeed, madam," Charlotte said.

"And it's always best to take note of what foods are good for your child as well and what makes them ill. Miss Bennet?"

Her sudden addressing me made all eyes turn to me. I was equally as surprised at being applied to.

"Yes, your ladyship?" I asked, a little silently.

"As a child, you had favorite dishes yourself, didn't you?"

"Well," I said, "yes, I did."

"It is natural."

She turned her attention back to the pregnant ladies and began to appeal to them.

I didn't need an explanation, but I knew. Deep within. That was the furthest that she could exert herself. It was her way of saying thank you for saving her daughter's life.

And to think, it was Lady Catherine's arguing with me that led to me seeking Lizzy and Darcy.

It was that which led to Mr. Darcy going downstairs to compose a letter to Colonel Fitzwilliam.

It was my going to tell him that Lizzy was in the bedroom that led to me walking up the steps at that particular moment.

It was my walking up the steps that led to me meeting Anne de Bourgh.

And that led to me saving her life.

If all those moments had not happened, if something had been different, then Anne de Bourgh would have died. It was a heavy fall, a terrible fall, and she would not have recovered from it.

All these circumstances led to this one moment.

It all led to saving a life.

By sheer happenstance, Anne de Bourgh's fate was preserved.

Anne de Bourgh would now live.

And her fall was the one to save us all.

Chapter Fourteen

THE NIGHT BEFORE CHRISTMAS

The night before Christmas did not go as one had planned. There were no frightening ghost stories to be told.

Rather, we remained around Lady Catherine, as she told us stories of Christmases that were long past. When she finished her stories, she called on Miss Darcy to play while wishing for her to sing a Christmas carol.

Naturally nervous to sing alone, Georgiana agreed to play while someone sang with her.

Charlotte and Elizabeth agreed to sing while Georgiana applied her talent to the instrument.

We all assembled, while the three ladies went to the instrument and began to perform 'Joy to the World'.

The performance, done by the firelight, and with the Christmas tree standing in the main parlor, was enough to stir the sense of goodwill and cheer amongst us all.

When it ended, we cheered merrily, and Lady Catherine expressed her wish to hear another song.

"I am not against the notion of it," Georgiana said, "but

aunt, I am a little in the mood for dancing. I know that we have not men enough, but I was wondering if you would allow us to dance a reel. It just feels correct."

"Well," Lady Catherine said, looking around the room, "I do not find it altogether agreeable. I never believed that these hallowed halls of Rosings should lend themselves to such gaiety."

"Dancing is not a serious enough activity for the sacredness of this establishment," Mr. Collins said.

I sighed. I had wished to dance.

Mr. Darcy seemed to notice this, so he leaned forward, and whispered over my shoulder.

"You wish to dance, don't you?" he asked me.

"Yes, I confess that I do."

"I had a feeling."

Mr. Darcy stood up.

"Aunt Catherine," he declared, "music is your delight, but for some of the ladies, well—it is Christmas Eve. Surely, you remember the gaiety of standing up to a partner at such a merry time. And besides, I have never seen you dance yourself. Rosings can shed its solemnity and aspire to moments of levity at such a time. It's the season for smiles."

"Also," Mr. Bingley added, "some of us men admire the activity as well and are far from objecting to dancing. And if it is a concern of lacking men, then it must be recalled that three of our ladies are in a delicate condition."

"Sadly, so," Jane acknowledged, "we cannot dance, at present."

"But that should not stop the company from enjoying themselves," Elizabeth supported. "Charlotte and I can play while the rest of the company dances, and Jane can turn the page for us."

"And," I added, "if there are still not enough men, some of your servants can be produced to assist us."

"To have a servant stand up with you ladies," Lady Catherine declared, "that is highly improper."

"A servant man has been known to dance as well as gentlemen," I added gently, but not as a means to be contrary. "It is just...this is the time of year not to care for stations."

"And our Holy Redeemer has believed in meek..." Anne said.

Her sudden speaking made everyone turn to her. Alert and surprised. When she and Mrs. Jenkinson had finally joined us, she had been silent the whole time.

"Yes, Miss de Bourgh?" Enara encouraged.

When seeing us all look at her, she suddenly grew apprehensive.

"Well," Anne said, "never mind. It is nothing."

She looked back down at her hands, and I could tell that she didn't wish to contradict her mother. Her mother was, after all, her mother.

"It is just," I continued, "it's such a wonderful time of year...to forget station."

"Imagine," Georgiana supported me, "if some servants dance with us, it can be said that we embraced the spirit of giving."

"Well," Lady Catherine said, not fully giving in, just yet. "First let us see who is standing up with whom, and then we can apply to see who else is required."

This was accepted and Enara, Georgiana, Lady Catherine, Mrs. Jenkinson, and I were the chief ladies to have partners. Mr. Darcy, Mr. Bingley, Arthur, and Mr. Collins were the main men to stand up with us. Since Lady Catherine was not inclined to dance, at first, it made the choice easy.

Since the Boulanger worked perfectly with the song 'We Wish You a Merry Christmas', they sung it as we danced the first set. The dancing proved to be the perfect sort of diversion that allowed the Christmas cheer that we wanted.

When we ended, we clapped for Elizabeth and Charlotte. But inevitably, when one dance ends, another dance is always demanded to occur. I confess that I was part of the voices that encouraged another set. In the corner, Anne de Bourgh sat.

"What of you, Miss de Bourgh?" I asked her. "Do you not care to dance?"

This sudden question made Anne stand more alert in her seat. But once she adjusted to it, she smiled slightly and began to stand up.

"Anne's health still prevents her from dancing," Lady Catherine declared.

"Oh, very well. My apologies."

When Anne de Bourgh saw me retreat away from her, she stood up.

"Oh," Anne said, "but Mama, I think I can brave one dance."

"If Miss de Bourgh finds that it does not suit her," Arthur Philips said, "then she can always sit down." Not even waiting for Lady Catherine to object, Arthur walked up to Miss de Bourgh and offered her his hand. "Miss de Bourgh, I would be honored."

Anne blushed, slowly took his hand and she stood up gently.

When doing so, Mrs. Jenkinson looked a little nervous, Lady Catherine looked slightly bewildered, and the rest of us were merely curious.

Her ladyship was not left to wonder at her daughter's

nerve for more than a few seconds before Mr. Bingley approached her and offered her his hand to dance.

Lady Catherine was amazed. I daresay that she had not been asked to dance in many a year. But the flattery that comes to being asked always takes hold, she accepted Mr. Bingley's offer and stood up with him.

"If we are to dance," Lady Catherine said, "we should do Sir Roger de Coverly."

Mr. Darcy took Enara's hand to dance, and that left only Mr. Collins to be between Georgiana and me. To spare Georgiana from having to dance with my tedious cousin, I asked one of the servants if he was willing to stand up with my sister-in-law. Since he was a young and handsome man, the servant felt this compliment very keenly, and Georgiana was not against his offering his hand.

"Well," Mr. Collins declared as he approached me, with a jovial look, "my fair cousin, it is my great pleasure to stand up to the quadrille with you."

"Thank you, cousin," I said, accepting my fate. As I took his hand, over his shoulder, I saw Georgiana mouth the words 'thank you' to me. Well, if one of us had to suffer, it might as well have been me.

~

To give Elizabeth and Charlotte a rest from playing, Mrs. Jenkinson offered to perform herself, while Charlotte and Elizabeth sang beside her. The music began, and soon into the dance, Mr. Collins stepped on my foot.

"My dear cousin," Mr. Collins said, "I apologize."

"It's well, sir," I replied.

"For a second, I was just thinking if you remember, when we danced together, at Netherfield Park."

"Oh, is that what you were thinking?"

"Yes. Do you remember it?"

"I remember it very well."

You stepped on my frock and tore the bottom of it. Mr. Collins, how could I forget?

"I declare, I do not think that I could ever remember a happier moment than that evening. And now to know that by going there, not only was my happiness sealed, but now to know that my cousin is responsible for saving Miss de Bourgh's life! You have made me very proud of you, Kitty. I never thought I would be so, for, when we first met, I did not think you would become such a lady. But now, you have proven to be of immense value. From myself and Mrs. Collins, we do indeed appreciate your coming here."

His insult was followed by a compliment. Usually, he worked by way of the reverse of that, but such is life. I thanked him for recognizing my actions, unlike Lady Catherine, who was still silent on the matter. But that was as far as it had gone. Mr. Collins was of the opinion that I had little value until I saved Anne's life. Now that I had done something that benefited him, and his reputation by association with me, I was now within range of his respect and notice. I was, as he put it, of value. But this was another game that I did not want to play. Especially on the night before Christmas.

"And returning back to our happy time at the Nether-field Ball," he continued, "it was all so enchanting. For there is where I met my dear Charlotte. Indeed, I was quite enraptured from the very beginning."

"You were? I had not known this, for I do recall when you first considered my sister, Jane, and then you proposed to my other sister, Elizabeth, when you discovered that Jane was soon to be engaged."

"Oh, that!" He chuckled nervously. "Yes, that moment of my own misdirection did occur. Naturally, feeling called upon to do what was right, by duty and devotion to one's family, I was aware of the injury that I caused your household, from the entailment."

While that was a matter which I had considered, time and age had allowed me to view it from another perspective. Yes, Mr. Collins was ridiculous. Yes, none of us could ever entertain the idea of marrying him—excepting Mary, for a time. However, there was a kindness and nobility to the idea that he did try to consider our feelings.

"But when your sister refused me," Mr. Collins responded, "she was indeed providing a kindness. Not only did it give me the chance to choose the perfect wife by way of my dear Charlotte. However, she also quitted me of any guilt or ill-feelings for when I inherited Longbourn. The matter was settled, all in my favor, and I daresay that God has been very good to me."

"Yes, he has," I said. Since it was the night before Christmas, I thought it best to bestow a kindness toward him. "Mr. Collins, I shall be very honest with you. I despised the idea of you inheriting Longbourn. Perhaps, inside of me, I still do. However, here and now, I wish for you to know that I do appreciate the honorable inclination to have married one of us, so not to turn us out of our own home. That was kindly meant and very good of you."

He smiled at this concession, for it naturally would have swelled his pride and self-assurance. However, I was not about to abandon who I was fully. While I did want him to feel that his good intentions ought to be praised, I still did not want him to believe that he was beyond any sort of reproach. As such, I could not help myself but naturally recall another occurrence that gave me some bitterness.

"However," I said, "while you are a clergyman, often our Holy Book does teach forgiveness. Does it not?"

"It does indeed," Mr. Collins said, cheerfully. "Truly, I am happy that you have now bent your mind to more serious application. When I first met you, as well as your younger sister, your intentions were more angled toward less proper subjects."

Ah, there was the Mr. Collins that I knew and despised! I knew it would show its ugly head eventually. It is nice not to be disappointed, and it made what I had to do all the easier.

"Well then, Mr. Collins," I said, "if that be true, then I think I have been reading our book in a more thorough way than yourself."

He looked at me with a look of incredulous discomfort. "Eh?"

"Well, our New Testament teaches forgiveness, yes?"

"Indeed, it does. Most admirably written."

"And you are a clergyman who preaches of such matters, very thoroughly."

"You are very keen to notice."

"Thank you. Well, I do recall, when my sister, Lydia, had her unfortunate plight, you advised my father to abandon her, and leave her to the product of fate. Well, when you wrote to him, where were your teachings of forgiveness? Of telling a man to abandon his child, due to youthful folly, under the excuse of morality, when that same morality orders you, as a clergyman, to be there for such young people? And not against them."

When I said that, Mr. Collins missed his dance step and made a mistake in our dance.

When he regained his proper footing, Mr. Collins stuttered, completely perplexed on how to respond to what I said.

"Well," he continued, "in such matters, the matter is complicated in a way that you do not understand."

"Do not tell me that I do not understand, by assuming that you are more intelligent than I am. I have spent a great portion of my life with people telling me that I do not understand merely because they think they are wiser than myself. Whenever that happens, they fall flat upon their face. Pray, do not assume that your education makes your ways of comprehension superior to mine. It leads to improper pride, and pride leads to hubris, and you result in creating a sword that you fall upon. I *do* know what I am about. And I tell you this now, do you know why clergymen were invented? Do you know what your purpose is?"

"I am certain that I do, in a very cemented way. It is to preach and practice the sanctity of our incredible lord and savior. It is also to bring the souls of my congregation to a better way and prepare them for God, and heaven beyond."

"Well, if that be the case of your profession, how can you prepare souls, when you are preaching to parents to abandon their children for making mistakes? That is not fulfilling the act of forgiveness, nor is that bringing sinners back to the world of morality. It is only exiling and estranging families away from each other. And forgetting the preaching of our religion. I find that I cannot agree, sir. And that, I feel is *common sense*."

Mr. Collins was appalled by my speech, in a very subtle way. However, he could not disentangle himself from the dance, because it would be improper for him to insult Mr. Darcy's sister-in-law, Miss Darcy's friend, and Anne de Bourgh's savior.

"Therefore," I said, "I give you both praise and criticism. Again, I thank you for having initially wished to save our family from being homeless and destitute, but never tell a parent to abandon their child, because of strict maxims that is not fair to the longevity of their bond. Very few mistakes are worthy of permanent exile. I do not approve of my sister's actions, but it was not worthy of banishment. It was worthy of chastisement. As a clergyman, if you teach forgiveness, I ask that you understand it. And I look forward to your sermon on Sunday's service."

The dance came to an end. We bowed to each other, and Mr. Collins was probably happy to be quitted of me.

When it came to him and me, a leopard cannot change its stripes.

~

When the Collins' departed, Lady Catherine wanted us to sit down for a little longer before we retired.

As we walked back to the parlor, having just seen Mr. and Mrs. Collins to the carriage that Lady Catherine had arranged for them, I felt an arm brush against mine.

Turning to my left, I saw that it was Miss Anne de Bourgh.

"Miss de Bourgh," I said.

"Yes."

"Well...did you enjoy your dance with Mr. Philips?" I asked her.

"Yes, I did. I—I did. Very much."

"Very good."

"It...it was my first dance."

My eyes widened.

"What?"

"Yes. It—it was my first dance."

"For a first dance, you didn't miss one step."

"I would prac—practice by myself, when no one was noticing."

"I see. Well, I am happy that you were able to have such a delightful experience, and on Christmas Eve as well."

"Yes. It does feel like a miracle for me." When speaking gentler, she lowered her tone. "I heard how my mother spoke to you... after the incident. I don't know why she spoke so. And I also fear that I have been remiss in showing my thanks. But I am doing so now. Thank you. It is quite possible that you have saved my life. I will not forget it."

"Miss de Bourgh, I thank you for caring for my actions," I said, "but also, no thanks are required at all. I did what was the right thing to do, and all I can say is that I am happy that you are well now."

"I am sorry...if I have been cold since you all have arrived."

"I understand that it is just your way. You are naturally quiet."

"It is not just that. I never learned how to converse easily with strangers. My illness and my state of life has never put me much in the way of learning social etiquette, as it has with you. I just want you to know that my silence is in no way a disrespect toward you or your family. In fact, I..."

"You what?"

"I envy you."

What a confession!

What a thing to hear the daughter of a great lady say!

And it could not have come as more of an astonishment.

"Me?" I questioned. "You envy me?"

"Yes, I do."

"How could that be?" I asked. "You are wealthy, and I am poor. Your family is of nobility. Mine is not. I have no importance in the world, but what I create for myself."

"You are pretty."

"You are not unhandsome."

"But I am not remarkable. You are. And you are not perpetually ill and seem to be free of having to remain in the same house day in and day out. You act like a woman who has gone to places by yourself."

Ah. The harsh luxuries of Anne de Bourgh's life! She was born to wealth, but that wealth came with many trappings.

She was given a body, but her illness trapped her inside of it, and her spirit never was able to rise to any sort of independence.

Even when one is rich, there is confinement.

When one is poor, there is confinement.

When one is stricken with ailment, you are confined to the bed.

When one has a brilliant constitution, one is confined to tend to the ill in their family, or to constantly be employed.

It seems like, no matter what path we are given in life, we all lose.

But for Anne de Bourgh to have been blessed with so much, and then for so much to be taken from her—she might never be given a chance at the life that she had been born into.

"You have much of your life that I ought to be jealous over," I said, "but maybe that's not what you want to hear. Miss de Bourgh, you have your second life. You can do much with it and cast off envy. Tomorrow is Christmas. When that happens, humanity can say well done. And we can feel born again. We can say that we are almost out of the dark."

She did not cry at my words, but her eyes grew misty.

"Well then," Anne said, at last. "As you say... as you say. But in the end, at least let me feel like I am in your debt."

"You are not."

Then suddenly, I had an idea.

~

Sometimes, it is best to relieve people of the debt they owe you.

Other times, it is best to remember it.

But only if nothing mercenary could come of that.

And I had the perfect notion.

"Miss de Bourgh," I contradicted my previous assessment, "you say that you are in my debt. Then I will ask for one favor, and that will put an end to what you owe me. It is a favor that is simple, is free, is moral, and only requires a lady of the house to help me."

"A favor?"

Her eyes widened in wonder.

"If you are worried that I will ask for something that is painful, it is not. It has to do with tomorrow."

"Tomorrow?"

"Yes."

Anne looked ahead.

"It is just that no one has ever asked me for a favor before."

"Well, then this is a new experience for you."

She breathed in heavily.

"What is this favor?"

"It is a Christmas tradition of our family. My sisters and I would do this every year, on Christmas morning. But two of my sisters are not here. And we are not at home. Also, my sister, Mrs. Darcy, really wants to reconcile with this part of the family, and to make us all feel united. This might help."

"What is this tradition?"

I told her about it, and when I finished, she was amenable to the plan. In fact, for the first time, I thought that she looked excited.

She agreed to help me, and that was all that I needed.

"Anne," Lady Catherine called to her, "come sit by me."

Anne obeyed and went to her mother. Lady Catherine looked at me quickly, then looked back into the fire.

I proved to be everything that she did not want me to be. She still might never fully forgive me.

As we sat down in the parlor, I was giddy of knowing that tradition would not die.

In life, there is always so much change that some things need to remain constant.

With us Bennet ladies, this was such a thing.

Skipping up to Elizabeth, I whispered into her ear.

"Our Christmas tradition is alive."

"It is?" she whispered back.

"Yes. It is. Tell Betsy and Sarah. And I will tell Lucy."

"Oh, you may depend on me for that."

"I know that I will."

I rushed over to Jane, gave this confirmation, and she was delighted.

"Oh, that is too wonderful," Jane replied to me. "I will tell Enara."

"Thank you."

In the back of the room, I saw Georgiana standing by the window. Going there, I joined her as we watched the snow fall.

"We will have a white Christmas," she commented.

"Yes," I said, "we just might. I am glad of it."

"I don't know, but when I look at the snow, I feel as if I can go anywhere, and everywhere."

"Yes, so do I. I think it's because the snow comes at the end of a year and at the beginning of a new year. It always makes one feel born again, and as if they can start over."

"Precisely. Kitty, I want to start over."

"Georgie...me too. But until then, I got something that I wanted."

"And what is that?"

"A tradition. And it's time that you were a part of it."

Chapter Fifteen

CHRISTMAS DAY

reams. Sometimes, they come.

Other times, you close your eyes, hours pass, and when you wake up, it was as if you had only blinked since the last time that your eyes were open.

On the night before Christmas, I had no dreams. And I guess that I would have had it no other way. For when I woke up the next morning, I was as alert as ever.

It was the light.

That is what awoke me.

As was her usual custom in the morning, Lucy entered, drew back the curtains and the sunlight fell into my room. Usually, I was already awake, however, this morning, my body and my mind must have been exhausted. For the first time, the sun's light upon my face is what woke me.

"Lucy!" I exclaimed.

"Begging your pardon, miss," she said, "but I'm just so used to you being awake at this point, and Lady Catherine is very particular about the time."

"I understand," I said, rubbing my face, to help me

wake up. It truly did feel like it was only a second ago that it was nighttime.

"Miss," Lucy declared, "come and see."

Refusing to be sluggish, I jumped out of bed and dashed over to the window.

"I cannot believe it."

I woke up to find that it was snowing heavily. The ground was already white, and the tree branches had icicles hanging from them.

"It was snowing even before I woke up," Lucy said.

"I cannot believe it!" I laughed, grabbing her arms, excited, "I cannot believe it."

"Oh, it'll make a believer out of anybody."

"Yes, it just might."

I looked out of the window again.

"Lucy?"

"Yes, missus."

"Merry Christmas."

"Aye, Miss Bennet. Merry Christmas."

Filled with the rave that comes from being overjoyed, I must've looked like a madwoman to Lucy.

"Last night I took a chance. Let's see if it will be productive!"

Grabbing my robe, I put it on as I rushed out of my room.

Going into the hallway, I went to every guestroom and knocked boldly on the door.

"Come out to a new morning!" I cried. "Come out! It's Christmas Day!"

I was not left to wait for long. Soon, Jane, Elizabeth, Georgiana, and Enara exited. Afterwards, I went to Anne de Bourgh's door, and I knocked on it gently.

"Miss de Bourgh," I said, "are you awake?"

Quicker than I expected, the door opened, and Anne

de Bourgh was there, already dressed in her robe and with her servant behind her.

"I was worried that you would forget about me," she uttered.

"Why would I do that?" Over her shoulder, I saw her servant, Bithiah. "Come too, Bithiah. Don't you dare leave us incomplete?"

Bithiah pointed to herself, astonished.

"Me, miss?"

"Yes," Sarah said, dashing into the room and pulling Bithiah's arm. "This is Christmas, Bithiah. Don't be a dunce and come along!"

Ah, Sarah and Betsy. There is something to be said for headstrong women.

All the ladies of the house, and our attending servants, filed into the hallways and we each linked hands.

"Since there are too many of us to be a circle in the hall-way," I said, "we are going to be like a chain. Miss de Bourgh will lead us!"

With us forged together, into one chain, our husbands and relatives stood in their bedroom doorways, rubbing their eyes as they watched us.

With all eyes on Anne de Bourgh, she felt the compli-ment of it. Gathering her courage, she began to sing:

'Hark the herald Angels sing'

We all joined her as we began to skip through the hallways.

Glory to the newborn King,
Peace on earth and mercy mild,
God and sinners reconciled!
Joyful, all ye nations, rise

Join the triumph of the skies
With th'angelic host proclaim
Christ is born in Bethlehem!

When beginning a tradition in a home, you worry that the magic will not be the same.

That the very innocence that you had created will die.

As such, the wisest thing one can go into life with is no expectations. It is the only way that one can overcome being disappointed from the left, right or center. But we all cannot help but ignore our own maxims, sometimes, and go into situations with expectations anyway.

And those expectations were met.

Merrily, we skipped through the halls, singing to fill up all the hallowed solemnity of the place. For a quick second, Rosings Park lost all its elite grandeur and became a simple and lovely place.

As we were about to begin our next verse, we moved down another hallway that, to my ignorance, belonged to Lady Catherine. When hearing the noise, she emerged from her room, with her hair still wrapped up and tying her robe over her nightgown.

"What is the meaning of this?"

When seeing her daughter's cheery face, Lady Catherine squinted, as if she was doing her best to recognize her daughter.

"Oh, Mama!" Anne said, grabbing her hand, "come. It is Christmas Day."

"But," Lady Catherine stuttered, being pulled, too overwhelmed to put up a fight. "What's all this?"

"Just join in," Anne stressed, and she continued to sing, and we all joined in with her again.

Hail the heav'n-born Prince of Peace!

Hail the Son of Righteousness!
Light and life to all he brings,
Ris'n with healing in his wings.
Mild he lays his glory by,
Born that man no more may die;
Born to raise the sons of earth,
Born to give them second birth.

Since Lady Catherine was so overpowered by the sight of her daughter looking happy, she didn't remain in a perplexed state.

Instead, being the lady of the house, she felt it was her duty to remain in the front of the line, leading the procession. She joined in with the rest of us, and when we all ended, our men had followed behind, clapping for us.

"Well," Mr. Bingley declared, "now we can fully say Merry Christmas."

❧

We sat down to a late breakfast, and afterwards, we all joined around by the fire and tree to unwrap our Christmas presents.

Elizabeth and Darcy had bought me a shawl.

Jane had given me a new bracelet. All the presents that I gave were appreciated, but I never knew if they were what anyone really wanted. I always was a little apprehensive about gift-giving. For, no matter what, it's hard to give presents to a set of people who already have everything that they want.

I was the only one of us who had anything to wish for or want. With everyone else around me, they had the pin money to get themselves anything they wished at a moment's notice. Therefore, I would always be at a disadvantage.

We all were given a great surprise, however, when the men had a surprise for us.

"Since we were worried that you ladies might not be able to maintain your Christmas tradition," Mr. Bingley said, "we gentlemen had been preparing a carol for you all as well. Hopefully, this will be worthy of you."

We all sat down as the men gathered around the pianoforte.

"Forgive our coarse voices," Arthur Philips said, "some of us have not practiced under a master in years."

We all assured them that we were looking forward to their endeavor.

Arthur sat down at the pianoforte and began to play.

"I didn't know Arthur knew how to play," Enara whispered to me.

"I forgot that he ever did," I whispered back.

As Arthur began to play, he, along with Mr. Bingley and Mr. Darcy began to sing 'Oh Come All Ye Faithful'.

Their three voices were deep and masterful, and they sung it with such incredible strength, that despite myself, I was almost moved to tears.

When I turned to see Elizabeth and Jane, they were unable to be anything else but emotional. Be it from their natural affection for their husbands, or because being with child made them prone to sensibility, the tears were doing everything to escape from their eyes and roll down their cheeks.

When they finished, we all clapped and stood to shower them with our compliments.

Mr. Darcy, who was not accustomed to being so much on display, could not help but blush.

"Mr. Darcy," I whispered to him, "you betray yourself."

"Do I?" he responded.

"Yes. Your cheeks are turning red."

Instinctively, he began to touch his cheeks, as if that would help remove the crime of being a blushing husband.

I laughed.

"You laugh at me?" he asked.

"No, you dolt. I laugh with you."

Darcy did something he did not often do: he half-smiled.

"Merry Christmas, Kitty," he said to me.

"Merry Christmas, Mr. Darcy. I want to believe that you have gotten all that you wanted this year."

"Except for the occasional conflicts that came from the world pushing itself into our lives, yes, I did."

"Oh, you know as well as I do that you cannot help the occasional conflict. It helps to remind us all that we are needed somewhere."

"Do you like the world always finding its way back into our lives, even the worst parts of it?"

"I don't know, now that I come to think of it. I like the society, and all the interactions that come with it, but there is a certain amount of stress that it can place on a person. It's like it's a weight of heavy baggage that can oppress someone."

"It does do that," he said, "but Kitty, tell me, are you happy?"

"Do you know what?"

"What?"

"I am not certain that I have a good answer for that either. This holiday has been a series of ups and downs, for my part."

"I do not just mean this holiday, but in general. Are you happy?"

Why was he asking me this? Did he do it because the

spirit of the holiday moved him, or because he was worried about me? Or did Elizabeth tell him to see about me?

"Mr. Darcy, I confess that I will always be a little apprehensive here, and that does dictate much of my happiness. However, you know what? Here and now, I am very happy."

"That's good. And thank you for saving my cousin's life."

Ah, now it comes down to it! I saved Anne's life, and now he might have felt even more drawn to the idea of caring for my feelings. I was not offended, because it was only natural.

"It was the right thing to do. You are welcome." For some reason, I felt also drawn to the spirit of bestowing gratitude. "Mr. Darcy, I really must thank you."

"For what?"

"For everything. For taking me in. For not telling me that I was not good enough for the Colonel. For not slighting my friendship with the Colonel or Finlay. And for protecting me. I have said it before, but now, I feel that I must say it, more than ever."

"You're welcome, but the advantages are manifold. My sister adores you, Kitty. She's had quite a few friends in her life, but none of this size before. You are the proper companion for her. She needed a woman of her age, who was not stricken with insufferable pride or obsession with connections. She just wanted a true friend, and you gave her that. I owe you for that as well."

"She is the best friend that I have ever had. You owe me nothing for that either."

We both looked at each other, awkward. Then I laughed.

"Oh, for the love of Mab!" I declared. "Both of us will not accept thanks, will we?"

"We are making terrible work of it."

"Mr. Darcy!" Elizabeth called to him.

We turned to her.

"I think that I wish to have my husband explain his good singing voice, and why he hid it from me," she said.

Mr. Darcy turned to me.

"Your sister calls me."

"Run to her."

"All I know how to do is walk quickly."

"That works equally as much."

He nodded to me.

"I am proud of you," I said to him.

When hearing that, his eyes relaxed.

"Really?" he asked.

"Yes, I am."

"I am proud of you as well."

He went to Elizabeth, sat down with her, and placed his hand on her stomach, to feel its size.

Now I saw why Mary fell in love with Mr. Darcy. She saw the hero underneath. Thank goodness *that* love didn't last.

Elizabeth was the right Bennet sister for him.

Regarding myself, only time would tell who I was meant for...if I was meant for anyone.

Chapter Sixteen

THE REQUEST

L ater that evening, when it was time to retire to bed, I was sitting down at my desk, writing in my journal. Lucy was arranging a bedwarmer under my sheets, to help me remain comfortable as I slept.

"Writing about what happened today?" Lucy asked, over her shoulder.

"Yes," I responded, almost finished writing my entry. "Did you enjoy our procession through the hallways?"

"Yes." She laughed. "I hadn't had such fun like that on Christmas Day, in years."

"I never got the chance to ask," I said, still writing, "what do you servants do on Christmas Day? Because it's not as if you are given a day off. It's one of the busiest days for the household."

"Well, it's difficult. Most of us don't get the chance to go home on Christmas Day to our families—usually. But we servants learn to understand the benefit of helping one another. If there is a servant who has a lot of family, us single women and men will take up the course of the work on the holiday."

"Oh, so that way, the servants with families can have Christmas Day off?"

"Yes, miss. And then, when they return, they take our shift, and we can have an extra day off."

"That makes sense. Proper scheduling really does help the world go around, doesn't it?"

"Aye, miss, so much so that we spend most of our lives doing just that: scheduling. Promise me that you won't write too late, miss? I don't want you straining your eyes."

"I promise," I assured her, "I am almost done."

"Good, and I'm happy you had a good Christmas—"

We were interrupted when there was a knock on the door.

Lucy gave me a look.

"Must be Georgie," I said.

"Yes, of course, it is," Lucy answered, going to the door.

"Actually, it's not her," I said, recognizing the knock. "Be prepared."

When she opened the door, she jumped back immediately and became more formal.

"Lady Catherine."

I sat upright in my seat.

Lady Catherine entered, still wearing the gown that she wore at supper. Even her hair was still done up.

"Your ladyship," I said, guardedly, standing up. "I confess that I am surprised to see you."

"I can imagine so," she answered, looking at Lucy. Reading Lady Catherine's expression, Lucy excused herself immediately, and her ladyship and I were left alone.

~

Lady Catherine sat down.

So, I felt that there was nothing to do but sit down as well.

There we were, facing each other, and feeling all the weight of past incidents.

"Did you enjoy your Christmas?" she asked me.

"Indeed, I did. I thought that our Longbourn tradition would be lost, but it was your daughter who helped me maintain it."

"My daughter is a superior creature."

She was a protective mother, who was facing the young woman who protected her child instead of doing it herself. And it was a woman who she hated. I was willing to let her win her battles where she may.

"Yes," I agreed, "yes, she is. She looked very happy today as well."

"If she ever were to get well, I might send her to Pemberley one day. She might want to be in Georgiana's society. And she might be in your company as well. You both might wish to remain at Rosings Park after New Years. If you wish it, I can tell my nephew."

She wanted me to stay at Rosings Park now? This woman could not make up her mind about anything.

"Thank you, your ladyship. That is a great honor, however, I owe it to my parents and relatives in Hertford-shire, to see them again. I have not seen my mother and father for quite a few months now. It would be wrong not to return and spend some time with them."

"Of course. Respect for one's family is natural, and it does you credit."

"Thank you, Lady Catherine. Did you enjoy this Christmas as well? You looked happy to join our dance."

"It made my daughter happy. Therefore, it made me so. Of course, I want it understood that, in the future, Rosings Park is not the sort of establishment that shall entertain such frivolity. I only allowed such behavior because it was Christmas Day, and it made Anne content. But in the future, you will not do anything in my house, without inquiring to me first. And such activities will not be permitted. Do I make myself quite clear on the subject?"

I was tired, and I had no inclination to put up a fight. I just wanted this all to be over.

"Yes, madam," I said, "if I ever do visit Rosings Park again, it will be so."

"Good."

She stood up and began to leave. Then, she turned around and faced me again.

"My daughter is my prize possession."

"Yes, she is. I can tell."

"If anything were to ever happen to her, I don't think I could...but no matter. She is alive, and that is all that counts. I do not deny that the service that you have rendered has fulfilled my happiness. I am very—I acknowledge that I might have appeared ungracious before. Well, I am here to correct that mistake. You saved my daughter's life. As such, I thank you, Miss Bennet."

"You are most welcome, your ladyship. I could not have done otherwise. Anne has a good heart. I see that about her."

"Yes, she does. Her ailments keep many from noticing that about her. But her heart is very true. Now, you need your rest."

Now that she had reluctantly showed her penitence, Lady Catherine moved to depart again. She had her hand on the doorknob when I was seized with a realization.

Whether she liked it or not, her instinct would be to feel as if she was in my debt.

And I was in the mood to take advantage of that.

"Lady Catherine," I began, "I have to ask you something."

"Me? What, pray?"

"I understand why you wanted Anne to marry Mr. Darcy. It would have united both Rosings Park and Pemberley, while also supplying Anne with a husband who is constant and is devoted to family."

"Yes," Lady Catherine said, "it had all the proper ingredients to a perfect match for my child. And that, augmented by the romance of my sister and I planning the match since both our children were in the cradle—it was a dream and dearest wish of her and I for so many years."

"Disappointment had no choice but to be natural," I acknowledged, "yet I must request that you overcome it. My sister is the best woman for your nephew. You have seen them together, and you can see the love in their eyes. You see how she brings life to him."

Lady Catherine clutched the doorknob, leaned against it, and looked away from me, shuddering.

For a moment, I worried that she was suffering from a seizure.

I wanted to go to her, but I was scared to.

"Your ladyship!"

"I am well," she assured me, standing up straight again. "I am. Forgive me. My ankles suddenly grew weaker for a moment. That is all."

"Yes," I answered, accepting her lie.

"You are correct," she said, slowly and heavily. Every word that escaped her lips now felt like a burden to say. "They are properly matched."

"And my sister dared to come here, knowing your history with her, in hopes of establishing a relationship with the rest of Darcy's family. She was willing to face insults being hurled, and even asking me to sacrifice my pride, for the sake of family peace. I understood why, but my patience had limits, as you know. Therefore, I ask you now, madam, please accept my sister as Mr. Darcy's wife. You suffered a disappointment, I know, and it set you down. It hurt you. But be brave, Lady Catherine, and conquer your heart. Please, this Christmas, this is the only thing I want from you. Accept my sister as part of the family."

Lady Catherine did not answer me but only nodded and left.

Who knew what tomorrow would bring?

Chapter Seventeen

PASSIONS

The next day, Lady Catherine did the unexpected: she actually listened to me.

While maintaining her dictatorial manner, there was a kinder tone to her attitude towards my family. She spoke to me rarely, but I did not lament it. In fact, I understood her. Now that I did not live down to how she viewed me, the embarrassment was still too much for her to bear. And since I still was a little distraught from our history, and the change of the dynamic in our circle, I didn't know how to talk to her either.

But what I did notice was that people looked on me a little differently since I saved Anne's life. Our company seemed to look on me with a strange sort of reverence—or always in expectation of something. It was almost as if they assumed I would do something or say something clever, every now and again. Only Jane looked at me in the same manner as she had always done so, and I could not think why she was different.

The days leading up to New Years passed very casually.

We visited Hunsford Parsonage, where Charlotte and

Mr. Collins showed us the presents that Sir William Lucas and Lady Lucas sent to them.

On Sunday, we attended Mr. Collins's church service, and listened to his sermons. When reading from a holy chapter, he forgot his place twice, stuttered a few times during his lecture, and repeated the same line a couple of times. Repetition for effect is one thing, but he was doing something else entirely. And it didn't work at all.

When the sermon was ended, we complimented him on the service anyway, because sometimes, the truth is not the right thing to do.

But there were highlights to the remaining days.

For after Christmas, there are often the rush of letters arriving, and messages that we must send.

We received two letters from Colonel Fitzwilliam. The first was addressed to the entire family. Since he was another one of Lady Catherine's favorite relatives, she ordered us to read the letter out loud. It spoke less of himself, and more of his expectation to see us again.

The second letter he sent was meant specifically for Georgiana. When Lady Catherine heard that, she gave Georgiana a very distinct nod.

"Your cousin writes specifically to you, Georgiana," she observed, "that is delightful. After all these years together, a bond would naturally grow between you."

Georgiana thought nothing of this comment, but I did. When wishing to walk among the snow, I offered to walk with her. When we were getting our heavy capes on, gloves and bonnet, I nodded to her.

"Ah, her ladyship is at it again."

"At what again?"

"Matchmaking. But this time, she is making it with you."

"With me?" Georgiana grew fearful when she saw what I was speaking of. "No, Kitty, no!"

"Oh, yes. She is a wealthy woman with an unmarried daughter, who did not get the husband that she wanted. Therefore, she has nothing else to do but marry off the other single lady in her family."

"Colonel Fitzwilliam is like an older brother to me. He's one of my guardians."

"Yes, he is. And she also is a woman who tried to marry her daughter off to her nephew when they were children."

"Oh, dear god," Georgiana said, "just the thought of marrying a close cousin of mine—all of that feels so wrong! Ewww!"

I laughed as we walked along the snow in the fields surrounding Rosings Park.

~

Once we were far enough away from the house, Georgiana sat on a tree stump and read it.

"Ah," Georgiana said after a minute. "I knew it."

"What is it, Georgie?"

"He writes to me for two reasons. First, he does care for my welfare, but second, he knew that I was the best means for sending a secret letter to you."

She handed me the letter, with her finger pressed where the message for me began.

"There," she said, "read the romantic nonsense."

"Nonsense is a very underrated subject, if you ask me," I said, taking the letter and looking where her finger had been, "there is something to be said for nonsense. Personally, I think we ladies and men of leisure speak much of it almost every day. If we didn't, then what would we have to say?"

I sat down next to her on the stump.

"No," I said, "you don't have to look away when I read. The Colonel doesn't say anything that I wouldn't have told you later."

"Good. I don't like it when people read things over my shoulder, but I like doing that to others."

She leaned over my shoulder, and we read together.

And now, dear Georgiana, please do me the service of delivering this part of the letter to Kitty's direct hand and not to the general public. It has been a long December, for my part, and I have not been able to enjoy the comforts of family being near me.

If all of that is to be denied me, then can you, my wonderful cousin, give me this one moment of unveiling my sensibilities to your companion. If you do me this service, then I will now begin...

Kitty, is that you?

Are you there?

I pray that you are, for my heart is heavy, as well as my time spent away from you all. Whenever I went to Pemberley, I always felt as if I was falling into the very best comforts of life. Yet, the little bit of time that I spent there, with you, was a joy that I think I will never know.

I miss you, my perverse and wicked friend. I miss the very thought I had of you, of envying anyone who comes near you, or speaks to you with any sort of intimacy.

This winter has been cold to me. My duties as a soldier have given me no joy, and I feel as if it is all a drudgery.

Would that I were wealthy, Kitty!

Yes, I know, we have spoken of this time and time again. How much I repeat the things that I say.

How often I run from you, only to come back, and then say all the same words again and again to you. But I see your face now—I know that look. You are about to forgive me for everything.

I smile in knowing that is how you would react. I rely upon that constant forgiveness, that consistency of affection.

And yes, I dream of you. In my heart, in my thoughts, and in my bed. I think that our passion would be something worth the earning.

But I provoke you—not my scandalous words, but the fact that I say it with no guarantee of it ever coming true.

Finally, I feel like I might be prepared to be a husband.

And yet, I cannot have my wife.

But if you can do me the service, of writing to me once more—through Georgiana—for just one moment, please call me your great love. Call me your great passion. Call me the man that you preferred to all others.

Even if it's not true.

For a moment, imagine me as the only man in your life.

I'm sorry for asking you to dream of something that might never come true.

May God bless you, and merry Christmas.

R.F.

When I finished the letter, I closed it gently, and handed it back to Georgiana.

Feeling cold inside, I barely moved, not even giving Georgiana a glance.

"Kitty?" she asked me.

"I am the worst," I hissed. "I am the absolute worst!"

Standing up, I ran away from her, and through the woods.

"Kitty!" Georgiana cried. "Stop!"

"I can't," I cried back. "I don't want you to see me now. I don't want anyone to look at me!"

"Don't be foolish!" she called after me.

She was right. I was being foolish. And yet, why could I not stop?

I ran further and further away, and soon, all my dreams came rushing back to me.

Of myself running through the woods, and Georgiana accompanying me.

The coincidence of reality rushing into my dreamworld was so terribly frightening. And also fascinating.

When I felt an ache in my stomach, I stopped, leaning against a tree branch.

Behind me, I heard Georgiana's footsteps. Panting, she had reached me, and I heard her gasping for air.

"I'm sorry," I said. "I am so sorry."

"Why did you do that?"

"I don't know," I said, "I felt that if I ran, I could escape it."

"Escape what?"

"The confusion. I felt like I could put it all behind me and find a clearer way. But I was fooling myself. I'm still close enough to affect them both. Just like I was foolish enough to feel as if I could choose between them."

"You are torn again?"

"Yes."

"And you weren't until this letter? Then... Kitty, did that mean that you had chosen Finlay all this time, and it was Colonel Fitzwilliam that you did not prefer?"

"Georgie, you know that I will never tell, for fear of offending both. Either way, I was deluding myself. I still care for them both, and it will still be that way until I learn to govern how I feel. The Colonel has a profession that puts him in danger. Finlay was born low, and a military life is all that he knows. I know that I cannot control that. Death courts them both. We never think of that because it's a reality that is just too awful to consider. But I must think of it now. Finlay's life is danger, but I feel like he will always survive it. He has such a will to him, and he has survived so much. However, with the Colonel, it just feels different, somehow. I just... I cannot explain it, but I feel his mortality more. I know that it's irrational, but I just do. He needs to find an heiress, someone like Anne de Bourgh."

"Richard could never love Anne," Georgiana scoffed. "And she could never love him."

"I know. What I meant was someone like her. He needs someone to get him away from that sort of life."

"Even if he did marry such a woman, he still might not give up his profession. He might still wish to maintain his avenue of employment, to consistently gather revenue. He still might have to go into battle if there is another war."

"Of course, there's going to be another war. There's always another war! This is Britain. What is with the world and war being the only thing that everyone understands? Why must it always be that a man can only earn money if he risks his life in the process? What renown is in that?"

"It's not fair, I know."

"Oh, I have a headache."

"Of course, you have a headache. Kitty, if the Colonel was to move on, and marry another woman, would that make you happy?"

What a unique question to ask me. It was unique because Georgiana knew, as did I, that the answer was not easy. Nor was it singular.

"Yes, and no. Yes, I would be happy, because he would be able to have the life that he deserves. But no, because I worry that he would marry her, considering her dowry before anything. I don't want him to be that sort of man.

"It is well to be rational and marry, with consideration of a woman's dowry. But that needs to be an enhancement to her charms, and not her ONLY charm. Then I would be happy because he would release me from the pains of being so torn between two men. He would force me into a better way.

"But also no, I would not be happy, because I would miss him. But I would get over it. I'm used to getting over things. No, it's time I stopped laying in a desperate sort of limbo, and I did something about it. They need their freedom of me. Complete separation. It's the only way that they can make the right decision. If they can't move on, I will help them."

"Kitty, I am about to propose a very frightening aspect that you might have overlooked. If you spend your life this way, then you might not catch either one of them. If both move on, then you will lose two men you love, and end up with none."

"Maybe that is well. I daresay that I might fare at being a sister to great women as opposed to being a wife. I am more used to the first identity than the second. Life might be simpler that way. But love... why is love never simple? Why must it always be so complicated, so tangled, and so tainted?"

Georgiana sighed.

"I don't know. After all that is bewitching about the emotion, and it is the one thing that eludes so many of us. It is never simple, never neat, or even sometimes never solvable."

"Too many things in life are like good dreams: fleeting and often not able to fully be in one's grasp."

"Very true. You are right."

"I am?"

"Yes. You are. Maybe you do need to get away from them. Maybe you do need to give both men a fighting chance of moving on, because maybe..."

"What?"

"Kitty, I am going to say something that might prove disagreeable to consider."

"I know that you do things to consider my welfare," I rushed out, urging her to get on with it, "now go on."

"Well, maybe it's time to consider that neither man is the right man for you."

My eyes widened at this notion. For a split second, I wanted to scream at Georgiana. How could she propose such a thing? Both men were perfect for me. They simply were two perfect men at the wrong time and with the wrong size of income. As I was. But then, a few seconds after all these sensations rushed through my mind, I had to reevaluate. What if Georgiana was right? What if neither man was the right man for me, and the three of us were wasting our lives? That would be a horrible thing to consider.

"Do you hate me for suggesting it?" Georgiana asked me.

"For a second, I did. Then the rave of irrationality passed on and sense is back into my mind. I think that your idea makes sense... but it also would be the scariest thing of all."

"Yes, it might be. However, you don't need to commit to this now. In fact, I am about to be a hypocrite and tell you to do the reverse. Colonel Fitzwilliam needs something good for him this Christmas. He couldn't spend it with family, and he needs some kindness. Write back to him and tell him what he wants."

I collapsed into myself, feeling all the tension fade, for the moment.

"Good. Because that's what I wanted to do. Whatever I do tomorrow, for today, I want to make him happy."

"Let's go back to the house. Quickly pick up your pen

and paper and give the Colonel the Christmas that he needs."

"I'll worry more about this tomorrow then."

"Oh, don't worry about tomorrow either. Worry about it next week."

"I like that better. Besides, I have New Years to go through. I'll make my resolutions then."

~

When we returned to Rosings, Georgiana began her letter back to the Colonel. When she finished, she secretly handed it to me so that I could add my own words to it.

At first, I didn't know what to say. I wanted to give the Colonel everything that he wanted, but I also didn't want to encourage him.

But Georgiana was right, and so were my instincts. He knew the fact of our lives, and therefore, he knew the reality. He just needed a dream.

Picking up my pen, I began to write. At first, I wrote about common things and how Christmas had gone, and how we were going to Longbourn after leaving Rosings. But once the subject became tenderer in text, I trusted my instincts.

> *...my poor Colonel. I see your face now and what I would give to soften that look, to ease the tension on your fevered brow. It was unfair for you to be taken away from us. If any man deserved to be among family now, family that loves him, that adores him, it would be you.*
>
> *Colonel—I will call you Richard now. Your title will not suit what else we have to say at this point. I write this not to confuse you, not to offer you hope for an outcome that will never be, but to give you the truth that you need.*

Dearest Richard, I adore you more than words could say. I miss your company, my rattle of a friend, and you will always be a part of my affections. There is no way that I can ever tear my feelings from your image, and here and now, I want you to know that, wherever we go, and however separate we will be, you will always be a great love of mine.

I want you to marry someone else, Richard. I want you to be happy, wealthy, and free of the sorrows of life. I want to give you all these things, because I will not be the baggage that holds you down.

I am not the woman for you in the next year, or the year after that. I cannot give you a better life, because I don't have the money to give you a better life.

But for the moment, here and now, I am the woman for you. I am the lover for you. I am your wife. Let us have this moment. Because we will not have the next.

I love you, my fair cousin.

Your Kitty

When I finished, I handed the letter to Georgiana, and it was sent.

Chapter Eighteen

NEW YEARS' DAY

On New Years' Eve, Lady Catherine had planned a most interesting' party.

She had arranged for the Fairfax family to spend two days with us. This included Mr. and Mrs. Fairfax, their two sons and daughters.

This led to the servants having to work even harder than usual to prepare more rooms. Georgiana and I were asked to share one room, to make room for the two Fairfax sisters. This was readily agreed to, and soon, on New Year's Eve, we awaited the arrival of this family.

They arrived on time, were punctual, and we were actually quite happy to see them.

The Fairfax sisters didn't have much to divert them, regarding to not having any beaus to flirt with. For all men in our company were happily married, and therefore they only had the pleasure of seeing and being seen by the illustrious individuals in our company.

I did not regard them as being idle and shallow for wishing to have any men to dote on them, because they both were young. One was sixteen years old, and the other was fifteen. They were at the age where one was drawn to the opposite sex for every moment of the day. That is the age when one is very ready and eager to be fallen in love with.

Despite that there were no prospects at the party, they were cheery and pleasant young ladies. They talked, and listened, which was good enough for me. They still were willing to please and be pleased by everything that they saw.

After all, where one wealthy married man was, another single man of extensive wealth could be associated with him.

The brothers were another matter entirely.

Roger and Walter Fairfax were two brothers who also were very much ready to fall in love themselves and were eager to make a match. For they were older and at the time in life where a young man has overcome his wanton ways and is more amenable to settling down with one woman.

"At such a time in one's life," Roger told Georgiana, "I find it to be the perfect time for a man to acknowledge that he is good enough for a wife. Before that, I am not so very certain. Sometimes, a man needs to have more time in growing up, accepting that he is not complete unto himself. Do you recall the song in Shakespeare's 'Much Ado About Nothing'? The particular lyric 'Sigh no more, ladies, sigh no more'."

"I know the rest of it, I believe," Georgiana listed, "it goes something like 'men were deceivers ever'."

Together they began to recite the rest of the song, which naturally was to Roger Fairfax's delight:

'One foot in sea, and one on shore,
To one thing constant never.
Then sigh not so, but let them go,

And be you blithe and bonny,
Converting all your sounds of woe
Into hey nonny, nonny.'

"I thought I was the only one who memorized those lyrics," Georgiana exclaimed, giddy. "Shakespeare did us proud with that one."

"Well," Roger responded, "let's see how good you were at remembering the rest of it."

"I think I can accept that challenge."

Georgiana cleared her throat and continued her recitation.

'Sing no more ditties, sing no more
Of dumps so dull and heavy.
The fraud of men was ever so
Since summer first was leafy.
Then sigh not so, but let them go,
And be you blithe and bonny,
Converting all your sounds of woe
Into hey, nonny, nonny.

Roger Fairfax cheered for her.

"Bravo, Miss Darcy," Roger said for her, his eyes warm, "you have impressed me once more."

"Well, I am glad to have made you proud. And you adhere to what the Bard said? Do you believe his advice to us ladies, about the truth of the male mind?"

"Oh yes. I am not such a coxcomb that I deny the reality of what it's like to be a young man. Very few young men shift about the world always knowing what they are, or what they are about themselves. When I was nineteen, I was quite the rattle. I know it now, but at the time, I thought that I was perfectly right with how I treated ladies. But I was a right shame. I really was."

"Well, at least you admit to it. Some people in life never acknowledge the villains that they once were."

He nodded. "Precisely. Self-awareness is one of the best gifts to have. I am glad that I met you now, and not when I was your age. At that time in my life, I would do everything in my power to endear myself to the opposite sex and then offer them nothing in return. My words were empty. My pleasing looks were fleeting. And then, I would never understand when ladies would be bitter when seeing me again. I thought that they were in the wrong. It took years to see what I was doing. 'Men were deceivers ever'. Shakespeare was telling the truth about quite a few of us. Now that I am older, I know what constancy is."

"Be happy that you found your way there, in the end," Georgie said. "Now that you have, you are worthy. Promise me something."

He caught her gaze. "I would love to."

"Whatever your course in life, always apply this consistency of sincerity to relationships. When a person puts it into their mind to engage a heart and offer nothing in return, one can do a great deal of damage."

When she said that, I blinked, recalling Henry Crawford and the damage he did when he engaged Maria Bertram's affections. He was a man who had the skill to produce rapture in a woman's bosom and then abandon her when he had obtained his conquest.

To look on a romance and see it as a conquest—yes, that was a great evil. I had a hard time feeling very bad for Maria Bertram, because in the end, she was the one who committed to the ultimate betrayal and put herself in her situation. She did not have to marry Mr. Rushworth. However, now I did understand what she was feeling.

Henry Crawford had, viciously and carelessly, found his way into her heart. It led to her ruin. Love! The most powerful emotion in the world, besides 'hate'. For like hate, it has the power to build up and also destroy.

~

While Roger Fairfax and Georgiana talked, Walter Fairfax observed them. After he was able to untangle himself from Lady Catherine's inner circle of an audience, he sat near me, and we looked at his brother and my sister-in-law together.

"Two people who cannot be separate from each other," Walter said, "don't my brother and your sister look comfortable together, in such a way?"

"Yes," I acknowledged, "they do. Then again, that is Georgiana's power: she can make someone comfortable."

"She's approachable, just as yourself."

"You find me approachable?" I asked.

"Oh, much."

"Well, when it comes to having conversation, one cannot be agreeable alone. There has to be two to cause a proper discussion."

"You compliment me. Heavens rejoice! She complimented me."

"One compliment, Mr. Walter Fairfax," I said, "you really must not get too big for your breeches."

"I will not."

"Good, because if you did that, your trousers would start ripping at the seams."

"I need new trousers anyway."

"I think you should look better in your original ones."

He looked at me pointedly.

"Are we truly talking of clothing now, or something else entirely?"

I gave him an 'oh, really?' look.

"Mr. Walter, honestly? Is that where your mind goes?"

"I thought that was where your mind went. Forgive me, I am being positively horrid. I don't want you thinking I am a rake. Really, I am not. I just got excited for a moment and took the discussion too far. We should change the subject to something better. Something more proper."

"And just for saying that," I said, "we will now have no idea of what to talk about. Have you ever realized that whenever someone says that they will change the subject, conversation becomes forced, and no one knows what to say after that?"

"Yes. I really rode us into the fishpond, didn't I?"

"Don't worry. One has no choice but to stumble a bit. It's the first step to learning to walk. And then when you learn to do that, you can run."

"I just realized something."

"What?"

"I do not think that I have ever seen a young lady run."

"Never?" I asked, my eyes widening.

"No, never."

"That is beyond me. Your sisters had to have run when they were children."

"My sisters are not women, Miss Bennet. They are my sisters!"

I laughed, and that made everything lighter.

"I think," Lady Catherine said, "that the young people are very much wishing to dance a reel. Am I correct?"

"Oh!" Miss Fairfax declared, "I dearly love to dance."

"I do as well," the younger Miss Fairfax said. "We never get to enjoy the activity enough."

What a chance it was.

From Lady Catherine not wishing to allow dancing at her parties, to now incite the activity, it did show her growth.

Walter and Roger stood up with Georgiana and me, Arthur danced with Enara, and Mr. Darcy and Mr. Bingley danced with the Fairfax sisters. Mr. and Mrs. Fairfax also desired to dance as well, and they showed that age did not confine a person to the side of the room. Many elders still possess dancing skills and, to be married for over twenty years, and still wish to dance with one's spouse offers the best display of domestic felicity.

Mr. and Mrs. Collins remained with Lady Catherine, Anne, and Mrs. Jenkinson, ever to be their constant companions.

Betsy played the pianoforte for us, and the dance began.

As we danced, mirth and energy found its way back to our company, and it offered us all half an hour of diversions. Since it was the sort of dance that allowed us all the chance to talk, Walter Fairfax was most attentive at pressing some hints to what he desired.

"Look at Miss Darcy and Roger," he said, chuckling as we took each other's hands and skipped around the other couple. "They even dance well together."

Out of the side of my eye, I saw Georgiana laugh at something that Roger Fairfax had said.

Rather than appear coy, or play ignorant, I felt that I had nothing to lose by being direct. After all, I enjoyed having Walter's good opinion, but I did not need it. Therefore, if I lost it, I felt that I was not losing anything that would tear at my inner peace.

"I know what you are about," I said perceptive, but still playful.

"Oh, do you?"

"Yes, I do. Your brother is at the age where he is ready

to make a good match. And my sister-in-law is the perfect sort of lady for him to align himself with."

"And if I did feel that, am I wrong? Look at them. They are splendid. Their tempers are so much alike."

"As alike as two people can be who have only met in two social settings. For, you cannot deny, Mr. Walter, that when two people meet twice, that is not enough to determine a true affection."

"But it can be the beginning of it."

"That is very true, but alas, it cannot be put to the test. We leave Kent in three days' time, so may your brother enjoy Georgiana's company while he can."

"And what's to say that he will not make her an offer?"

I laughed.

"Is that a laughter of approval," he asked me, "or do you mock me?"

I gave him a studied look. "Oh, you poor boy. I mock you very much! Your brother proposing to her now would be like allowing himself to climb a mountain with no equipment. It would be the worst sort of climb there would be.

"Women are like men, in this case, and yes, we are ready to fall in love. But, Mr. Walter, it has to be a great deal more than that. Georgiana is like me. She is passed the age where one falls in love too quickly. We learned to be cautious. A woman must know the man she chooses, through and through. He must be like the rocks beneath us, and the wind that whips about our hair. Such a step as marriage must be tried and tested before one jumps into it. One has to experience the burning passions of love. It is to burn, to be on fire. But one also has to experience the smoldering sort of love—the knowledge that the passions last for more than one week, or a month. If you are to align two souls into one, make sure they are one first."

At this point, Walter was merely staring at me.

"Oh." I sighed. "I gave you quite the speech, didn't I?"

"Yes, you did. But it was not unwelcome." His voice became gentler. "There is a way for such a bond to be maintained. I have a solution."

"A solution? And I gather you thought a great deal about this solution?"

"Yes, I did. Surely you do not have to leave Rosings Park so soon. If you were to ask Lady Catherine, I am sure that she would invite you and Miss Darcy to remain for another month complete. And, due to the service that you rendered Miss de Bourgh, it is more than sufficient. In fact, maybe Miss de Bourgh would prefer to have the company of ladies her own age. At such an age, young ladies are vital to each other. And as for us Fairfaxes, well, yes, you are quite correct. Two days is nothing, for a love to grow. But a month, Miss Bennet... a month!"

"Yes, a month can give way to many revelations and other things," I acknowledged, "but, Mr. Walter, family is family. It's precious to Georgie and me. Right now, going to Hertfordshire is the best thing for us to do."

When I said this, he looked disheartened, but I had to tell him the truth. And I did it in the best way that I possibly could.

"Of course," I said, "Georgiana can feel differently. Your brother may ask her, but I believe she and I are of the same mind."

"And if she wants to stay," Walter said, "what of you?"

"I will not leave her here. I will stay with her."

Walter sighed.

"You're going to ask your brother to appeal to Georgiana, aren't you?" I asked him, unafraid.

"I will not tell you."

"Very well. We all must have our secrets."

~

That night, Jane, Elizabeth, Georgiana, Sarah, Betsy, Lucy, Enara, and Anne de Bourgh and I were sitting in her bedroom, in front of the fireplace. We all had on our nightgowns, our robes, a shawl over us, and our hair was also done up in curling paper or caps.

Each of us had a twig in our hands that Betsy was so kind to collect for us from some trees.

In the corner on the side of the room, Mrs. Jenkinson sat there, looking through some lace. Every now and again, she looked up at us, apprehensive.

"Never fear, Mrs. Jenkinson," Jane assured her, "there is nothing pagan about what we are doing."

"Then what are you doing?" Mrs. Jenkinson asked us.

"Making resolutions."

"Just please keep your eye on the time," Elizabeth asked her.

"Yes, I am," Mrs. Jenkinson said, checking her timepiece that was on the table. "It's three minutes to midnight."

"Thank you, Mrs. Jenkinson," I said, "now we should begin."

"Do you do this every new year's eve?" Anne de Bourgh asked us.

"We always do something similar," Elizabeth said, "but this time, I felt like doing something a little more unique. Lucy, you are at the end. You can start first."

So flattered to be a part of it all, Lucy raised up her twig to the fireplace.

"From last year, I will forgive myself for when I lied about something that I should not have lied about. My past shall be burned, and I start anew."

She threw her twig into the fire.

The next was Sarah.

"From last year, I promise to forgive myself for always arguing with Betsy in public areas. From now on, I will only do it in private rooms where our employers don't see us."

Betsy hissed.

"You prat! That was what I was going to say!"

"Well, I beat you to it."

"Ladies!" Elizabeth chided. "You both have the same repentance. And right now, you are arguing in front of us, so your resolution is not working."

"Oh," Betsy said, "right. Very well, we both said it."

Together, Sarah and Betsy threw their twigs into the fire.

The next was Georgiana.

"From last year, I promise to forgive myself for falling in love with the wrong person. From now on, I will consider what feels right and true."

She threw her twig into the fire.

The next was me.

"From last year, I promise to forgive myself for all the times my indecision hurt others. This year, I shall take back my life and make the right decisions that benefit more than just myself."

I threw my twig into the fire.

The next was Elizabeth.

"From last year, I will forgive myself for being afraid of the idea of having a child. I did not fathom the idea that I would have to share my husband with another person in my life. But now, I will cast such thoughts aside and love my child."

That was a surprise!

The next was Jane.

"From last year," Jane said, "I will forgive myself for when I let my gentle temper or passive habits result in my not protecting my sisters or helping those who need it. This year, I shall find my voice."

Another surprise.

She threw her twig into the fire.

The next was Enara.

"From last year, I shall overcome my fear of returning home, and worried that I will regret returning and not loving it as much as I remembered."

She threw her twig into the fire.

The last was Anne de Bourgh.

We all looked at her. With the firelight illuminating her pale skin and her thin frame, she looked like a light elf, with the light drawing her forward, but the darkness pulling at her back.

She shook a little, and then she raised up her twig.

"From last year, I will forgive myself for always being afraid. Every moment, being afraid, and hating myself. This year, I shall no longer do that, and I shall not be afraid anymore."

We all were so quiet as she raised up her twig and threw it into the fire.

"Ten seconds!" Mrs. Jenkinson cried, excited.

"Nine," I began.

"Eight," Elizabeth said.

"Seven," Jane listed.

"Six," Georgiana said.

"Five," Sarah said.

"Four," Betsy said.

"Three," Lucy said.

"Two," Anne de Bourgh said.

"One!" Mrs. Jenkinson cried. "It is now the new year."

"All past mistakes are gone," Jane instructed, "all errors are forgiven. We are born anew. Another part of us will now begin."

"Happy New Year!" we all declared.

Chapter Nineteen

LONGBOURN IN THE NEW YEAR

B etween local family visits, entertainment at Rosings, and visiting the Collins' at Hunsford parsonage, the rest of our time in Rosings Park went without any sort of family discord.

I will not pretend to say that Mr. Collins reformed during the rest of our visit. His pride and self-conceit probably would not allow it. However, he did learn that he would not have a parrot with me, and I would not repeat everything that he said or believed.

Charlotte proved to be content with her lot in life when informing me that she only wanted a comfortable home and to be able to be mistress of it. And since, due to Mr. Collins's duties, both husband and wife spent so little time in each other's company, Charlotte had the best life that she could have hoped.

For my part, I wondered at it. To be married in such a fashion, to rejoice in not being too often in your husband's company—well, I would find it to be a droll sort of business. And yet, between my parents and the Collins', I couldn't help but wonder if that was the fate of so many. Is that what marriage ultimately leads to? A settled and eventual indifference, where both husband and wife are in each other's lives, but they are separate, even when they are together. Is marriage not to be the fairytale that it is often dreamt of being?

It is perfectly natural to begin a wedding with hopes, dreams, and happiness. My sisters, and their marriages, are still young. So, I cannot measure the longevity of domestic joy through them.

But then I think of my aunts and uncles, and the continual respect that both spouses have for each other. Also, Lord and Lady Fitzwilliam had a great admiration and consideration of each other's talents.

Maybe Charlotte is right: happiness in marriage is entirely a matter of chance.

It's all to do with luck. And that is the gravest of frightening aspects. I've never been very lucky.

~

The day of our departure came, and I really did find myself looking forward to the idea of returning home after so long. I knew, of course, that my visit there might end with me wishing that I had never gone, but it didn't hinder my present expectations.

With all preparations made, our company breakfasted early, and Lady Catherine and Anne de Bourgh were kind enough to see us off.

"When the time draws near," Lady Catherine said to us as our carriages were being prepared, "I shall visit Pemberley and Godfrey Park. It is proper for me to be there when both ladies are having their laying-in."

Elizabeth and Jane thanked her for this, and I stood back and watched. Lady Catherine did not need to say it, but she did say it in her own way: she now accepted us. Never again would she disparage or belittle Elizabeth for marrying her nephew. Peace, in the family, had been found.

"Anne," Lady Catherine said, "come and say farewell to your family."

Anne stepped forward.

"I... I am glad that you all came to visit," she began.

"It was our pleasure," Elizabeth said, "we are glad that our company was not an eyesore to you."

Anne smiled gently, then she looked directly at Georgiana and me.

"You must come again for the next Christmas, so we can do this all again. And, if you were to visit earlier, that would be preferable."

"We will visit again," Georgiana assured her. "Depend upon it."

"Good," she replied, imploringly, "we shall look forward to it."

"Darcy," Lady Catherine said, "since the young ladies are near the same age, I would prefer if Kitty and Georgiana are always of the company when you come. It would be best if we planned this visit in May, when the weather is more congenial."

How the tides had turned on me again, after turning so much against me before.

I was invited back to Rosings Park. I—the blight on the company, the ugly ink spot on the fine bit of paper that was our company...was now invited to return especially.

All that was due was to thank Lady Catherine and agree eagerly to this. Georgiana and I did so, more so because of the look that Anne gave us. Evidently, she was lonely.

We expressed every desire to make good on this plan, and Anne's eyes lit up when we accepted.

As our carriages took off, we watched the mother and daughter as Mrs. Jenkinson waved to us.

Anne de Bourgh took a few steps forward, watching us depart with a wistful eye.

"The poor girl," I whispered to Georgiana, "she just needs friends, better health, and room to breathe some breaths of liberty."

"Yes. We can't give her the last two, but if we do have the chance to visit again, we can give her the first."

"Do you think she will ever have the energy to attend a whole ball?"

"I should imagine not, but if she did, I am certain that Aunt Catherine would not take the risk. Anne is her only child and only heir to Rosings. She must keep her safe at all times."

"It must be hard, to have such a great house, all that fortune, and to have only one child who was not born with the best constitution."

"Yes, she must. Kitty?"

"Yes?"

"I think Anne de Bourgh misses us already."

"You think so?"

"I know so. For her sake, we do have to accept visiting again. I know my aunt can be difficult to be around, but she means well. We must go back."

"I know. We will."

This was a difficult thing to consider because it might have gotten in the way of something I had been planning to do. But I would not mention it now, for it might never come to fruition. After all, it was a whim of the moment. But time would tell.

Either way, so had ended our Christmas in Rosings Park. Who would have known that it would have ended so very well? Truly, I had never expected it.

We did break our journey at Bromley. Afterwards, we travelled the rest of the way to Hertfordshire. When we rode through Meryton, I felt my spirit rise with familiarity.

Every now and again, a shopkeeper had exited their business, along with a few shop boys, as they were closing.

When seeing me wave at them, they smiled, waved back and I saw them all whispering. By tomorrow evening, it would be all over Hertfordshire and Meryton that we all had come home. Despite the last bit of light that lingered over the horizon, I saw my aunt and uncle Philips's house in the short distance.

Tomorrow, I would go there, despite that we were to dine there for dinner.

But the sight of home! Even if some of the memories were not always pleasant, it still provided the warmth of familiarity and familial bonds.

Whatever our history, I did miss my parents. I doubt that father would have missed me very much at all, but hopefully he would have had some kind words to accidentally say.

For a second, as I rode on, I was reminded of when all of us Bennet sisters had walked into town together. Unmarried and all in expectation of a visit into Meryton as being the highlight of our day. The times were simpler. But I suppose that is the price that one pays as they age. The prospect of innocence dying is inevitable, and we rush for use and complacency to accept us.

But for the moment, it was still the new year, and all was fresh and new.

We passed by Lucas Lodge, and I eagerly looked at the windows.

"Maria might be home!" I cried.

And certainly enough, as if my mentioning her name was like a siphon that urged her forward, on the second floor, Maria appeared in a window. She was looking down, to see the carriages that were rolling along.

It might have been too dark for her to see who I was, but I waved anyway.

Her eyes lit up and she waved down at me. Maria, I have come home!

In that time, I would get to see Diana Long as well. All of this added to the charms of coming home at this most special time.

Further down the road, we rode, until Longbourn finally came into view.

"There it is," Arthur Philips said to me, "welcome home, Kitty."

"Yes," I said, "and are you prepared for Mother's excitement and Father's wit?"

"I am. I find great amusement in both because family fussiness is the best kind of fussiness."

Chuckling, I looked back at the house and didn't take my eyes away from it.

When we parked in front of the house, the door opened and soon, our mother and father emerged from it.

"Mama and Papa." I sighed. "For the life of me—there they are."

"My goodness!" Mama cried, "you have come."

Father stood behind her, a look of amusement on his face. They both were there, as they always were.

"We were worried that you had been overset," she said, as our men helped us down from the carriage. "Or that you had been attacked by highwaymen."

"Nonsense, Aunt Bennet," Arthur Philips said, "we have made very good time."

"Oh, Arthur, you are returned back to us. And look, Mr. Bennet! Our girls are home."

We all embraced her as she took in Lizzy's and Jane's girth.

"Oh, look at you both," she cried, "my girls are going to have children of their own. Mr. Bennet, is this not the best thing in the world?"

"Yes, it would be so," Mr. Bennet replied, walking forward, and showing great affection to his two eldest daughters. Since Mama and Papa were spending their primary focus on their two eldest, who were the most cherished, I remained by the wayside, stood in the back of the crowd, and waited my turn.

For some reason, Georgiana sensed my insignificance, so she patted my hand.

"The eldest are naturally the ones that get the most attention," Georgiana noted, "especially when they are the ones with child."

"Thank you," I said, "I'm used to waiting."

After showing affection to my two eldest sisters, Mama addressed Mr. Darcy and Mr. Bingley, offering them all the compliments in the world, and welcoming them back to her humble abode.

This was all done in her traditional way of being, and I could tell that Mr. Darcy was doing everything in his power to bear her words with equanimity.

Mr. Bingley was kinder about it.

"Now," Mrs. Bennet said to Mr. Darcy, "where is that talented sister of yours?"

"I am here, Mrs. Bennet," Georgiana said, "next to Kitty."

Thank you, Georgiana, for showing that I was being regarded as being an afterthought.

When hearing my name mentioned, a quick streak of

discomfort flashed across their faces again. I knew that look. My parents had known I was there the entire time but were afraid of how to receive me. Or they were afraid of how I was going to receive them. Either way, it was still strange to not be given the proper warmth when one returned home.

"Oh, Kitty," Mama said, "what nonsense do you do, dear, in hiding in the back like that? Come forward and be happy to see your parents." She fussed about, to make it appear that she merely didn't see me. Rushing up to me, she embraced me as well. "Longbourn has not been the same without you and your sisters. If only Lydia was here, I would have all five of my daughters under one roof. Is that not so, Mr. Bennet? Do you not wish that Lydia were here?"

"Our youngest daughter is happy where she is, I believe," Mr. Bennet replied, "she always looks so attractive at that distance."

Everyone looked at him, and either widened their eyes, or suppressed a smile.

"Well, Kitty," Father said, "you are looking very well. Very well, indeed. Miss Darcy and you seem to almost have the same look about you. That is greatly to your benefit."

I sighed.

Out of the side of my eye, I saw Mr. Darcy roll his eyes.

"It is quite cold outside," Elizabeth said smoothly. "Let us all go in."

"Yes," Mrs. Bennet ordered, "let us go in then. Oh, dear Arthur and Mrs. Philips, you both are a welcome addition to our party. You can tell us all about Australia again. I still marvel at the animal, the kangaroo!"

Immediately, I looked at Mr. Darcy, Mr. Bingley, and Arthur.

Each of them had a different expression at this.

Arthur was amused by it.

Mr. Bingley smiled, diplomatically.

Mr. Darcy was not amused.

We all entered, Mr. and Mrs. Hill immediately came forward and began to take our things as Betsy, Lucy and Sarah were arranging for our luggage to be brought inside.

As I looked around, I felt the warmth of familiarity encompass me. Despite the chilly reception, I still felt happy to be home.

"Since Mary and Lydia are no longer living here," Mrs. Bennet explained, "Longbourn will not be in want of comforts or room. There is room enough for everyone. Mr. Bingley and my exquisite Jane will remain in Jane's room. Mr. Darcy and my Elizabeth will remain in Lizzy's older room. Elizabeth, I want to let you know that I have not changed the room at all, so you will have that same feeling whenever you arrive again."

"Thank you, Mama," Elizabeth said.

"And Arthur and Mrs. Philips," she said, "you both shall have my dutiful Mary's older room. The sheets and bedding are brand new. I know that your parents were unable to have your older room repaired in time."

"Thank you, Mrs. Bennet," Enara said, "I am sure they will be to our liking."

Lastly, Mama turned to Georgiana and me.

"And Kitty and Miss Darcy, this is the only offense that I shall give. But it is not our fault, I assure you. We would wish to give you every luxury in the world, but to be sure, we are not so grand as Pemberley, I know."

"What is it, Mama?" I asked. "Is it that Georgiana and I will share my old room?"

"Well, Kitty, I was going to mention it myself. Miss Darcy, we dearly wished that you could have your own room, however, that is not to be so."

"I am not so very fine that I cannot share a comfortable bedroom with a good friend," Georgiana said, "therefore, there is no need to apologize."

"See, Mrs. Bennet?" Father said. "All those words, only for it to be so very settled. We really must learn to be economical with our apologies. Ten words a minute. Ten words a minute."

"Well," Mama continued, ignoring Father, "you will be happy to know that there will be dinner parties every day that you are here. Truly, there will be diversions aplenty. Nothing less could be done for the masters and mistresses of Pemberley and Godfrey Park. You all do us great honor. Now, tell me everything about your Christmas. At Rosings Park too!" Mama chuckled. "My daughters must have found that to be a wonderful experience. Was it, girls?"

We all opened our mouths to speak, but she overrode us.

"I am sure that it was a splendid affair. I want to hear every detail, my dears. Every detail."

"I too would like to hear the entire story," Father said, "once you all have a moment to speak."

"Oh, Mr. Bennet," Mama said, "I know the truth. I know that you don't prefer to hear tales of social scenes, and actions at great houses."

Father turned to the rest of us.

"My wife knows the depths of my mind in every respect. She speaks for me now and might speak for me all throughout this evening. Before I keep quiet, because Mrs. Bennet speaks better than I, I must again look on my daughters and admire them."

He turned to Elizabeth first. Then to Jane.

"Elizabeth and Jane, you both look well thus."

"Thank you, Father," Jane said, patting her stomach.

"You both possess the glow that ladies often have when

a child grows within. Mrs. Bennet, you had that same look."

"Oh, did I, Mr. Bennet? No, indeed, you tease me. I must have looked horrid."

"You said it, my dear, not I."

"Oh, Mr. Bennet!"

"I tried to compliment you, but you wouldn't let me."

"You would give everyone the impression that we spend the day teasing each other or sounding so droll." She turned to the rest of us. "Indeed, that is not so." She looked at Arthur and Enara. "We spend our days in perfect bliss, especially in knowing that our daughters are so well-settled. Arthur understands me. Do you not, Arthur?"

"I do indeed, madam," Arthur said, "when my parents discovered that Enara fell in love with me, my mother looked happier at me—happier than she had looked in three years."

We all laughed, but finally Father turned to me.

"And you, Kitty. I can see, by the very way that you sit, that you are falling into the blooms of womanhood. To see my daughters so grown up, it makes a man ask where the time goes."

"In the air," Elizabeth said, "and into the atmosphere, while the rest of our persons must remain on the ground, and age like dirt must turn into mud."

Mr. Bennet chuckled.

"There's the wit that I miss so very much. Mr. Darcy?"

"Yes, sir."

"I heard that you have the most incredible library in the country."

"It has had the benefit of years of additions to it. If you wish to ever come to Pemberley, you can spend your days there and only retire to your room for sleep."

Mama clapped her hands.

"We have been invited to Pemberley! How merry!"

I could sense Mr. Darcy groaning secretly. But there was nothing for it. After all, when it comes to a husband, they always come with a wife.

We sat down to supper. Georgiana and I didn't speak much the entire time because my parents directed most of the comments to the married couples.

We weren't upset about it, because we both were very hungry, and the comments focused more on discussions about being wives, mothers, and fathers. Georgiana and I lacked experience on both counts, and we sensed, now more than ever, that the gulf between single and married ladies can be very large. Even when they find common ground, the world seems deemed to cause distance between them through the focus of motherhood on one, and the lack of motherhood on the other.

After supper, Mama had arranged for us to have baths drawn, and she gave us time to retire early, since we were exhausted from traveling.

When I had changed into my nightgown, Georgiana was taking her bath. Alone in my old room, I was able to move around it, reflecting on being back inside of it again.

My room was also kept the same as it had been. I wouldn't have wanted it any other way. There are some things in the world that need to remain the same and in your own power. A room of one's own... oh, yes! A room of one's own.

While I was undoing my hair, there was a knock on my door.

"Come in, Mama!" I called. "I am decent."

The door opened and it was mother.

"How did you know it was me?" she asked, closing the door behind her. "I will never understand it."

"It's not just your knock that I am accustomed to," I

said, "but also your footfalls. I heard you even before you came to my door."

"Well," she said, "that makes all the sense in the world. If anyone is to know my walk, it had better be my own girls."

She came in and sat down on my bed.

"Well, Kitty," Mama began, "I was hoping to catch you alone."

"Well," I assured her, "Georgiana has just gotten into her bath. So, you have a few minutes."

"Kitty, I have a question."

"Go on."

"Have you missed me at all?"

~

Have you missed me at all?

Now that was the question!

When hearing it, I stopped undoing my hair and I looked at my reflection in the mirror. Behind me, I saw my mother sitting on the bed, looking at me intently.

Never before had she asked me such a question.

"You take a while to answer it," she said.

"Because I cannot help but wonder at it," I said.

"How so?"

"Because I cannot help but wonder if you have missed me."

"Oh," she pressed, "I have. I have very much. I would beg you to not even consider it the reverse."

"Well, judging by the cold reception that I received, what else am I to think?" I asked her, not afraid to cut to the quick. "You ask me to miss you, when you have shown no signs of missing me."

"It is not that."

"Then what is it? I come home, after being away for months, and you and Father—"

"It is not for want of missing you."

"How am I to know that? Lydia and Jane were your favorite children," I continued. "Please, don't pretend to be otherwise. You made it clear, very often. As did father with Elizabeth."

"I love you all, equally."

"You attack me for coughing."

"I was out of spirits, at the time. And I took it out on you. That was wrongly done. I know that now. Kitty, I realized that we must have been very cold when we saw you, but it was not due to want of feeling."

"Then what was it? You keep on talking around the matter, but not directly to it."

"We didn't know if you would be happy to see us."

I shifted in my seat as I turned and faced her directly.

"What?"

"Kitty, what do you expect?"

"What do you mean by what do I expect? I thought you would be happy."

"We were, but we were also scared."

"Scared?"

"When last we saw you, you weren't pleased with us. You reminded me of my shortcomings as a parent, I have spent months dwelling on that—oh, Kitty! That was too unkind of you."

"No, it wasn't too unkind of me. It was me being brave enough to tell you what you are too afraid to know. But when I came home, I was happy to see you. You know why? Because I was willing to begin again. But here you and father are, as you always will be. I was willing to overcome past grievances and start over, but you are so much caught up in the past."

"Well, I just don't understand what can make you happy."

"Be kind to me and accepting of me. That's all that I ask."

"You will look on life differently when you get married, and you become a mother. Life looks very different from where one stands, domestically. That's another thing. You have been at Pemberley for so long. I do so wonder why you are not at least amidst a courtship yet."

"What has that to do with anything?"

"You will see. It makes all the difference in the world. When you get married, you will understand me better and everything that I am. But when will you marry? I don't understand why you delay the matter."

"I don't marry because I don't want to right now. I need more time."

"Kitty, is it possible that maybe it is because no man has asked you? I would not be ashamed of you."

I groaned.

"Stop it!" I cried. "Just stop it!"

Mama was silenced.

"Kitty, why are you so upset? Why do you always get so upset now? And you have become so disobedient. I am the only mother that you have."

"Madam, you gave birth to me, and I thank you for that. But that's as far as my gratitude goes. It does not mean that I must live my life compromising myself to complete obedience. First, I must choose *my own* life and order my own life. And I will."

I stood up and moved away from her.

"It was a mistake," I uttered.

"What was a mistake?"

"Me coming here. If I could have stayed with the Gardiners…"

"Kitty, you break my heart. You are not wishing to see me? How could you do such a thing to your poor mama?"

I turned to her, cold. I was so angry that I could not stand for anything else.

"You said the same thing when Lydia ran off with Mr. Wickham. And you got over that, tolerably well. In fact, you seemed to forget the whole horror of the experience. Therefore, I think you will get over this all equally so.

"And if you came here to perform Father's business, because he was too indifferent to face me himself, then you can tell him yourself. I am not here to blindly obey anymore. I have seen too much of the world and have made too many of my own decisions. I will no longer be incorrectly dictated to. If this is too much for him, or for you, then you can keep your distance, as he has done already. I came here, happy to see you. But I will not compromise myself. Not anymore. Can you be happy with that? I hope you can. I did miss you. But that's as far as it goes. Can't you all just love me and be done with it?"

"I do what is best for you."

"What is best for me is for you to listen to me and let me feel as I feel and think as I think. I hurt no one by doing so. Can't you give me that?"

Mother looked heartbroken.

"Mama," I said, "I don't ever wish to hurt you."

"I just...we used to get along so very well. I don't understand what changed."

"I told you what. Are you listening to me? Mama, please."

"I just don't think we can ever go back."

Despaired, she got up and left me alone.

I sat down, feeling my headache coming on.

New Years at Longbourn.

And this is how I began it!

Chapter Twenty

ROMANCE RETURNS

When Georgiana returned from her bath, she found me in a pitiful state. Taking one look at me, she knew that something was wrong. Therefore, I told her everything that had occurred.

"It was as if I was on a runaway cart," I said, "and I could not get off. How could things go so wrong so quickly?"

"Kitty," Georgiana said, "in your defense, they began it all wrong. They were very inattentive to you when you arrived, and then your mother brings up marriage as if it's a bag that a person can swing about them and then, suddenly, all the answers come. I think your parents don't understand you because they can't. I really do think that their minds don't bend themselves in the direction that makes them know what sort of person you are. They seem to have an image of you in their minds, and that image is not real. It's what they want to see."

"And you know it. Then why can't they? They are older than us. Should they not be wiser than us?"

"Age can bring one of two things: experience and

wisdom, or rigidity of thought and immovably stocky opinions. An old dog has experiences, but it can't always learn new tricks. I suggest that you wait tomorrow to see how matters unfold. Maybe your parents need to sleep on the situation, and then when they wake up, you can start anew with them. Time helps things. But wait till tomorrow, then we will see what we will see."

Betsy came in.

"Miss Bennet," Betsy said, "it's time for your bath."

"Go on," Georgiana said, "we can talk about this when you return."

I kissed her cheek.

"Thanks, Georgie."

I went to my bath.

Once more, diving into the warm water gave me the release that I needed. Nothing can make one more purged from the failures and disappointments of the moments before, like a warm bath to make you feel as if you have been washed away from all that.

My mother was probably telling Father everything. But that was in another part of the house. Here, in the comforts of being underwater, I was far away.

As I dunked my hair, Lieutenant Finlay and Colonel Fitzwilliam passed across my thoughts. Their kind eyes and their firmness of opinion fortified me. They would not be ashamed of my outburst, because they relied upon my own newly found firmness. They did not fear my spirit, or my place in the world—if I had a place. Like Georgiana, I knew if I were in their company, I would be in the presence of people whom I would not feel ashamed.

When I finished bathing, I returned to Georgiana immediately, and we spent the rest of the night talking about the matter. Eventually, we grew tired and fell asleep, each exhausted from the remains of the day.

The next morning brought the reaction that was perhaps the most expected.

Georgiana and I went down to breakfast where everyone was happy to see us, excepting my parents. Or at least when it came to seeing me. Mother and Father smiled and greeted me, but they clearly were anxious, and they looked on me like a spooked animal. They were apprehensive about making any sudden movements toward me, so all their approaches were general phrases:

'Good morning, Kitty.'

'Did you sleep well?'

'Tonight, we are dining at the Philipses. Your aunt and uncle will be happy to see you. They always are, you know.'

'You must miss seeing the officers there.'

'Remember when you and Lydia would often go there? You always returned with such a glow to your cheeks.'

'You and that sister of yours.'

I suppose they really did wish to pretend as if last night never happened. That, sadly, was the best that I could hope for. They were two people who never could learn how to approach personal matters of this nature, for they spent their entire marriage not understanding each other. Sometimes they make progress. Other times, no—regression. They get better, and improve, then they fall back to older ways. What a fool I was for ever hoping that they could rise above what they always had been. If I ever made any progress with reaching them, it would now come to an end.

After breakfast, Georgiana had some letters to write to her friends in Scarborough and to Emma Watson.

Giving her time alone, I said that I would take that time to visit Lucas Lodge and call on Maria Lucas. So not to have any others volunteer to walk with me, I told her to tell everyone else where I had gone.

I threw on my pelisse, bonnet, scarf, and gloves and

dashed out of the house as quickly as I could. It is such a shame that one must rush away, out of secrecy, from one's own home just to have an appropriate moment alone.

The cold hastened my pace, and sooner than usual, I arrived at Lucas Lodge, where Lady Lucas saw me eagerly. Soon after I arrived, Sir William Lucas entered to tell me that Maria had gone to visit Diana Long, and that she wouldn't be returned for an hour.

"But before you go," Lady Lucas said, actually happy to see me, "can you tell me how my dear Charlotte does?"

"Yes," Sir William Lucas said, "being the mistress of Hunsford Parsonage already gave us great pleasure, but now to know that Charlotte is to be a mother."

"She does well," I said, "and her stomach is as large as Jane's and Lizzy's. You will see them both very soon, so you will be able to see the matter for yourself. She asked us to give you her regards. I think she misses you both, but she does the service of 'clergyman's wife' very well. In the time that we were at Rosings Park, I never met any of Mr. Collins's parishioners who did not think very well of her."

"My dear Charlotte," Sir William said, "always doing the sensible thing. But I declare, in all my life, I never thought she would be associated with a great patroness such as Lady Catherine de Bourgh."

"And you were at Rosings Park," Lady Lucas said, "my husband tells me that there are some rooms that put him greatly in mind of St. James's Court. It makes me eternally curious."

"Oh, my dear, I believe that I am correct," Sir William said, "am I not, Kitty?"

"Sir William," I said, "how did you know that I have been to St. James's Court?" I rolled my eyes. "Oh, yes. Mama."

"When she heard that you all had been in town," Lady Lucas said, "she gave us every detail of the matter."

"Well," I said, "Sir William, I can give some authority on the subject. Lady Lucas, there are some rooms in Rosings Park that Sir William is quite right about. Some of the rooms do remind a person of St. James's."

Sir William clapped.

"See, my dear?" he said to his wife. "I was correct."

"Yes, Sir William," Lady Lucas said, "you were."

I took my leave of them, promising that I would call back again in a couple of hours.

As I put on my bonnet and Sir William and Lady Lucas bid me goodbye, eager for me to return soon, I smiled at the brief visit.

Ah, the never-ending cycle that revolved around Lucas Lodge.

Sir William still spoke of St. James's Court and connected it back to everything that reminded him of it.

His wife had to listen to it and understand that her lot in life was a circle that remained surrounding her husband's fondest memory, and daughter who was married to a ridiculous man who happened to serve a great lady.

And yet, I smiled. Because, I might have missed all of this.

As I stepped down the house's front steps, at first, I turned to go back to Longbourn.

Although, that was not what I wanted. I felt the restlessness that often stirred me into the opposite direction that I was supposed to go.

I wanted to go to Meryton. I had every intention of seeing aunt and uncle Philips before we dined there. Also, I would be able to visit Mary and Mr. Atkins without the rest of the family being present. A dinner party gives something for us all to look forward to. But it doesn't allow intimate discussion.

Therefore, I found myself making a left and walking to Meryton at a brisk pace.

"Kitty!" I heard Aunt Philips call from the upstairs window.

When I had arrived at the Philipses home, Aunt Philips saw me from the window. She opened it and waved to me.

Eagerly, I waved up at her.

"I know!" I cried, "I'm six hours early."

"I wouldn't have had it any other way," Aunt Philips said. "Dennison! Open the door. Kitty is here."

The door opened before I even wrung the bell, and I was met with Dennison's older and kind face, his simple way of talking and his lopsided grin.

"Miss Bennet!" he said, "It's a great pleasure to see you again."

"And you as well, Dennison."

"I declare," he said as he let me in and I handed my bonnet, pelisse and gloves to him, "you have turned into a proper lady. You and your sisters already were a set of pretty faces, but now you are quite grown up."

"Not too grown up, I hope. I would hate to be called stodgy."

"You aren't stodgy, not for my life."

"Kitty is here, Mary," I overheard Aunt Philips say upstairs.

Dennison led me to the parlor, and I was not left waiting long. Soon, Aunt Philips came down the stairs and entered with all the congeniality that was what I hoped to find when I came. Her manner was the most maternal thing that I had encountered when I had come home, and finally I felt the Christmas cheer return to me.

"Kitty!" she cried, and I rushed into her arms as she

folded them around me. "Oh, my lovely girl. You have found your way back to us, at last. You just missed Arthur and Enara. They just left."

"Oh, Aunt Philips, how I missed you and uncle."

"I hope that you missed me as well."

I turned to who said that, and my sister, Mary Atkins, had just come down the stairs.

"Mary!" I cried.

"Yes, Merry Christmas, Kitty."

Mary embraced me as well and we laughed as we danced around.

"You look handsome," I said to Mary, and it was true. Sometimes love does make a woman glow. Mary was positively beaming. I always said that she didn't always wear the most becoming gowns. This time, she was wearing a simple dress that flattered her look, her hair was done up better, and she looked happy.

"Me?" Mary said, pointing to herself. "Well, you are just being kind."

"I'm not." I turned to Aunt Philips. "Tell her that I speak the truth."

"She does, Mary," Aunt Philips said. "Love has helped you on, and you look very pretty." Aunt Philips turned to me. "Who would have thought that our Mr. Atkins would be the cure for her. Then again, it does make a great deal of sense. After all, I married my father's clerk. I suppose that it was only a matter of time before one of my nieces followed my footsteps."

"And the biggest surprise was that it was me," Mary said. "I should get Mr. Atkins. Kitty, he will be happy to see you." Mary touched Aunt Philips's arm. "Does Uncle Philips know that Kitty is here?"

"He doesn't. Bring both men. Uncle Philips needs a reason to abandon his work."

"He always does."

Mary left, and Aunt Philips immediately bombarded me with questions about Rosings Park. I only finished telling her about our first day there, before I heard the thunderous footsteps of the men of the household.

Soon Uncle Philips and Mr. Atkins came charging into the room, with Mary behind them.

"My dear Kitty!" Uncle Philips said loudly.

"Merry Christmas, uncle and brother!"

I reached out as Uncle Philips took my hands in his.

"Welcome home, sister," Mr. Atkins said merrily.

"Kitty," Uncle Philips said, "before you tell us anything, I must know. You are still single and happy. You are not engaged or swept off by any of those ton-totties who are so puffed up with foolish notions of self-importance that they are mere coxcombs?"

"No, uncle," I said, laughing, "I am not. I still am very much my own woman."

"Good, good. Remain that way and hold on to your bloom. What do you say, Atkins?"

"I say that true love is the only way to go, as long as one can do it, with respect to practicality," Mr. Atkins said. "But nothing less than a worthy soldier would do for Kitty."

"You think you know me, do you?" I asked, shrewd.

"Oh, I know that I know you very well," he said, eyeing me keenly. He was thinking of Finlay. And he knew that I was often thinking of him. Why did the men in my family have to know me so well, excepting my father himself? It was so ironic.

"Well," I replied, diplomatically, "I shall let you win this round. But only on the grounds that you are correct, and I will not pretend otherwise." I looked at my uncle. "While I do want to tell you how our Christmas has gone, I must ask, because I am dying of curiosity. Did you receive my last two letters?"

"Concerning the Bertram family and their property in Antigua?"

"Yes."

"Oh, I received them all, and I also received a letter from Sir Thomas Bertram himself."

"You did?" I asked, my eyes widening.

"I did indeed. Well, your suggestion has forced your vulgar uncle to gain some life in him yet. I am awaiting some more news on the matter."

"Don't tell me just yet," I pressed. "I want to be kept in suspense for a little longer."

"That is how I wished for it to be, because the news is favorable."

"Good," I said, relieved. "Tell me no more. Wait till all is confirmed."

Good news during the twelve days of Christmas. That was all we needed.

After I told them all about some of the chief highlights of my time at Rosings, I thought to tell them no more, because I wanted to wait till dinner. My sisters, Georgiana and Enara would have stories of their own, and it would be best not to spoil anything.

Mr. Atkins could not remain long, because he had to finish reading some papers for Uncle Philips. Aunt Philips's cook was having some troubles in the kitchen, so Aunt Philips and Mary had to go and tend to it.

This left Uncle Philips and I alone for a few minutes.

"Well," Uncle Philips said, "now that we are alone, tell me, Kitty. Are there any secrets that you need advice on? If there are none, then don't create any. But I just figured that I'd ask in case you were afraid to voice them."

"How did you know that I had secrets?"

"You visited us by yourself, despite knowing that you are dining here this evening. You only ever do that when you have something that you need to tell, or you need to run away from something else. Am I right?"

My emotions betrayed me. Exasperation and pain must have filled my eyes because he saw a problem in them.

"What happened?" He lowered his voice. "Does it have to do with those two indecisive men that you stooped to fall in love with? Do I have to write to either one of them for doing anything foolish or inconsiderate to your feelings?"

"No," I said, but I might as well have wept the word. "It has nothing to do with them. Right now, they keep their distance. And that is good. It will help me sort out my feelings over time. No, the problem is not with them."

"Then what is it?"

"Uncle, I was happy to come home. But I am astonished with how quickly everything can fall apart."

Uncle Philips looked ahead.

"Is it your parents?"

"Yes."

I told him everything that had happened the night before. When I finished, he groaned.

"I know that you think that I exaggerate," I said, "but..."

"I know that you don't. I know my sister and brother-in-law. Kitty, I know them. And what you have described is precisely how they are. I suppose that what I have to say will not offer much comfort, but I am being practical now."

I waited for the lecture. Even though Uncle Philips had

always stood by me, I did go against my parents and was disobedient.

"The fact is, after all that is bewitching about the idea that some people can change over time, that is not always so. Some people are forever trapped in their own ways. Your father has always been a mixture of quick parts, cynical wit, and sarcasm. Marriage to your mother has only brought out that tendency of his even further.

"Wit can easily turn to bitterness if one is married to a person that they do not respect. It reaches a point where that's all they know, and superiority of mind is what they cling to. Your mother was once a vibrant and good-humored woman who was not as intelligent as your father. This led to her entering the marriage with good spirits, but an undeveloped mind, and a character that was still not defined. Her sister, my wife, was older than her, so I found her when she was ready to marry. Your mother was not ready to be a wife yet. She needed a few more years in her.

"Over time, she became a woman who was no longer respected or loved by her husband. To not have your spouse's respect or love can easily destroy a mind. Especially a mind like your mother's. She will cling even more to whatever she can control, and she will hold fast to it, with the mean understanding that has developed from being a disrespected wife. As such, you have an unequal match made between two people. That inequality will lead to how they assess every situation. They will not see matters for how they are. But rather, they will watch it from a view they have set in their minds.

"The reason that your mother and father cannot see you properly, and see what is inside of you, is because they do not reflect upon their own character, and they cannot see what is inside of themselves. Therefore, they have set up an image of you in their minds, that cannot be fully done away with. Even when it seems like they are improving, their instincts will fall back into a sort of default. They will still see things as they once saw them. Your father looks at you and sees a frivolous young woman who is among the silliest women in the country. He improves, but then he forgets. Your mother looks at you and sees you as another daughter of hers. She loves you, but she was wanting a son when she had you. And so, you just became another child in her family who could never live up to Jane's idealism and Lydia's good humor. Neither of them saw you as a young woman, looking for happiness and acceptance, who was trying to discover herself. Their abilities do not stretch so far as to see you in any other way than their own perspective. Even when they improve, the default perspective is still there."

"Then," I said, "it's as Georgiana said. They can never fully understand me. Even when I thought that they were improving."

"Yes. There is that chance. That's why your mother kept talking of marriage. At this point, that's all she knows. You are the daughter who is single, and since she has spent so much time trying to have you all married off, now this is all that she can relate to with you. But you are beyond that, and therefore, you are beyond her conceptions."

"I just... I thought that they would not be so cold when seeing me. Lydia eloped and Mama received her merrily. There was no awkwardness when they met again. I return after telling her and Father how I felt about things. They understood, initially, and now they look on me like I am a foreign concept."

"Lydia is married. Your mother understands marriage. You questioned her parenting skills and your father's as well. They are not used to being questioned in that regard. They are not accustomed to liberality of mindset in that way. At least, not when it comes from you. So, when you do speak out, they will take note of it for a while, but then they will regress. And go back to the beginning, taking you with them."

"Do you think that they will never fully see me?"

"I want to believe that they will, one day. They have made progress in some ways. But, if they do not make a complete development in the matter, I don't want you to allow it to affect you. Respect your parents, Kitty. I want you to understand that. You should always respect those who gave life to you. But I don't want you to be led in the wrong direction."

I sighed.

"I cannot stay at home," I said, "can I?"

"No, you can't. I suspect that you still have some more roads to walk down."

"How do you know that? You are correct. I feel that I do need to walk down some more paths. But truly, how did you know that?"

"You have the same look about you that Arthur had when he went to join the Navy. That restless and wandering look is not an expression that is confined solely to us men. Women have it as well. When I look at you, I see a female version of my son. And so, I guess that's why I favored you. Because I felt that I knew you."

This confession warmed me. Especially since it helped me consider what I had been contemplating before. I still was not sure if I would do it, but Uncle Philips was right. I could not stay home.

"Well," I said, sighing, "I appreciated it. I always did, uncle."

"Also, you and Mary are very good sort of girls. And you both looked like your Aunt Philips when she was young. That helped."

"Oh, I didn't know that."

"Yes. You do, especially. It's hard not to love the younger version of your own wife. Well, as long as you like your wife."

"And you love Aunt Philips."

"Yes, I do. Kitty, don't tell her I told you this, but I wish that I die first."

"You cannot bear the idea of life without her."

"Precisely. I would be lost. As selfish as that sounds."

"That's the sort of selfishness that can always be forgiven."

Mary and Aunt Philips returned, with cakes for us.

Soon, my visit came to an end. I expressed my joy in seeing them soon for dinner, and I set off for home.

Taking a shortcut, I didn't keep to the roads, but rather, I went across fields and along some light woods. This way, I could visit Lucas Lodge one more time before I returned home.

As I walked, I saw a rider riding down the road. At first, I thought nothing of it, because I was a slight distance away. But naturally, one's curiosity always gets the better of them and I looked at the rider who rode casually along.

No, it couldn't be?

But it was!

"Colonel Fitzwilliam!" I cried.

When hearing his name being called, he slowed down his horse and looked around to where he heard my voice.

Through the trees, I began to run.

"Colonel!" I cried, "It's Kitty who calls you! Look to your right."

He looked to where I cried, saw me, and then his eyes

brightened up. Immediately, he dismounted, pulled his horse off the road and along the wood, tied its reins around a branch, and then he dashed toward me.

"Kitty," he uttered as he drew closer.

I could not believe it. Of all people to come, there could not have been a greater surprise.

Since he was coming toward me, I decided to remember decorum and remain in my place. Eagerly, he moved along the trees, moving branches from above him so that he could make progress toward me.

"You found us," I whispered, desperately.

"Yes, I did. I missed you."

Rushing toward me, he grabbed my waist and smiled down at me.

"Did you miss me, my wicked friend?" he asked.

"Oh, Colonel," I said, falling into him. I rested my face against his neck as he wrapped his arms around me. Pressing my hands against his chest, I felt the same warmth that I always felt whenever we held each other.

"Come," he uttered, "we are too close to the road."

Obeying without thinking, I let him lead me further into the wood, where the trees were thicker, closer together, and no one was in sight at all. Indeed, the winter was much in our favor. Due to the cold, no one wished to take a walk anywhere, excepting myself. How much I had been rewarded for it.

When we reached a safe distance from the road, Colonel Fitzwilliam rested me against the tree and wrapped his arm around my waist again.

"Colonel Fitzwilliam has returned to Hertfordshire again," I uttered.

Romance returned to Longbourn.

Chapter Twenty-One

REINFORCEMENT

"Yes," Colonel Fitzwilliam said, under the cover of the wood, "I have."

We looked deeply into each other's eyes.

"Once more, you do not make it easy to overcome my affection for you," I said, getting to the heart of the matter.

"No, I do not. Would Kitty have me apologize?"

"Even if you do, you know that I would forgive you."

"No matter what."

"No matter what."

"Still content to forgive me for anything?"

"I cannot help it. I will never let anything be said against you."

"And I will be your defender."

He raised up his hand and ran his fingers down the side of my face.

"I received your letter," he said.

"Then it is my fault. I gave into you so easily that I allowed myself to call myself your wife, didn't I?"

"You obliged me. I know that it is difficult for you to say no to me, and I suppose I took advantage of it."

"We are both so terribly weak, aren't we?"

"Weak enough to allow you to kiss me?"

I sighed.

"Colonel, I don't want to encourage you anymore. I will not be a bad influence, no matter how sorely I am tempted."

"Are you certain?"

How beautiful he was in his plainness. When looking up into his eyes, where his expression was deeper than an ocean, I could not withhold anything from him. I never could before, and it would be the same now.

"No," I professed, "I am not certain. I know that I do want you to kiss me. I know that I do want your affection. But I also know that I am torn between affections, and I will not encourage you to waste any more time on me. I am not good enough for you."

"Let me be the judge of that."

I sighed. Instinctively, I raised my fingers to his face and pressed my fingers against his lips.

"I am sorry that I am not rich."

"And I am sorry that I am not. Kitty... may I kiss you?"

"If you do, I will not have the strength to resist you again. Richard, I need to have that strength. I... I... dear lord, I missed you so much."

I collapsed into him. He held me as we crouched down onto the ground and the Colonel held me in his embrace.

"Have you come to stay?" I asked him.

"Yes, I have," Colonel Fitzwilliam said, "I will remain at the inn. But I cannot remain for long."

"We will only be here for three days," I said, "stay until then."

"I can do that. Duty calls me away soon after that. I was only given these four days to myself because of the holidays."

"And you decided to spend it with us."

"I had to know how things were for you at Rosings."

"They started out very ill, then things took a little turn, and it ended well. It's a long story. Thank goodness we have three days of time."

He chuckled.

Slowly, he ran his hand along my stomach.

"Richard," I said, sighing, "please, be strong enough for the both of us."

"Kitty," he said, unbuttoning my pelisse and seeing my gown underneath.

"I shall give you a minute," I allowed, unable to deny him anything.

"Thank you," he said, diving his hand down the front of my gown and thrusting his fingers within. I cried out, burying my face into his shoulder so that my exclamations were stifled. Feeling his hands delve under my stays and cup around my breasts, I had to control every part of my being. The ecstasy of it was too overwhelming, and I welcomed it with such intensity, that I wondered when I was going to gather the courage to make him stop.

He was on the verge of tilting my head up to kiss me when I finally remembered myself.

"Richard, we must stop."

"I will, if you say that you are my wife."

"I will be making it harder on you to move on from me."

"Let me be the judge of that. Tell me!"

"I am your wife."

Colonel Fitzwilliam sighed.

"Richard, you promised that you would stop."

"You do not take pleasure in this."

"I take all the pleasure in this. I would not stop you, for the world, if I was allowed. But please, Richard."

Instinctively, he reached down below my gown, reached around the back, and pressed my bottom firmly.

I shrieked, to which he had to cover my mouth.

"Tell me that you would not want me to go away," he uttered.

"Only if you tell me that you will understand why I— why I care for you too much to be the ruin of you. Only if..." His touch was so wonderful that I was slowly losing the gift of speech.

"Fine," he said, "I promise. Now tell me."

"I do not want you to go away."

Sighing out, he gently kissed my forehead and then he ceased.

"I know that you love Finlay," he said, "but for the moment, please pretend like I am the only thing that matters."

"I want better for both of you. While you are here, I shall release him. Just like when you are gone, I will release you." I realized that the only way that I could encourage him was to give him an ultimatum. "If you promise me, Richard, that you will try to find another woman who is worthy of you, I will give you something."

"What?"

"I will give you another moment like this. And then I will kiss you."

He held me tighter.

"Do it now," he hissed. "We might not get another chance."

"But you must promise me."

"Fine," he uttered harshly, "I will try to fall in love else-where. Now, can I?"

Happy to give in, I leaned forward and kissed him.

～

Finally, I was able to feel the bliss of being so far gone, so much falling into my passions, that I wondered how I had gone through so much of my life, not experiencing something of this incredibility before.

Colonel Fitzwilliam pressed his lips against mine for longer and longer, and I lost all sense of time and the space around me.

He dove his hand under my bodice again, and rubbed his hands deeply against my chest, cupping my breasts in his hand. Afterwards, he ran his hands down my leg, under my gown, ran his hand along my leg, up my thigh and finally he dove his hand inside of me.

I cried out in his mouth as he stroked his hand further and further within me.

At last, he stroked me so much that I cried out, my back spasmed and I collapsed against him.

Out of breath, I leaned back as Colonel Fitzwilliam kissed my neck.

"I love you," I could not help but utter.

"And I love you. Can you really find it in you to let me go?"

"Did I not say that I love you?" I repeated.

"Yes, you did."

"And that's why I have the courage to let you go. Richard, I'm not letting you go. I'm giving you up, for a better chance at life."

"My perfect wife—that will never be."

"Yes. Will never be. Thank you, Richard, for thinking I was perfect."

By the gift of providence, we had been completely unseen the entire time. There were no lookers-on, no spying eyes to force us into a union that we both were ill-suited for, and so, we were able to stand up, dust the snow off ourselves and walk through the trees completely unnoticed.

We reached his horse. Colonel Fitzwilliam untied the reins, and he escorted me along the road. This gave him time to explain why he was here, and me time to calm my burning passions.

"The deserter did not prove to be innocent by any means," he explained as we moved along, "it turns out that he deserted because he left many debts behind. He was fleeing the debt collectors."

"Oh," I said, rolling my eyes. "And I was hoping that your soldier was innocent."

"Sometimes, they are. But every now and again, there is one rotten apple in the bunch. And sadly, that is the one that we all remember in life."

"Well," I said, "I will always remember the good as well."

"Yes," he said with a smile, "I suppose that you do." When he looked into my eyes, his expression grew wistful and remorseful.

"You look upset with me," I observed. "What have I done to warrant that look of yours?"

"No. It is just that our past actions are sinking in."

"And the guilt is returning to you."

"Yes, I suppose that it is."

"It is creeping into my mind as well."

"I did it again. I enticed you, took advantage of your love for me, and then I just had to drive you into my desires."

"I was not good at resisting, again," I admitted. "We are so weak, aren't we?"

"We are human. Despite our better instincts, we will always be that way. I confess that I grow more and more apprehensive about Finlay being your first big love. I suppose there is something of the possessive wanton about me. I wish to push my affections into you further and make it the more dominant affection in your eyes."

"Your aunt told me to stay away from you."

When I confessed this, he turned to me so abruptly that he hurt his neck.

"She what!"

~

When I finished telling him everything, to the point where Anne's incident forced Lady Catherine to accept me, Colonel Fitzwilliam was bitter.

"I love my aunt, but she had no right to speak to you in such a manner. Kitty, I am heartily sorry that she addressed you as thus. It was very wrong of her, and I apologize, because I know that she won't."

"She has overcome her anger toward me."

"Not because of any enhancement of mind, but because you saved her daughter. She is obliged to accept you. What I wonder is how she ever learned of my affection for you."

"That's what I wish to know. But I suppose that it will forever be a mystery. At first, I was angry that she spoke so, but over time, I have been considering the subject. Between her, your brother, your parents, and common sense, I have come to accept that I was angry with her because, despite it all, she had a point. She addressed a problem that we have been afraid to submit to. Richard, I cannot cling to you forever. I must let you go. I will."

"Yes. And I must let you go. But not today, Kitty."

"No, not today. Today, I am your wife and will adore you terribly. But tomorrow, we must try."

"Yes, we must. We will fail, won't we?"

"Oh, we always do. But we must try anyway."

Eventually, we passed Lucas Lodge, and I asked him if he was willing to step in for a brief visit.

Since we were man and wife for a day, he agreed, and we entered to find Sir William and Lady Lucas happy to receive us.

At this point, Maria Lucas did return, and she wasn't alone.

"Mr. Liam Lucas and Diana!" I cried.

Mr. Liam Lucas and Diana Long were also present.

So eager to see them, I almost raced toward them, but I did my best not to tackle them.

"Kitty!" Maria and Diana cried.

"Well now," Mr. Liam Lucas declared, "aren't you a sight for sore eyes?"

"Sore or safe," I said, "I am happy to be a sight for anyone. I bring the Colonel with me."

They greeted each other, and I was not disappointed in my husband-for-a-day. Colonel Fitzwilliam always had the unique skill of making anyone comfortable around him. Sir William and Lady Lucas occupied his attention, while I was able to speak to Maria, Diana, and Mr. Lucas.

"It feels like ages since we saw each other," Diana cried.

"Of course, because it has been an age," I said. "Two of them, point of fact."

"I was going to say three," Mr. Lucas declared, "but who's counting?"

"I am sure that you are not," I replied, teasingly.

"Still a tease?"

"Liam!" Maria cried. "Kitty does no such thing. She is merely friendly."

"Thank you, Maria, for defending my good name."

"Oh, but it was no offense at all. In fact, it was a compliment."

"A compliment?" I echoed.

"Yes," he confirmed. "I like a woman who knows how to tease. They keep life interesting."

"Then may you find your modern-day Cleopatra," I said, "she was the expert at such matters."

"Well, Mr. Dixon has that done very well. But, for my part, I still am not to be so easily satisfied."

I squinted.

"Mr. Dixon?"

"Yes," Diana Long informed me. "Oh, you didn't know? But of course, you didn't. You just arrived so perhaps no one told you the news yet."

"I am glad of it," Maria said, "we are the first to convey the good news. Kitty, what do you think? Mr. Dixon is going to be married."

My mouth dropped open.

"Mr. Dixon is getting married?"

"Yes, he is. Is it not wonderful?"

Looking back at my history with Mr. Dixon, remembering when he proposed to me, to our argument, and even to when we reconciled, he never mentioned a new infatuation of his. But perhaps it was a sudden sort of love.

All I knew was that this was the most wonderful news of all.

"Yes, it is," I answered. "This is incredible. Is the lady anyone that we know?"

"Her name is Miss Georgette Simpkins. She moved in with her cousin, who is lately with child, around three months ago."

"What sort of woman is she? Is she kind? Is she handsome?"

"She is not a great beauty, but she is not unpleasant to look at either," Maria Lucas said, "and there is something attractive about her."

"Some women are more striking than beautiful," Diana said, "she has a striking countenance."

"As someone who has met her," Mr. Lucas said, "I can assure you that she appears to be a kind and amiable person. But sometimes, we humans are very good at putting up facades."

I laughed.

"Well," I finalized, "I daresay that is the best news that I have had all day. I am very happy for him."

"So am I," Maria said, "so am I."

Eventually it was time to depart for Longbourn. The Lucases and Diana Long saw us off, very good-naturedly, and expressed their joy in seeing the Colonel again.

As we walked away, Colonel Fitzwilliam noticed that I was smiling.

"You look happy," he said as we walked back to Longbourn. "Does that mean that your guilt has dissolved?"

"It is distracted, because of some news that I have just heard."

"What is it?"

"Colonel, it is the sign of a heart healing. Miracles have come to Hertfordshire."

Chapter Twenty-Two
MY ANNOUNCEMENT

T hat evening we dined at the Philips', and it could not have been a merrier gathering.

First, the joy on my aunt and uncle's faces when they saw their son and daughter-in-law again was priceless. Aunt Philips practically wept aloud with happiness, for she had not expected to see Arthur for at least a couple of years.

Colonel Fitzwilliam was also a welcome addition to the family, and my aunt and uncle saw no need to worry about the unexpected addition to the party.

"And if there is no seat for me," Colonel Fitzwilliam said, "never fear, I am a soldier. I am accustomed to eating while standing."

"Not at all, sir," Aunt Philips said, "there is always another chair to be found, and we always plan for extra helpings for food."

"Dennison," Uncle Philips called, "bring in another chair for the table and things rearranged."

"Yes, sir," Dennison said, tending to it at once.

We sat down, all attention and eagerness. Accidentally, we all began to talk at once, and that made us laugh.

"We ought to begin with your visit to Rosings Park," Colonel Fitzwilliam said, "for I am eager to know of the holiday that I sadly missed out on."

"Oh, poor Colonel," Enara said, "you missed out on some incredible experiences. First, did Kitty have time to tell you? She saved Anne de Bourgh's life."

The Colonel turned to me, along with my aunt, uncle, Mary, Mr. Atkins, and my parents.

"Indeed?" Colonel Fitzwilliam asked, feigning surprise. "Kitty, what?"

"Yes," Aunt Philips said. "What is this, Kitty?"

"Oh," Kitty said, "I did little."

"Not true," Arthur continued. "Kitty belittles her act of heroism. Miss de Bourgh was about to fall down the stairs. A fall down some stairs is already a very fatal thing for the average person. But with Miss de Bourgh being a sickly and slight sort of creature, it would have been disastrous. Kitty caught her before she fully fell, at the risk of falling herself."

"Why didn't you tell us this when you visited earlier today?" Mary asked.

"I promise," I said, "I didn't do it by way of ignoring the issue, I swear. It's just, for some reason, it never seems to come to my mind to talk about it. Or maybe it's because people looked at me differently when they learned that about me."

"About your heroism?" Mr. Atkins said. "You didn't want people to admire your courage or intuition?"

"No, it's not that. I do like being appreciated—I suppose that is my vain side."

"We all have that side to us."

"Yes. What I refer to is the look of having expectations

placed on one. When you save a life, it's almost as if you become responsible for that life. And you feel as if people look at you in a way that displays..."

"Reverence?" Jane said for me.

"Well, yes."

Jane took a sip of her coffee.

"As is, you are perfect, and that perfection is antagonizing to you. It makes everyone look at you differently and always expect you to be the best at things. To have high expectations of you. And that is too heavy a burden to bear, isn't it? It's daunting. Especially since you just want to be seen for being as human as any other, while still being worthy of being loved."

When Jane said this, you could hear a pin drop. We were all so silent.

"Yes," I uttered, quietly. "That's precisely how I felt. You understand?"

"Yes, I do."

"Do you understand me because you have felt it before?"

Jane blushed, but she didn't respond. I realized that it was dreadful to ask her about that, even though it was a family party. Therefore, I rushed out my next sentence.

"Well, yes, I did feel that. Which is strange because I do usually like having people's good opinion of me. Vain again."

"And common again," Mr. Atkins said.

"But the fear of being revered for one's heroic deed leads to everyone putting you on a pedestal," I continued. "I suppose, maybe I don't talk about it because I know that I would fall off that lofty height eventually."

"While I would say that it's not your fault if people place you into an ideal, but theirs," Jane continued, "I know that the world will not see it that way. Now you know why

I always didn't censure or despise your spirited nature. I wanted you to enjoy your youth and the freedom that comes from knowing that you didn't have such limitations."

"Oh," I said, "I didn't know that, Jane."

"Well, there was no proper way for me to phrase it."

"That's true wisdom, Jane," Uncle Philips said, "you and I have more in common than I thought."

Jane smiled and looked down at her lap.

"Oh, and now you are returned to being the one that is praised," Uncle Philips said. "It's a never-ending cycle with you, isn't it?"

"Well, I shall not weep over my lot in life," Jane said, "it's a better lot than most. But Kitty, you did a good deed, but don't worry, we still know who you are, and will not place you on that pedestal."

"Very wise again, Mrs. Bingley," Colonel Fitzwilliam said, "and I propose a toast that is more like a promise. To Kitty, who saved my cousin's life, but we will still look on her as we always did before."

"To Kitty!" They all toasted and then they drank. I sighed.

"Oh," I said, "well, thank you. Now I can say that I am ready to talk about it."

"What was it like?" Mary asked. "When you caught Miss de Bourgh?"

"You want the truth."

"Well, why not?"

"In fact, when I did it, it was like I was not even thinking. Rather, it was like I was just acting on impulses. All thought left and pure instinct took over."

"That happens with men amidst battles," Colonel Fitzwilliam said.

"It does?"

"Yes, it does. Sometimes, men have been known to be

so driven by impulse, that they were shot in their leg, and they didn't even know that they had been till after the battle ended."

"Truly?" Elizabeth asked. "All that pain and the body overrides it?"

"Yes, it does. Because the body is acting on pure driven instinct and that power makes one override the painful factors. Or that's why some soldiers rush into battle with no fear. The instinct takes over and their fighting side begins to come into effect. That's what you were feeling, Kitty. The instinct to protect took over, and your mind shut down."

"As with soldiers," Elizabeth confirmed, "to know the mind of the fighting man, can be inside of a lady in a drawing room. Well, it certainly does bridge the gap that is placed there."

"Yes," I said, "it does. I didn't know that was what I was feeling. Then I didn't feel for quite some time. Later, all these emotions came racing back to me. But the main emotion was—"

"Fear?" Colonel Fitzwilliam guessed.

"Yes. I was scared."

"That's the natural reaction that occurs later. You are afraid about all the possibilities. What if you missed catching Anne? What if you dropped her? What if you fell with her?"

"Yes! All those fears rushed back to me."

"Your mind returned. It doesn't mean any less of you. It just shows, that in the heart of the moment, your instincts will take over and you will be brave."

"That's something about myself that I never knew."

"You don't?" Mr. Darcy asked. "You've acted this way before. You just didn't notice that about yourself."

"But still," Mama cried, a little breathy, "Mr. Bennet,

did you hear? Our daughter saved Lady Catherine's only child and heir. Well, Kitty, I am proud of you. Aren't we, Mr. Bennet?"

"Yes," Father responded, a little bashful, especially since he couldn't think of anything witty to say back. "We are."

"Well," I said, gently, "thank you, Mama and Papa. That... that means a great deal to me."

"And to think," Mama continued, "that now that you saved her child, Lady Catherine must feel like she is quite in your debt. Think of all the handsome rich men that she will introduce you to. I see a large house and large estate in your future."

And once again, we had been brought back down to the painful reality that I must be wed soon. I looked at the Colonel, who was upset when hearing this. How could I spare his feelings?

"But, for the sake of your feelings, we can talk of other matters." Mr. Darcy turned to the rest of my family. "Wait till the ladies tell you what they did on Christmas Day."

"Oh," Mama said, "did you do your usual tradition?"

"This time, it was grander," Elizabeth said. "Kitty asked Miss Anne de Bourgh for a favor, and Miss de Bourgh repaid it by making it a larger event than usual."

Jane and Elizabeth told our family the story, with Enara adding touches every now and again.

I sat there, silently, reflecting on recent memories that were undergone.

The narrative shifted from our Christmas caroling, to New Years Day, and the entire meal was spent with recollections of Rosings Park.

While cards were brought forth, and the tables were arranged for us to sit down to a game of Whist, Aunt Philips turned to Arthur.

"Son," she said, "you did very well to come and visit us

before you set sail, but it is as it always is when parting with one's children. It's very difficult to endure it."

"I know," Arthur said. "I have made poor work of being a loving son. Yet, mark my words, I will return as soon as everything is settled and making the journey back home is convenient. The only regret that I have in this scenario is that my lovely Enara here has had the good fortune to meet my parents, but her parents will never be able to make my family's acquaintance. I think they would find you all to be the most agreeable creatures in the world."

This gave me the opportunity that I wished for. For weeks, I had this secret desire and had been feasted on by dreams that I didn't know what they indicated. But, for many days now, I knew. I knew what ought to be done.

"Well, would a cousin suffice?" I asked.

Everyone turned to me.

"What?" Mama echoed. "Kitty, what cousin do you speak of, pray?"

"Of myself." I turned to Arthur and Enara. "For quite some time, I had been wondering that maybe it would be better for one of your family to come acknowledge Enara's family. I was wondering if you both would wish for me to come with you and join you on the voyage to Australia."

Enara cheered, standing up. This was supported by Arthur, who rushed to me, gay.

"Kitty, you remarkable little imp!" he cried, taking my arms, and swinging me around. "What a thoroughly good idea!"

Enara embraced me as I laughed merrily.

"That is the most wonderful news in the world!" she cried. "My family would look forward to your coming. And we don't have to worry about you coming without them being ignorant of you joining the party. We always have a guest room that is easy to prepare. Often guests come and go from the place, that we are used to more than one addition to our party."

I sighed, happy that they enjoyed the idea of it. Inviting oneself is never proper to do. One must wait to be invited somewhere. But if there was anything that I learned from Lydia's encounter with Mrs. Forster, was that I was the one who would not often be invited anywhere. As such, I knew that, maybe, I had to take matters into my own hands. It all could have fallen in front of me, and I would have been met by a very civil rejection. I would have been humiliated and mortified.

Therefore, it was more than pleasant to see the reverse occur. My self-invitation was met with eagerness and acceptance. The light in Enara and Arthur's eyes was proof of that. Finally, after weeks of secret planning, it all came true.

There was only one problem: there were other people in the room who had power over my actions.

"But," Mama cried, "that is quite out of the question."

Our enthusiastic cloud was quite dissolved at this decline.

"Out of the question?" I repeated. "Why so?"

"Kitty," Mama said, "it is too dangerous a journey. Mr. Bennet, tell her so."

"Oh," Father said, "forgive me, I am called to make a decision. For a moment, I did not think that Kitty was serious."

"What about me did not sound serious in that moment?" I asked him, pointedly. When he saw that I was insistent, Father leaned back in his chair, wondering what the best way was to attack me.

"Kitty, your mother is correct," Father said, "it is a dangerous journey."

"More dangerous than the journey that Enara must

make?" I countered on my parents. "If she can brave the journey, why am I more important than her?"

"It is different," Father said, "Mrs. Philips is a married woman. You are single."

"All the more reason for me to go," I added. "I am single, unmarried, and have no child to leave behind. My health has improved very much over this last year, I am at the stage in my life where I am as strong as I will ever be. Also, I have learned to become more of use to others. I propose that I am the perfect candidate of the family to go. And Enara and Arthur are amenable to the plan. Therefore, what is the reason for keeping me here?"

"Because you have not consulted us about this at all," Mother said, "I find that very hard. Very hard indeed."

"I did not include myself in their voyage out of disrespect toward yourself or thought that it indicated any disobedience. I am traveling, with family, to another country, where the Rileys have every right to become acquainted with us."

Colonel Fitzwilliam shifted in his seat, uncomfortable.

"Kitty, while I understand the inclination to want to visit the Rileys, I can understand your parents' discomfort at not being consulted first. It must be proper to always appeal to one's parents before inviting yourself somewhere."

I was disappointed with him supporting my parents' stance, but I was not surprised. In fact, I predicted that he would do that and did not despise him. After all, I knew the source of his viewpoint. Also, I knew that I would have to apologize later.

"Yes," I said, "you all are right. But now the subject has occurred, and it cannot be undone."

"Kitty," Jane added, "it is a difficult matter indeed."

"Very much so," Mr. Darcy added. "Kitty, life on a ship

is very different than what you are accustomed to. Enara has grown used to that style of living because she has undergone it before. But you will be deprived of pleasures that you are not used to."

"Precisely," Mama added. "You do not know if you are capable of suffering under seasickness. The food on the voyage will upset you. And your cough might return."

"These are all possibilities that I might encounter," I said, "but I find the positives of the adventure to greatly outweigh the negative. I could learn to adapt to a new way of living. I can see the ocean, face differences, gather a wider knowledge of the way of the world, and meet the new family that we have."

I looked at everyone in the room.

"I would have thought that you all would understand how important it is that we establish a connection between both families. Especially at this time of the year, where we preach of goodwill toward man and love for our fellow people as we head closer to the grave. Are these but words that are spoken in the church and we ignore them when we leave it?"

I ignored looking at Colonel Fitzwilliam because I knew that I had quite betrayed him. He had come to see us, and I was announcing my desire to leave England for at least three months. The poor man did not know that I was doing it for his own good.

As for the rest in my company, they all were caught up in the logic that they didn't want to confront. All, excepting aunt and uncle Philips.

"Sister," Aunt Philips said to my mother. "While I am the first to always confirm that a child ought to be obedient to one's parents, I do not believe that our Kitty joins my son to be disagreeable or difficult. Rather, I think she does it out of devotion to Arthur and Enara. I cannot help but feel the compliment of it."

"Well, of course, sister," Mama said, "you know that your family is of great importance to us, and I value it as highly as my own. It is just that I don't believe Kitty is quite up for the journey, as she believes herself to be."

I groaned.

"I am right here," I said. "There is no need to talk about me as if I were in the other room."

"And what must be considered," Uncle Philips added, supporting me, "is that Kitty is right. We should have one family member to go and meet the Rileys. Kitty is the best candidate for it. And she is a young and independent woman."

"She still depends on her father's supporting her," Mama said.

"Is this what you really wish, Kitty?" Elizabeth asked me suddenly.

Everyone turned to her.

Bracing myself, I tried to maintain my courage.

"Yes, it is."

"Then I will supply you with the pin money that you might need when you go, and your ticket purchase."

Once more, everyone turned to her. For some reason, Elizabeth always had a habit of making everyone accept her way of thinking. From when Mama was against having her walk three miles to Netherfield, to Mama being against her refusing Mr. Collins, Elizabeth always won. There was a finality to her tone, a determination that made everyone take her seriously. It was a skill that I had yet to fully acquire.

And so, I knew that my plan had been accepted.

I would go.

"Really?" I said to Elizabeth. "You would do that for me?"

"Yes, I would. You deserve it, and you, Aunt, and Uncle Philips, have a point. One of us should go and meet Enara's family.

"She turned to Papa. "There will be no expense on your part. And Mama, Kitty will be in Arthur and Enara's company. And as to danger, leaving Britain is no more or less safe than remaining in it. Experience has shown us that a young lady can find danger among officers in Brighton, or around the wrong sorts in other towns. Therefore, danger is always possible. The only way that a young lady can avoid danger, altogether, is if she never leaves her home."

"And we Bennet ladies have always left home," Mary said, "and come back, through it all. I agree with Elizabeth and the rest. Kitty has every right to go."

"This all can be discussed later," Father said.

"But they will not be here for long," Uncle Philips said, "therefore, maybe it ought to be settled."

Father gave Uncle Philips the disagreeable eye, and Uncle Philips did not take heed to it.

"Let's weigh the circumstances," Uncle Philips said. "For it takes time to prepare to travel. A great deal needs to be done. If Kitty goes, there is no expense to you, Mr. Bennet. Her sister has volunteered to pay her way. If Kitty goes, she has my son as a chaperone, and my son—your nephew—has proven to be a brave man who has faced many a danger. He will keep her safe, at the expense of his own life. My new daughter's family ought to be recognized by someone in our family, and my wife and I are of an age where we cannot make the journey. This is the time of year where one is supposed to open their hearts to their fellow creatures."

"Precisely," Arthur confirmed. "Aunt and Uncle Bennet,

I would appreciate it if Kitty comes with us. I find it to be a great compliment. Do you not trust me? Do you not believe that I will do all in my power to make certain that Kitty remains safe?"

"But there are different diseases in New South Wales," Father said, apprehensive. "You cannot protect her from that."

"There are diseases in England that take lives," Arthur continued, "both nations pose those same dangers."

"I will risk it," I confirmed, still ignoring Colonel Fitzwilliam's eye. "And if sickness does take my life, amidst the journey, then neither Arthur nor Enara is guilty of it. It is the way of life, and I will face it."

"The young always think that they are immortal," Father sighed.

"I wish that I was," I refuted, "but I know that I am not. But still, I wish to go. Father and mother, won't you give me your blessing?"

Mama and father looked at each other, resigned.

"Very well. Kitty, you may go."

I sighed, relieved, and Arthur, Enara, my aunt, uncle, and Mr. Atkins were happy for me.

The rest of the company was in a different state of quiet acceptance, or disgust at my leaving. I wished to take the latter reaction as their sign that they would miss me. But I did not want to flatter myself or puff myself up. They were probably angry at my impertinence.

Fortunately, my news was not the final announcement of the evening.

"We wanted to wait till near the end," Mary said, "to give our announcement. And I think it was properly earned."

Mary and Mr. Atkins looked at each other.

"Family," Mr. Atkins announced, "for we are all family

here, my beloved Mary and I have the most delightful news. Elizabeth and Jane, you have begun a trend in this family, that my wife and I are happy to repeat."

Taking in Mary's glowing countenance, it all now began to make sense. Indeed, perhaps I should have known before!

"Everyone," Mary said, "Dr. Johnson has been to see me, and it is confirmed. Mr. Atkins and I are going to become parents soon, for I am with child."

To say that the room was now filled with joy was enough.

"Three daughters with child!" Mama cried. "Oh, Mr. Bennet, we will be grandparents three times over."

"Yes, so it would seem."

"What is the saying? All good things come in threes."

"Living life by phrases, that is how Longbourn functions. I suppose."

They kissed Mary on the cheek.

"Oh, Mary! This is wonderful news indeed. You have done your duty. You stay here and have settled into your proper place. You do not run off and break your mother's heart."

I flinched, knowing that I was being slighted in every way.

"Well," Mary said, "thank you, but different women have different paths."

I smiled, looking at the floor. She was being kind to me.

"Let us focus on the good of this moment," Mr. Atkins added, helping to smooth the way. "Mr. Darcy and Mr. Bingley, we are to be fathers."

"Yes," Bingley said, "welcome to the role, Mr. Atkins. I think, like us, you will take to it admirably."

"I hope so, Mr. Bingley. Indeed, I hope so."

The rest of the dinner party was focused on Mary and Mr. Atkin's happy news.

My 'awkward' announcement had been all but forgotten as we discussed the child of the happy couple, and of course, the party directed its attention to Elizabeth and Jane's bloom.

"Well," I said, when I managed to get Mary's attention, "I should have known. You were looking lovely in a way that you usually never allow yourself."

"I don't see it," Mary said to me, "truly, I don't see it at all. But if you say so."

"I *know* so. I am happy for you."

"And I am for you," Mary said to me. Then she lowered her voice. "Kitty, usually I am not the sort to believe in being disagreeable towards one's parents or being disobedient. But in this case, you are right. I think you should go to Australia."

"You do?" I whispered back, equally as quietly. "Really?"

"Yes. One of us should go to recognize the Rileys'. And also...this is important to you, isn't it?"

"Yes, it is. How did you know?"

"Because I know you. Out of all of us, you are not the sort where a neighborhood is your world. I am happy here in Hertfordshire. I don't need any other place. It's the same with Lizzy at Pemberley, and Jane wherever Mr. Bingley is. Lydia was most at home wherever she could be seen with advantage. But you...you are restless, aren't you?"

"Yes, I confess that I am. But it's more than that. My going is as much selfless as it is selfish. Although you are right. I have wandering feet."

"You need to see more of the world."

"Yes, I do."

"Then go to it. Hold fast to it. Mr. Atkins and I will support you, as well as aunt and uncle Philips."

"You will?"

"Of course," she assured me. "I know you and understand you. I will defend you."

My heart swelled at the kindness of it. Between Jane's understanding me, Elizabeth's financing and encouraging me, and Mary's willingness to stand by me, I felt loved again.

"Mary, that was all I ever wanted from you."

"I know that now. When it comes to wisdom, I suppose it is like anything else: better late than never."

When the party ended, our carriage was drawn at the same time as Colonel Fitzwilliam's horse being brought.

The whole evening, I had never gotten the chance to speak with him in confidence. Due to the hustle and bustle of arranging everything, Colonel Fitzwilliam was separate from the rest. That gave me the chance to approach him as he was leaving.

"Colonel," I said, "Richard, I—"

I cut myself off when I saw him look on me with bold defiance and anger.

"What more have you to say?" he asked. "Something else to make me despise the sight of you?"

I blinked, overwhelmed with his declaration. I knew that he would be upset, naturally, but this was a side of him that I had not seen. It broke my heart for only a few seconds before I rallied and remembered my nerve.

"You must hear me," I said desperately, "you will hear me, Richard."

He ignored me, quickly bid us goodnight kindly, and quitted the house.

I hated myself. But I also was angry with him for not giving me the chance to explain myself.

But I was not going to give up. He was a fool to think that I would!

We returned to Longbourn, had our baths, and soon Georgiana and I were lying in bed, staring up at the tester canopy.

"You really are going to New South Wales?" Georgiana asked. "You will be gone for months."

"I know," I said, "but it's the right thing to do. Not just for myself, but for my family, and for both men. Especially the Colonel. You know why."

"Yes, I do know why."

"I will miss you," I said, "and don't worry. I'm not that selfish that I would ask you to go with me, just because I'm not used to you being too far away from me."

The sheets ruffled when Georgiana turned her head and looked at me.

"You want me to go with you?"

"Yes," I said, "but I am not going to ask, so don't feel guilt over not going with me. It is dangerous, and I know that it's not something that you would be interested in. Besides, you have many friends in England already. That will give you the chance to find your way back to them again, especially since I have been a very greedy friend."

"You haven't been that. Or rather, I've been equally as greedy. In truth, I was upset that you wanted to go to Australia because I thought that you weren't thinking of me. But now that I know that you were but merely didn't want to impose your intentions on me, well, I am not against you inviting me along."

Could this be? Could my friend really be that incredible that she would follow me into the unknown? It was a dangerous thing to have so much influence on a person, but I could not think of it. Yes, my selfishness was taking over me again, and I felt as if I could not overcome it.

"You really would wish to come?" I questioned. "Georgiana, I would like it if you did. But it must be understood that New South Wales is a land that is not only very different, but life might be harsh. It's a land that we colonized, is where our convicts were sent, and is being rebuilt into a proper civilization, but it is not there yet. We will be journeying into the unknown. I am not against that. In fact, I am looking forward to it, mishaps and misadventures and all. But are you sure that you are willing? I would hate to have influenced you to go somewhere that would be antagonizing you at every turn."

"I know what is in store for me. I know that I am leaving the comforts of English civilization to see the pains and labors of a land being utterly changed. I know that I might see the horrors of life. And yet, through all that, I still feel compelled to go."

"Then you know what I feel? I know that ships have been known to meet with tragedy on the high seas. And yet, I want to go. I know that the Rileys might not prefer my company. And yet, I want to go. I know that, while there, we will be met with rough and harsh wilderness. And yet, I want to go. I know that we may face disease that might take my life. And yet, I want to go."

"Precisely." Georgiana laughed. "I know that something horrible could happen, and yet I am not afraid."

"I think it's because we know what adventure is. But Georgie, are you sure? I must ask once and for all. Do not be influenced by me wanting you to come. There—still want to join Arthur, Enara and I?"

"Yes, I do. Besides, we will not be entirely lost from society. Remember, Emma Watson is going to be on the same ship that we will be on. She books passage on The Lilia. When we arrive, we not only have the Rileys, but we will meet the Watsons. That will be interesting because Emma has many brothers and sisters."

"That's true."

Georgiana mistook my two words as an indication that I was not optimistic about it.

"You will like Emma Watson. Actually, what am I saying? She was raised to be refined and might not possess the very spark that drives you. Maybe you both will get along, or you will not. We will see. I only ask that you give her a chance."

"I will," I assured Georgiana. "But Georgie, you must understand that it's as you say. I knew Emma Watson to be refined, having an air of decided fashion. I think I am not going to suit her company, because there is a coarseness about me. I speak as I find. Ladies like that usually do not prefer ladies like me. I just fear that she will not like me."

"If she does not, I will stand by you."

I smiled.

"Georgie, that's all I need."

I closed my eyes, content. Between Jane, Lizzy's, Mary and my aunt and uncle's support, and knowing that Georgiana would be in my company, now I felt even more certain that I was on the right path.

And all my dreams could finally be put to rest.

Until my eyes opened when I remembered another source of intense discontent.

"Georgie..."

"Yes?" she asked, her eyes closed as she was about to fall asleep.

"I have another problem."

"And by that, you mean that Colonel Fitzwilliam rode all this way to see you, and us, only for you to leave England for months?"

I closed my eyes, feeling the guilt that she deliberately was trying to push on me.

"I suppose that I deserve that," I said.

"Yes, you do. I know why you did what you did, but yes, you do deserve that. Did it make you feel guilty?"

"Yes, it did."

"Good. You should feel that too."

"Now I need to fix it."

"You need me to help you, don't you?"

"Yes, I do. I need to make amends for the agony I put Richard through. Tomorrow, we need to go to the inn, and I need to speak to him."

"Very well. I'll have the carriage drawn tomorrow."

"Thank you."

"Good luck trying to fall asleep."

"You know, very well, that I am not going to sleep well at all."

"I know. Good. You deserve that too."

She was right. I did deserve it.

It took hours, but sleep found me... an hour before it was time to wake up.

Chapter Twenty-Three

AMENDS

The next day, Georgiana and I informed the company that we were going to the inn, to visit the Colonel. If I had asked to go alone, my parents would never have allowed it. After all, the Colonel was an officer, and my father still didn't trust me with that lot.

Before going, I wrote a letter, by way of express, to be sent to Mrs. Forster. It was to inform her that I was to leave for Australia shortly, and to tell Finlay about it. I paid for the express messenger myself, so that Lieutenant Finlay would know about my departure before I left England.

Before Georgiana and I left for the inn, however, Mr. Darcy took me aside.

"I know why you go," he informed me.

"You do?" I asked. "Did the Colonel tell you about his unquiet feelings toward my announcement?"

"He didn't need to. I saw it in his eyes. But I also know that you are going there to make amends with him."

"Yes, I am. Before you think that my going to Australia is done out of carelessness for his love for me, it is not.

Believe this or not, I am doing this *for* him. Absence from me will help him. I should explain."

"You don't need to. I am happy that you are thinking about the matter in so realistic a way. I do not say this lightly. But this is a difficult situation for you, and for him. I just... Kitty, I need you to do something for me."

"What?"

"I need you to encourage him to—I need you to break his heart."

My stomach suddenly became filled with a harsh anxiety and as if water was boiling within it.

"What?" I whispered, harshly.

"Kitty, his love for you is intense. I am happy for him and for you, in that you both have found such a great passion. However, you and I both know that he needs to move on from this."

I sighed.

"It's a terrible thing," I said, "how much this is killing me. I can't tell you the agony of wanting to release someone that you are in love with."

"Actually, I know a little more about that than you know. For months, I tried not to love your sister. I know what you are feeling."

"Yes, I think you do." My heart was breaking, and I knew that it showed in my eyes. "I know why you ask this of me. But could you have said the same thing to Elizabeth? Could you have broken her heart?"

For a moment, Mr. Darcy's stern brow gave way, and I saw a contemplative expression. A look of gentle confusion that might have shown heartache.

"No," he said, "I could not have."

"Precisely. That is why Colonel Fitzwilliam, and I continue to always be running in circles around each other. Why we indulge this vicious cycle that we refuse to progress away from. It's because he and I cannot hurt each other. If we hurt the other, we hurt ourselves. Look at me. I choose to go to Australia, partly for his sake, and I broke his heart. Now look at me. Here I am, rushing to make amends. Because I cannot bear to hurt him. Do you know, Mr. Darcy, that I spent the entire night being unable to fall asleep? I could not rest for hours, knowing that Colonel Fitzwilliam was alive, in the world, and thinking ill of me."

"I know that it's difficult," he said, rubbing his lips. "Yes, it must be agony for you. It's painful because you both are quite perfect for each other."

"Yes, we are. And so, it hurts to know that we are actually not."

"I know."

Mr. Darcy turned away from me.

"Georgiana told me about her wish to join you, to Australia."

Holding my waist, I steadied myself. I was prepared for his reprobation, his reprimands, and his refusal.

"I know that you must be upset with me wanting her to come with me," I said. "But—"

"I gave her my permission to go with you."

I brightened up immediately.

"You did?"

He turned back to me.

"Yes, I did."

Excited, I rushed up to him and hugged him. At this point in our relationship, Mr. Darcy was accustomed to my public displays of familial affection. No longer awkward at my actions, he simply wrapped his hands around my shoulders, returning the embrace.

"I did not expect that." I laughed.

"I can see as such. At first, I admit that I was upset and

refused. Absolutely refused. The dangers of it. And for her to go where I cannot see her frightens me."

"I empathize."

"Often, we men appear as being very possessive. I want you to know how that sometimes, it just comes from a place of fear. We worry about you all. And when you go where we cannot follow, it is—it scares us. Because we know the dangers of the world. We know the horrors, and we know that you are not impervious to them, as we are not. But the more that I thought of it, the more that I knew it was best to accept it."

"What convinced you? What drove you to overcome your fears?"

"It was what you said the other night. There are dangers in England as well. A woman can become ill and die here. Danger is just a part of life. I cannot cling to Georgiana forever, or I might stifle her. But I will press upon you both to be careful. Please, take every precaution."

"I will. Excepting illness, which is beyond my control— I will keep Georgie safe. Any danger that might occur, I will get in its way. I will not let anything happen to her, for it will happen to me first."

"You promise this?"

"I do."

Mr. Darcy smiled again.

"I trust you," he said.

That small admission was another compliment that fortified me. To have Mr. Darcy's trust, well, that was no small feat.

"And I am sorry," he added. "I don't want to hurt my cousin, but I do it to protect him."

"I know you do. But still, I cannot fully hurt him."

"I know that you cannot. I didn't want to have to put something like that on you. But still, try and convince

Richard to find another woman. But if you still love him, which I know you do, then I understand if you let him know."

"I cannot help it. Thank you."

~

Georgiana and I traveled to the inn, where we requested to be shown to Colonel Fitzwilliam's room. The servant showed us upstairs, and the door opened to Colonel Fitzwilliam seated by the fire, with his jacket off. Since he was in his waistcoat, half-opened and his shirtsleeves were rolled up, he was naturally not expecting visitors. The servant closed the door behind us, leaving the three of us alone.

"Georgiana," Colonel Fitzwilliam said, standing up and rolling down his sleeves. When his eyes fell on me, his expression fell with it. First, he looked downcast. Next, he looked resentful. I wasn't afraid in the slightest.

"Kitty," he uttered.

"Richard," I said. "We are glad to see you. I... I wish to speak to you on a matter which I don't want you to be ignorant of for long."

"Ignorant?" he repeated, sternly. "In my opinion, you made yourself quite clear last night. And since you both are inclined to visit me before I was fully dressed or prepared to receive guests, I would ask that you wait downstairs until I am prepared to receive you."

He walked past us to open the door.

Enraged at his impertinence and disgust, I rushed up behind him and I pressed my hand against his fingers, on the doorknob, making him unable to open it.

"I will go nowhere," I declared. "Not until you hear me."

This action showed that I could not be anything else but myself. For I had quite pressed him against the door, which led to him pressing his back against me. The feeling of his body against mine was intoxicating. I just knew that I needed him to feel loved.

"Richard…"

Slowly, he removed his hand from the knob and placed it over mine.

Instinctively, I wrapped my other arm around his waist, and he rested his other arm over mine, as I held him.

"Please," I uttered, "as a woman who loves you, let me explain myself."

Colonel Fitzwilliam blushed and remained in my embrace, despite that I was significantly smaller than him.

"Georgie?" he said, over his shoulder.

"If you don't mind," Georgiana said, "is your bedroom ill-qualified for a woman to be in it?"

"We are cousins, and my room has nothing in it offensive to your eyes."

"You both will only have five minutes."

"Thank you," I said.

Quickly, Georgiana left the room, and our five minutes began.

❧

When alone, Colonel Fitzwilliam held my hands even tighter.

"Kitty, take off your pelisse."

"Richard, I promised that I would not do anything to encourage you or be a bad influence."

"Kitty. Take off your pelisse."

"Richard, I shouldn't."

"Kitty," he said, looking into my eyes, "take off your pelisse."

How weak I was!

Giving in, I removed my pelisse coat, gloves, and bonnet. Since I had worn my green floral gown, it had a lower neckline. Gowns that reached my neck were always confining and I despised wearing them. When seeing how I looked, Colonel Fitzwilliam took my arms, led me over to some chairs, sat down on one while I stood in front of him. Then he rested his head on my chest, with his arms pressed around my waist, holding me in place.

"Kitty," he said, "why do you do this?"

"I know that you think I am abandoning you," I uttered, thoroughly enjoying feeling the warmth of his skin pressed against mine.

"What am I to think? You allowed me to call you my wife and then you plan to leave for months? Is that not the very definition of inconstancy?"

"Don't ever accuse me of that," I said. "I have always been honest with you. When I say that I care for you, I do. And, perhaps, no matter where I go, or how far I run, I always will. And that is why I run. I have been warned and advised up hill and down dale, up countryside, and down city street. From your parents, your brother, your aunt, and even from other quarters. I am not good enough for you, Richard. And the only way for you to move on from where our hearts rest is if there was no chance of you to be in my company at all.

"If I remain at Pemberley or London, you will have no choice but to find me. And I will have no choice but to give in to you. At some point, we will breach propriety, and you will have no choice but to marry me. That will not be the fate you need. I must get away, to save us both. You know that I am right."

"Yes, I do. But Kitty, think on this. Imagine that when you are away, I do find another woman. She is a wealthy heiress who is precisely what I need for a wife, and she wants to marry me. What then? What will you feel?"

"The answer is simple. I will hate her. I will hate you. And then I will hate myself for giving you the life that you need. But when the smoke clears, my sense will overtake my sensibility, and I will be happy for you. I have every right to be happy for you. And I will look on you as one of my great passions. I will need time to be able to see you both together. But one day, I will know that we did right by each other and wished for nothing more. But for now..."

"Yes, for now..."

I raised his hand to my lips and kissed it.

"Your shirtsleeves do not offend me."

Colonel Fitzwilliam looked deeply into my eyes then he kissed my neck, ran his hands down my bodice and drove his hand into my gown, caressing my breasts. Lowering his lips downward, he kissed my skin along the edge of my gown, pulled my breasts to the surface and ran his lips over them savagely.

I almost cried out as it felt as if he was pulling my passions, my lifeforce and my strength from me.

Suddenly, standing up, he kissed me passionately.

"You will marry Finlay, won't you?" he asked angrily, between kisses.

"I don't know," I said, kissing him in return. "No man might choose me. I might find no one."

"Forgive me, but I hope you never do."

"I know."

"I am sorry!"

"I know. I know."

With one last lingering kiss, I had to separate us. Since he and I were both willing to fully consummate our feelings at any moment, I could not have withdrawn from him a second too soon.

Georgiana entered.

"Are you both friends again?" she asked.

Colonel Fitzwilliam and I looked in between each other.

"Yes," he said, trying to calm himself. "Yes, we are."

"Friends," I uttered.

"Yes. Friends."

Colonel Fitzwilliam offered to return to Longbourn with us. Readily, we agreed to this. Our burst of impropriety was precisely what was needed—in a perverse sort of manner—and Colonel Fitzwilliam was incredibly affable the entire way there.

When Mama saw him, she was all exclamations and eagerness. After all, Colonel Fitzwilliam made social events so easy and would smooth the way for any discussion that she would have with Mr. Darcy, who was a son-in-law that she had no knowledge of how to speak to.

Either way, the afternoon passed pleasantly, and amends had been made.

Even though it was at the expense of the Colonel and I being horribly wrong in our behavior again.

Whoever knew that, sometimes, wanton vulgarity is the answer to a problem?

Chapter Twenty-Four
THE END OF A CHAPTER OF MY LIFE

T hat evening, we were invited to dine with the Lucas family for a dinner party.

Sir William and Lady Lucas were on fine form to display their talents at hosting. Due to Mr. Darcy, Mr. Bingley and the Colonel being such distinguished men of consequence, Lady Lucas was very agreeable to my mother, and their silent habit of competing was quite done away. After all, despite Mr. Collins's patronage, when it came to whose daughters made the best matches, our mama had won. That left Lady Lucas to find her comforts where she may, and that was by being the best hostess.

Lucas Lodge looked lovely. There were still decorations, for we were at the end of the twelve days of Christmas. As such, there were even mistletoe hanging thereabouts.

In fact, there was a comical moment when Mr. Liam Lucas found himself under that very plant, with Elizabeth.

"Mrs. Darcy," Mr. Lucas said, amused. "We find ourselves in a very interesting predicament."

Elizabeth looked up and saw the mistletoe.

"A little more than carelessness, and little less than chance," Elizabeth responded, deliberately misquoting Shakespeare's *Hamlet*.

"Whatever are we to do?" he asked, leaning in to kiss her, which was immediately followed by Mr. Darcy standing next to Elizabeth.

"Not base one's actions off a plant," Mr. Darcy inferred, stoically.

"Quite right."

Seeing that the situation was about to become awkward, Georgiana nodded to me. Sensing what she needed me to do, I went over to where they were and pretended as if I accidentally stumbled in between the Darcys and Mr. Lucas.

"Oh, I do beg your pardon," I said, and Mr. Lucas had to catch me. "I do believe I have taken one too many cups of punch. Do forgive me, Mr. Lucas."

This was the welcome distraction that was needed, and Mr. Lucas focused on me while Darcy and Elizabeth made a silent retreat to the other side of the room.

"Oh, Miss Bennet," Mr. Lucas said, "you fell upon me in the most interesting of places."

I looked up and pretended to see the mistletoe for the first time.

"Oh, of all people," I said, "it would be me to be so unobservant. I give only one condition. A kiss on the forehead is all that I will permit."

"The cheek?" he challenged. "The cheek."

"Very well, Mr. Lucas, but only because we are longtime friends."

He kissed me on the cheek, and it was the briefest of kisses because someone tapped him on the shoulder.

He turned around and it was Colonel Fitzwilliam.

"Sir, the mistletoe is a large set. I think it requires more than one man to do the deed."

Mr. Lucas smirked and looked between us both.

There was nothing for it. No matter what, this was a spectacle. And I had just come in to remove the feeling of awkwardness between Mr. Lucas and Lizzy. But no good deed goes unpunished. Soon it would be spread all over Hertfordshire that the Colonel and I were in love and on the path to matrimony.

Oh well! What are we but to make sport of our neighbors and them to make sport of us in return? Hertfordshire had undergone quite a few rumors and scandals that us Bennet sisters went through. I daresay that they could stomach another one, and our good name would endure.

"I leave you to another who holds the mistletoe as being equally sacred," Mr. Lucas said to me, and he went over to his sister, Maria, where they were left to whisper together.

Colonel Fitzwilliam stepped up to me.

"You cannot escape," he said, smirking.

"I am too tired to run on the whole," I said, "for the moment, I will stand still and be here."

"That is as one would wish."

He leaned forward and we kissed. Due to a plant, it was the only time that he and I could exchange such intimacy, and it not be considered amiss.

Of course, the whole room might be watching us.

But, when one kisses who they adore, it is hard to be attentive to anything else. I'm certain that I was not. All I noticed was how wonderfully I felt in being so near the Colonel.

When we parted, the Colonel decided to do what he did best: compromise me and then save me.

"Never fear," he whispered, "I know how to save a lady's reputation after putting it in jeopardy."

He leaned away from me and addressed the room.

"Now," Colonel Fitzwilliam uttered, "are there any other ladies who are willing to line up under this very over-hang? I have a great desire to be put in the best of spirits."

All the ladies laughed in the room.

"Forgive my rakish habit," he uttered, "but as Mr. Lucas said, there are more mistletoe about. I think I can contrive to find you all under each one of them. You have been warned."

He gestured to me, and we went to one side of the room.

"Leave it to you to cover your true feelings with false ones," I said, "I marvel at you."

"In this society, that is the only way to be."

"Sadly, that is so. I feel that if everyone did anything with a shred of sincerity, the world would quite die of fright."

We moved over to Maria Lucas and Mr. Lucas and began to speak to them. I informed the siblings that Georgiana and I would be joining Arthur and Enara to Australia. They both were excited and immediately appealed to the Philipses to tell us what Australia was like.

"Georgiana is joining you on your voyage?" Colonel Fitzwilliam hinted.

"Yes, she is. Tomorrow we are going into town to collect clothing, items and apparel that will help us on our journey." I looked at him and saw the cloud that hung over him. "Richard, I promise that I will look after Georgie. I really will."

"I know that you will. I am glad that you are going with her. But I must stress upon this. Kitty, make sure that she is being guarded against fortune hunters. They are a dime a dozen here, to speak plainly. But they are not limited to Britain. In New South Wales, there are plenty of men who need a woman with a large dowry to help build their estates. I don't want her to be ensnared by them."

"Mark my words," I assured him. "I go there for adventure, but never to find love. And since romance can cause the greatest distraction in the world, I am free of it. As such, I will keep both eyes on Georgie's company, and make sure that she is not being sought after by pernicious suitors. I will advise her, to the best of my ability. But I also must entertain the fact that she might not listen to me. She is growing into her own woman, and it is best to let her. Yet, that won't stop me from doing the best I can to keep her from making a misstep that could ruin her entire future."

"Good."

"Believe me," I whispered even lower, "I have seen the pains that one suffers when one is in a match where both husband and wife are not properly suited. I would not wish that on Georgie."

"I know you won't. I trust you."

I smiled.

"Mr. Darcy said the same thing to me."

Colonel Fitzwilliam raised an eyebrow, amused.

"He did?"

"Yes. Never did I know that I would gain the respect of two men who was worth the earning. But stranger things have happened, haven't they?"

"Yes, they have. And I do not find it so strange."

"Colonel?" Mr. Darcy called him.

"Excuse me. I think my cousin calls me, to chide me for my invitation to the ladies to show preference for me."

"Good luck," I said.

"I will need it."

Colonel Fitzwilliam stood up and walked away.

As we sat down to dinner, I sat down next to Lizzy.

"Well," Lizzy said, "you and Georgiana are to go to Australia."

"I am happy that she wanted to go with me. I didn't ask her, Lizzy. Even though I wanted to."

"I know. I am happy that she goes with you. Look after her."

"I will," I said, "and this is the third time that I have made this promise, so you can believe that I mean it. I just fear disease catching her."

"And you?"

"I made the choice to go. If I fall from illness, it is my choice and mine alone. But with Georgie, I will feel guilty for the rest of my life. Lizzy?"

"Yes."

"There has been something that I have been meaning to speak to you about. I wanted to do it sooner, but between your condition and Mr. Darcy's often needing you, I never wish to intrude."

"What is it?"

"I just wanted to thank you, for paying for my ticket and for financing my trip to go. As well as lending your voice in support of my going. I will not deny that you are among the main reasons for which Mama and Papa have allowed me to go. And it has led to me asking this. Why did you support my scheme? Usually, you are not fond of my desires to go far and where there is no supervision."

"First, you have grown significantly over these past few months. You have learned to spot mercenary characters, you have not let your love for officers affect your judgment on what is ultimately prudent, and you have enhanced your senses on morality. Also, Georgiana loves you, and that peace between families is vital. But ultimately, I realize that I owe you a great deal."

"Me?"

"Yes. I, myself, never got the chance to thank you for urging Lady Catherine to accept me as Mr. Darcy's wife."

I felt my jaw drop open, in surprise.

"How did you learn about that?" I asked. "I never told anyone."

"You told Lady Catherine. And before we left Rosings Park, she informed Darcy and I about your last private conversation with her."

I marveled at that woman. She was such a mixture of sympathetic and apathetic traits. A combination of ultimate concern and ultimate egotism. A synthesis of compassion as well as ruthlessness. She proved that such extremes could exist in one person.

"She told you both."

"Yes, she did. She assured me that your kindness to Anne, your ability to include her, helped smooth the way for a place for me in her heart. Peace in the family. Kitty, you gave me something great. So, I give it back to you. I just worry that I put you in danger, out of my desire to help."

"I put myself in danger," I said. "You are giving me a chance at life. Now it's up to life to decide what it wants to do with me."

"Well, life has been kind to you, so far."

"Kind? Well, I am still alive and in comfort. So, there is that. But I would still say that it's been a mixture of fair and foul."

"That's not your life, Kitty. That's just life in general."

The next day, Georgiana and I were walking to Meryton together, to shop. We instructed the carriage to retrieve us in front of Ford's by three in the afternoon.

From buying more practical gowns, spencers, stockings, boots, parasols, umbrellas, lotions, soap, wash rags, etc. at each spot, we arranged to have our items packed where we would collect them at the end of our outing.

When we finished, we were a little exhausted, so we hoped to stop at my aunt and uncle's residence, which was so very close to the shops.

Aunt Philips was happy to see us because she had some news, and since Mary had gone to visit the Coxes, she was quite alone.

"Mr. Philips and Mr. Atkins have had a very busy morning," she said as tea and cakes were brought in. Georgiana and I dove into the refreshments easily.

"Busy?" I repeated. "In what way?"

"It is from an accountant in London. This concerns your letters concerning a Sir Thomas Bertram, of Mansfield Park."

"Really?"

This sparked Georgiana and my interest immediately.

"Yes. Now, I promised that I would never speak with you all, on that score, until Mr. Philips has had some more cemented news."

"Aunt Philips," I whined. "You draw us in, only to draw us out."

"That is so taunting," Georgiana said, equally as intrigued.

"I could not help it," Aunt Philips said. "He is reading the letter as we speak. In fact..." She called for Dennison and Dennison entered.

"Yes, ma'am?"

"Can you tell Mr. Philips and Mr. Atkins that Kitty and Miss Darcy have come to visit?"

"Very good ma'am," Dennison said, with a twinkle in his eye.

"And what is that look for?"

"Well, begging your pardon, mistress. But, from what I heard, Mr. Philips has gotten some very good news."

"Then go to it, man."

"Of course."

Dennison left, and we spoke of other matters for only a moment before we heard my uncle's thunderous footsteps.

He charged into the room, with Mr. Atkins behind him, holding the letter.

"My dear! Kitty and Miss Darcy, I come with great news."

"The news is success," Mr. Atkins said, looking around. "Where is my Mary?"

"Mr. Atkins, don't you remember?" Aunt Philips questioned. "She is visiting the Coxes."

Mr. Atkins tapped his head.

"Of course. Leave it to me to hear my wife in one ear, and then let the words leak out of the other. But I only do that when she speaks practically. When she speaks nonsense, I am completely attentive and excited. I was merely hoping she was here to receive the news first."

"What is the news?" I asked eagerly. "For goodness sakes, we are all sitting on pins and needles, with the way that we shift about."

"Success was the word put to it, was it not?"

"It was indeed," Uncle Philips said. "Kitty and Miss Darcy, as you know, Sir Thomas did write to me, under Pemberley's influence. I daresay, going there was one of the best experiences of his life. And it has forced me into being a man of action again. I found the perfect accountant in London who is to oversee arranging Sir Thomas's finances and transforming his property in Antigua to an establishment for hired labor."

"Truly?" Georgiana said, happily. "You've achieved it?"

"So far, all seems well. Now I must go to London to meet the accountant. His name is Mr. Carl Tucker. He is a respected accountant who I have had dealings with, in the past. He is remarkably clever at this sort of business."

"You will have to go to London?" I asked. "Well, the sooner the better, I say. Would it be best if you go with us when the family escorts your son and the rest of us on our voyage home? This way, you can see Arthur and Enara before they leave for years, and you can finish your business there while the rest of our company are in London."

When hearing this, Aunt Philips grew excited.

"That is a brilliant scheme!" Aunt Philips cried. "To see our son and daughter as they set sail. Nothing could be more romantic, Mr. Philips. I find it to be an infinitely preferable way of parting with one's children than watching them leave Hertfordshire."

"Well, since I am easy to convince," Uncle Philips said, clapping his hands together. "And since I feel my old eager feet remembering how active I was in my youth, why not? But this time, my dear, I will remember what I am about. I'm taking you with me."

"Oh, you better take me along."

"When I get home, I will ask my brother and Mr. Bingley," Georgiana said, "and see if you can remain in either of our townhouses while you are in London. This will give you the chance of being around family and not having to spare expense at an inn."

"That would be delightful," Aunt Philips said, "but I do not want to be an imposition. Especially by asking in such late notice."

"Mr. Bingley is not against such a scheme," I said. "He is a man who understands doing things in the work of a moment. Because he is the sort who quite likes to dash here and there very easily. I think he would not be against it. Especially since it is for such a good cause."

"Pack your clothes and arrange everything," Georgiana advised. "We will make short work of this and send a letter to you about our success when we go back to Longbourn. That is, if you can be spared from your services here."

"I can," Uncle Philips said, "since I have a clerk who I know will not burn down the house or business when I am away."

He turned to Mr. Atkins.

"What do you say, Atkins, my boy?"

"I say that I am sure not to light a fire when you go," Mr. Atkins said. "I just propose that I might only warm the coals."

"What does that mean, lad?"

"I have no idea. I was just trying to sound witty. Either way, yes sir, I will make sure to maintain your business and arrange all letters while you are away."

"This will give me the chance to see how you are at taking matters into your hand, and if you are the reliable sort, that I believe you to be."

Mr. Atkins gave us a look.

"Permission to say something witty?"

"Go ahead."

"Mary is here to regulate me. And when a man's wife is near, she is there to rein in his wilder aspects, by making him sit down and learn about the importance of muslin and meal arrangements."

"That's good enough for me." Uncle Philips said, looking at us. "Well, we shall know, by the end of the evening, if we are invited to go with you all to London, or not."

"You will be," Georgiana assured them. "Depend on it."

～

As we rode the carriage home, a notion struck me, that I found to be the ideal solution to Georgiana's situation.

"Georgie," I said, "let me propose something. I think it will help you."

"Help me?"

"Well, Colonel Fitzwilliam mentioned fortune hunters, and that, in your case, we had to be wary of them. And that reminded me of our unfortunate encounter with Mr. Atwell and Mr. Wright."

"Oh, yes," Georgiana said, rolling her eyes, "that sad episode of my life."

"Precisely. You and I both know that your wealth keeps men from noticing your true charms. Well, how about if we don't tell anyone about it."

"What?"

"Well, in England, you cannot escape your legacy, and your reputation as a Darcy. It's common knowledge. But now we are going to a whole different part of the world. You are not known there. You can go merely as a friend of the family, and we both can be known as women who are from modest households. Let it be known that you only have a dowry of maybe a hundred pounds a year. And that's it. That will frighten off any mercenary characters and you will be regarded as insignificant as myself."

"That is a brilliant notion," Georgiana said. "I go to Australia as a commoner, and that puts me both above and below the notice of any villain. If I am known for being attached to a watchful family, who cares about my safety, that's all that matters."

"Precisely."

The more that Georgiana thought about it, the more that she liked the plan.

When we arrived back at Longbourn, we had much news to relay.

Arthur and Enara were perfectly willing to introduce Georgiana as a woman of modest income, from a modest family, and that her connection to the Darcy family was distant.

When we made the announcement of Mr. Philips's success in assisting Sir Thomas Bertram, the company was in greater rapture.

"This is delightful," Jane told me, "because I have just received a letter from Mary Crawford. I can tell her about this news in my response. Despite the painful memories of Mansfield Park, she still is curious about all the goings on there."

"And I am certain that my housekeeper will be very good at preparing the guestroom," Mr. Bingley said. "I will send one of my servants to ride to London, posthaste, to inform her to have a room for the Philipses."

And we were proven correct. Mr. Bingley was a man who was very active and was quick to make up his mind about things in a hurry. Ergo, he was the easiest to adjust to another addition to our party in town.

Now that my aunt and uncle were coming, this idea naturally proved contagious. Mama also wished to attend, but due to the lateness of the invite, and the inability to pack all that was necessary to go into town within a day, father was able to convince her against it.

Especially since our last evening at Longbourn was going to end in a dinner party that mama had arranged.

While I was upstairs, choosing to wear my white muslin gown to dinner, with some hair pins with white rose ornaments at the end, the clock struck four o'clock.

Now that I had remembered myself, I knew what that meant.

It was the time of the last post.

And without being disappointed, I heard the post-wagon riding by.

Rushing down the steps, I ran out of the house, across the lawn, and down the road at the perfect time.

"Miss Bennet!"

"Yes, good afternoon, Mr. Dixon."

After all those months, Mr. Dixon and I met again.

The mark of a well-established relationship is that one can begin again, right from where one has left off. And that was where we were.

"Well," I began, "there you are."

"Yes," Mr. Dixon said, "here I am. And you, Miss Bennet, you are looking remarkably well."

"And you look happy."

"It's because I am."

"I know. I heard of your good fortune."

"You did?"

"Yes, I did."

I walked up to his wagon, he offered me his hand, and I sat right next to him.

"She must be a remarkable woman."

"She is. Her name is Georgette."

"Yes, I heard. A lovely name."

His eyes were lit up, but not in a forced habit. Rather, by an honest and open one.

"It is."

"Before I wish you joy," I said, "Mr. Dixon, I must make sure."

"Make sure of what?"

"Mr. Dixon, please do not hate me. We have reached a

point in our friendship where we are honest with each other."

"Very well. Speak your mind."

"I want to make sure that you are marrying her for the right reasons. Too many times, I've seen unequal matches. Or marriages that were founded because one thought that it was the best way to recover from an older disappointment."

"Put simply, you are worried that I marry her, to recover from not gaining you as a wife."

"I do not ask this out of vanity for myself. I know that you no longer love me."

He shushed me.

"I am not offended. From an objective standpoint, your question is valid. Sometimes, men and women do swing from one affection to another, to recover from when they were slighted from a previous affection."

"Yes. I know that you are strong, Mr. Dixon."

"But I am human. As human as any other." He tapped my hand. That was enough to show that his match was a true one, because he fully had accepted me as his friend again. "I can put your worries to rest. When I first saw Georgette, I didn't see her as a means to patch up the wounds of my broken heart. I just saw her. And that was it. That's when I knew that I was in love. All previous romances of my imagination faded away, and she became my reality. I wish that you could meet her. I am sure that you would like her."

"I believe I would. I pray that she will make you happy. You deserve it, Dixon. You deserve it very much."

"Thank you."

He looked ahead.

"Now that I have found my happiness, I can look at yours and be kinder. Jealous, I once was. Bitter, I once was.

Angry, I once was. And now, all of that is even more faded into the past than before. Be it Finlay or Colonel Fitzwilliam, wherever your fate lies, I wish you joy."

I laughed.

"After all this time, you and I have arrived at the proper place," I noted. "The whole, delightful, and astonishing reality of who we both were, are, and should be."

"Yes," he said, "Miss Bennet... Kitty?"

"Yes?"

"Thank you, for refusing me. By doing that, I had no choice but to move on. By moving on, I found Georgette. My fate could not be any other way. It is the right path that I was meant to take all along."

"Then go to it," I said, "and never regret it, Dixon. Be the good man that I know you to be."

"And you, Kitty. Follow your heart. It has proven to be the right thing, after all is said and done."

"Still friends?" I asked him.

"Still friends," he assured me. "Go around the world and back, and when you return, you will still find a friend in me."

"Mr. Dixon, you amaze me."

"How?"

"You stumbled on the perfect way to end this interaction. I am prodigiously proud of you."

I stepped down from the wagon.

"Always make her proud of you," I said, "and I will be as well."

"Then you will always be proud of me." He grinned.

"To work, sir."

"To adventure, Miss Bennet."

He rode his wagon along, and I called out to him.

"Merry Christmas!" I declared.

"And happy new year!" he called back to me.

I watched him ride along until his wagon disappeared.

When seeing Dixon fade into the distance, I couldn't help but look on this as another chapter of my life coming to a close. This was a time of my life where many things were being resolved, and new parts of my life were beginning.

That felt as it should be.

The new year really had come.

Chapter Twenty-Five

TO AUSTRALIA, WE GO!

I woke up the next morning, quite exhausted. The dinner party the night before had been a great success. The Longs and Lucases had come, and I could say farewell to Maria and Diana Long once more—and with good humor and goodwill on both sides.

We woke early so that we could arrive in London at good time. Mama and Father saw us to our carriages. When doing so, Father came to me especially, which was a great surprise.

"I know..." he began.

"Yes?" I continued, trying to help him on.

"I know what our refusal to allow you to go must have appeared like. It must have felt like we were confining you to our lives. And that we were reverting back to who we were before: where we were punishing you for Lydia's history."

I didn't speak but allowed him to continue.

"Well," he said, "I can assure you that it was not that."

"Then what was it?" I spoke. "And what drove you to say it while I am about to leave, and not at another time where we could have had a longer time to speak with each other about it?"

Father sighed.

"I know why," I said, "it is better to display your feelings when I have no time to comment on them, rather than allowing us the chance to understand each other better."

"Kitty?"

"What?"

"Let us end this well."

"But it wouldn't be real. It would just be an image. A falseness, to ignore what lies underneath. Well, Father, I will not let you. When you are ready to open up to me, and give me more time to do so, then I will listen. I will be gone for months, so you have time to learn."

He grabbed my arm.

"We didn't want you to go because we are worried about you," he uttered. "We worry for your safety, that you are walking into unknown danger, and we can't make sure that you are safe. We are scared because we love you. Because I love you. And your mother is scared, because she worries that she will never get the chance to get closer to you again."

Ah, the truth. The beautiful and agonizing truth that I had longed to hear.

"I appreciate that," I said, "but all you had to do was tell me this. Don't you ever see? That's *all* you had to do. I prefer that you worry about me. But you always do it too late, or when it's convenient for you. And when it's too late, you always do it ill, and then you suffocate my existence. And my identity gets lost in the process. Learn to care for me, even when it's not convenient for you, and then I will see your love for what it is. But we must stop dancing this same dance, over and over. We must go forward one day. If

I do return, please treat me better and remember this lecture."

My father blinked and he stepped back.

"You know the man that your father is," he uttered.

"Yes, I do. And I know what my mother is. Tell her what I said."

"I will. Despite an old man's desire to control his world, I do owe you that."

"Yes, you do. I will miss you both."

"You will?"

"Yes. You are my parents."

"Kitty, whatever happened this holiday, please believe me. Your mother and I love you very much."

"I know."

"We just need more time to learn how to show it."

From a short distance away from him, I saw Mama's anxious face, over his shoulder. She was evidently looking at us, hoping that Father would give her the chance to make our farewell smooth.

I smiled at her and waved. This was encouragement enough. She rushed forward and folded her arms around me, crying about how she would miss me terribly.

Whatever our past, I knew that she was telling the truth. At the remains of the day, our mother would cross an ocean if it meant that she could save us. She was merely born as she was.

Finally, it came time to depart, and my parents waved to us from their doorsteps.

Lord knows when I might see them again.

We left Hertfordshire at a good time and arrived in London by the early afternoon.

Darcy, Lizzy, Georgiana, Arthur, Enara and I went to Darcy's townhouse, while the Bingleys and the Philipses went to Mr. Bingley's home. Each of us was given rest and were arranged to take a bath, because tomorrow, The Lilia would set sail from the Thames.

Due to our brief time there, we joyously would not have time to meet Mrs. Hurst, Miss Bingley, or Mr. Hurst.

However, there would be dinner at Darcy's house, where our aunt and uncle Gardiner were invited.

Since they had no conflicts, in due time, a carriage arrived on our front steps.

Going down to meet it, I really felt our spirits rise as the door opened and we saw the Gardiners after so long.

Eagerly, we Bennets met them with such joy, and they returned our pleasures. Aunt and Uncle Gardiner were like constants. From their behavior down to their appearance. Naturally, it had not been long since we had seen them, so they weren't given much time to alter greatly.

But I suppose that is what enhanced our joys in seeing them. Sometimes, in life, change hurts. It can bring evolution, or it can bring agony. There are some things in life that a person wants to feel like it will remain the same. The Gardiners are such a folk. When they arrive, and you feel like they are as they always had been, you feel as if nothing bad could happen in the world.

"Kitty," they both said when they saw me, "so, you are to go to Australia?"

"Yes, I am, aunt and uncle," I said, "and try as you might, you will not be able to talk me out of it."

"Not at all, we assure you," Uncle Gardiner said, "In fact, we only wish to offer you joy."

"You do?" I asked.

"Of course," Aunt Gardiner said. "Exploration is something Britain has been doing for many a century. I cannot declare that the lands we explore have always profited from our visiting there. However, with this, I firmly believe that you will be a part of a new sort of exploration. And it will be to the making of you."

"Well," I said, "I never would have known that you would say such a thing."

"We have a way of being surprising, Kitty."

Since I was not the main attraction of the evening, the Gardiners focused more on Jane and Lizzy. This made sense, for they had a special connection to both of my sisters. Jane had come there, seeking refuge from her disappointment when Mr. Bingley left her. Elizabeth went on a holiday with the Gardiners, and that led to her meeting Mr. Darcy again, which had been the means of uniting them both. The Gardiners represented a magic about them, in Jane and Lizzy's eyes.

I was neither jealous nor feeling overlooked. I knew they loved me, and I loved them. It was just in a more complacent sort of manner.

They took in Elizabeth and Jane's girth, and they congratulated them, assuring them that they would be good mothers.

Afterwards, they wished to know about our time at Rosings Park, as well as wishing to know all about Aunt and Uncle Philips's business in coming to London.

While the discussion on Rosings Park was fascinating, the tale of the Crawfords, and Sir Thomas Bertram's life was the most fascinating. That is the great irony of life. Such awkward discussions about the Trade are always difficult to mention, and yet, when you speak about it, people are drawn in and enthralled. It's a dual reaction.

"I confess," Uncle Gardiner said, "that this part of your lives will always fascinate us, because of all the times that Mary Crawford and Mrs. Grant visited us at Gracechurch Street."

"Precisely," Aunt Gardiner added. "Whatever her faults, we were very much invested in her happy ending."

And that was another part of the tale that I had to accept I would never fully know everything about. Jane's relationship with Mary and Henry Crawford was something that Jane kept most of the history of, in London. She did not bring the whole story to Hertfordshire, and we had to accept that maybe that was how she wanted it. We all have the right to a few secrets, here and there. Jane was the sort to always have something that went untold. That might have been part of what made her fascinating.

The Gardiners spent the whole evening wanting to know everything, from when Henry Crawford stood trial at Pemberley, to when the Bertrams came, and Darcy and Finlay forced them to confront their painful realities.

Sitting there, I reflected on how magnificent Finlay was, in his defense. He stood his ground, like a man of spirit. There was fire in his eyes, and it lit us all up.

I never forgot my passion for him and never would. However, Colonel Fitzwilliam had done his best to establish such a strong physical connection to me that I could never forget it. That strong physical presence did not escape me in my final hours in London, but rather, the Colonel remained by my side for most of the evening. Sometimes, we didn't even speak. Often, we just looked at each other, and our eyes said it all.

I will miss you.

And I will miss you.

When Jane announced that Mary Crawford and William Price had gotten married, Aunt Gardiner sighed.

"Well, finally," she said, "all things come to the final point that they were always meant to arrive at."

"Yes," Jane said, "and who would have thought. After all

the schemes, of clinging to prejudices, of people falling in love with the wrong person to fall in love with, and to arrive at the proper conclusion for all. Mary Crawford married a Naval officer, despite her protests for the opposite. She grew, whether she wanted to or not. And she grew in the right direction."

"It just goes to show you," Elizabeth confirmed, "that everyone has a right place once they stop walking into all the other wrong areas of dwelling. How amazing we humans always are of getting in the way of ourselves, and then cursing life for it?"

"It makes me wonder," I whispered to Colonel Fitzwilliam.

"What?"

"Well," I said, "when I think of Mary Crawford, and her conclusion, it makes me wonder about her. At Mansfield, for so long, she was considered to be a bad influence and was almost villainous. But with some people, maybe they are not villains. They simply are heroes who were never given the chance to find their path to redemption."

"Now that is an interesting thought."

"Thank you. I am not saying that all bad characters can be redeemed. Yet, some just need more time. What do you think?"

"I think the same, by pure happenstance. We humans tend to fit the same model on each person. Ultimately, we do humanity a disservice when we do that. We don't take all the circumstances into account. That leads to us not always giving people the time to evolve in their own speed. Miss Mary Crawford was given Jane Bennet as a friend. Clearly fate gave her a second chance."

"Just like fate gave me you, Finlay and Georgie," I noted. "Fate gave me a second chance."

"And a third one, and a fourth one, and a fifth one," he joked. I nudged his stomach.

"Oh, shut it."

"Like you would want me to do that."

"Oh, very well, no I would not. But that doesn't mean that I would not punish you for teasing. I still will do that."

Quietly, he took my hand.

"Promise me something."

"What?"

"That late at night, when the darkness preys upon our wanton ways, and we think of love and lust, that you will think of me. That you will dream of me, under the cover of night, and in the depth of your desires."

"Will you promise me the same?" I asked. "This dark dream must be mutual or be nothing worth."

"It will be."

"Then I will dream of you. Even when I am awake."

In truth, I would dream of Finlay as well. But I would never speak of it. Finlay was parted from me, perhaps forever. Therefore, he would rest in my bosom. And there he would remain.

Colonel Fitzwilliam leaned into me.

"If I find fortune and wealth," he said, "I will sail to Australia, and you will be in my bed by nightfall."

"As long as there is a house around it, sir."

He smiled. That was the most encouragement that I would give him. I was too strong to give him any more. But I was also too weak to give him any less. For I meant it. Every word.

"No matter what happens," I promised him, "believe me when I say this. You are a marvel of a man, and you are one of the greatest loves of my life."

"And you are mine, my perverse Kitty. You are mine."

Eventually, the dinner party came to an end and the Gardiners offered us a hearty farewell.

Their coming into our lives was brief. But with them,

brevity was truly the soul of wit. And the quality of their coming bested the quantity of meeting others who lingered for longer.

∾

The next morning, I awoke from a deep sleep. Fearing that it would rain, and the day would be cloudy and feel doomy, I was happy to be wrong.

The sun was shining, and the clouds in the sky were thick, but non-threatening.

We all went to the docks along the Thames, and as we passed many other ships, at last, we arrived at The Lilia.

The Captain, an American named Joseph Archer, greeted us, and invited us onboard.

Now was the hour of farewells.

Aunt and Uncle Philips embraced their son and Enara. Aunt Philips wept, regretting that she would lose Arthur to the ocean again. They both told Enara to give her parents their regard.

While their farewell was very animated, Georgiana and I faced our family.

Jane, Elizabeth, Mr. Darcy, and Mr. Bingley each gave us such a heartfelt wish for a safe journey to New South Wales.

"We will miss you," Jane and Elizabeth said to us both, embracing us with intense affection.

"I am as excited for you as I would be for myself, if I could go," Bingley said to us. "You must write to us."

"We will," I assured them.

Next, Mr. Darcy came forward. To our surprise, he leaned down and kissed both our foreheads.

"Please," he urged us both, "look after yourselves, and come home. Georgiana and Kitty, I am not used to you both going where I cannot follow you and make sure you are safe. Please, don't break our hearts and have us lose you."

"We won't," Georgiana assured him. "We promise."

He looked on us both, with such apprehension that Elizabeth had to take his arm in hers, to steady him.

The poor man. He always loved Georgiana, but he had grown to love me.

"Come home," Elizabeth stressed. "Remember, our children need to meet their aunts. We will hold you to it."

At last, came the final farewell.

Colonel Fitzwilliam stood in the back. Moving through our company, I stood before him.

"Richard," I said, "now you lose your voice. Now you forget your courage."

"No," he said, "I just am about to ruin you, but since you are leaving, it will save you."

I read his mind.

"We must not."

"It will be the last time. We must."

Grabbing me, he pulled me to him, and he kissed me savagely.

"Richard!" I overheard Darcy groan, but there was nothing for it. Colonel Fitzwilliam had kissed me, and it would be a greater scene to try and stop us.

Once more, I could deny the Colonel nothing.

Because I didn't want to. He was the very best of me. And I would give that best away, one day. But for now, may the best find me, and enclose me in its comforts. Paradise given for a day.

And who was I, when in the presence of so many sailors, merchants, or passengers along the docks?

I was a nobody, of no consequence at all. What was

seen would be talked of for a day or two, and then it would be forgotten.

At last, Colonel Fitzwilliam released me, and I had to catch my breath, as I remained with my eyes closed, steadying myself.

"I love you."

"And I love you."

Behind me, I felt Uncle Philips's presence.

"Colonel, it's time to release my niece."

⁓

Embarrassment.

I just realized that Uncle Philips never saw me breach propriety before.

Now I remembered myself and I saw how I had allowed liberties to be taken and how I destroyed my reputation.

Colonel Fitzwilliam apologized to Uncle Philips, and I looked at my uncle, mortified. Prepared for him to have lost all respect for me, I could imagine what I looked like. Fortunately, Uncle Philips directed his anger toward the Colonel, and he took me away from him.

"What did I tell you," he whispered to me. "The man would rather ruin your name and offer you nothing in return."

"He was merely excited."

"And he forgot himself and didn't even think about how it will reflect on you. There is nothing for it, Kitty. I will speak with him after you set sail."

"Uncle, please, don't hurt his pride."

"I will. I am your uncle. It's my duty."

I couldn't argue with that.

"Now, we will say no more of this. Let me give my farewells."

He led me next to Georgiana and looked at us both.

"Kitty, look after Miss Darcy. And Miss Darcy, please look after my niece."

We promised him that we would.

"Go there for adventure and exploration," he said, "but not for love. Those places are filled with men who will view you both as novelties. People fall in love with novelties, but soon, that fades away, and you find that you are trapped in a match that you will regret. Please, I don't want you to suffer that fate. With marriage, there will always be deception, and a great deal of taking in. Choose a man that you know. Not one that you don't."

"We won't," I assured him. "We promise. We will not let that be our fate."

He kissed my forehead. Then he kissed Georgiana's.

"Brave hearts, dear girls. You are a Darcy and a Bennet."

~

The time came for us to board The Lilia. When we did so, we were met with two familiar faces.

"Emma and Mr. Howard!" Georgiana cried.

There, on the ship was Emma Watson and Mr. Howard.

"Georgiana and Miss Bennet," Emma Watson replied, as she and Mr. Howard walked up to us eagerly.

"This is too much," Emma said, taking Georgiana's hands. "You come with us. Now I shall not be afraid of returning home. For you are with me."

I stood back and prepared myself. I had to share my friend with another woman. Well, here we go.

Mr. Howard approached me.

"Miss Bennet, it is a great pleasure to see you once more."

"Thank you, Mr. Howard. I was under the impression that you were traveling with Mr. Osbourne."

"I was, but business took him and Mr. Musgrave on an earlier ship to Australia, and we will meet them there."

"Mr. Musgrave? You mean Mr. Tom Musgrave?"

"Yes, I do. They are close friends and Lord Osbourne invited Tom along. And he agreed."

Oh dear. I remember meeting Mr. Musgrave at the ball. I heard horror stories of him. For some reason, I sensed a sort of foreboding. But I couldn't place why.

I was not left to worry for long because soon, Captain Archer ordered the anchor to be raised, and slowly, The Lilia began to set sail.

Georgiana and I went to the edge of the ship and waved to our company.

Seeing us from a distance, they waved in return.

"Oh," Emma Watson said, "Do you see that rider there? He's rushing along the docks. Maybe he was a boarder, and he missed the ship."

I directed my attention to where Miss Watson pointed, and my eyes widened in excitement.

"Finlay!"

Lieutenant Finlay had ridden along the docks, on his horse.

He had come to say farewell, but he was too late.

"Kitty!" he cried.

All our company turned and saw him staring at me. Whatever scandal I had caused, I was leaving England, so there would be no time for anyone to care very soon.

"I'm sorry!" Finlay cried.

I knew what he meant. He was apologizing that he was too late to see me off.

"There is nothing to apologize for!" I cried. "You came!"

He rode his horse even closer to the edge.

"Do not forget me!" he cried.

"Never!" I cried in return. "Never in my life."

I almost wept at the beauty of it. He must have ridden all night to see me, and I could give him nothing but half my heart. But I would redeem myself. I was leaving. I was giving him his best chance.

Knowing that all I could give him was my final look, I raised my hand, by a wave of farewell, and let it rest there.

His eyes were wistful and he raised up his hand and waved to me as well.

Then I looked at Colonel Fitzwilliam, telling him farewell with my eyes. He understood.

I looked at both men and didn't tear my eyes from them until our ship was so far from the shore, that they faded from my sight.

"Who was that?" Emma Watson asked me.

"A friend," I said, "and two of the best men in Britain."

Georgiana came up behind me and rested her chin on my shoulder.

"And you say you are unlucky. You don't know, Kitty, that you have something to your life that is luckier than most."

"Time will tell," I said, "you have been right many times before. I will miss them both."

"I know. Carry their love with you, but don't let it leave part of your soul behind."

"It won't. We are on an adventure. Among it will be danger."

"Exoticness."

"Wonder."

"Alarm."

"Curiosity."

"Kindness."

"Cruelty."

"Dirt."

"Savagery."

"Civilization."

"And the unknown."

"Onward we go."

"Yes, onward we go."

Our world was behind. The new worlds were ahead.

Exploration is like a fire. A fire had a duality to its nature.

Fire brings warmth, light, and sometimes a means to see the right way when you are lost.

But a fire can also burn, be dangerous, and it could kill.

Georgiana and I were walking into a fire. Whether it was to warm us, to bring light to us, or to burn us, we didn't know. But into the unknown, we would go.

Come what may.

Epilogue

On the shores of the Thames, the Darcys, Philips', Bingleys', Colonel Fitzwilliam and Finlay stood. As The Lilia grew smaller and smaller in the distance, Fitzwilliam and Finlay were the last to remain. Side by side, they both watched as the love of their lives sailed further and further away, until she ultimately disappeared.

"It's like she's fallen off the edge of the world," Lieutenant Finlay said.

"Yes," Colonel Fitzwilliam agreed. "It does feel like that. As if an abyss has swallowed her up, and she will never return. But we have to tell ourselves that she will."

"She's left us."

"Yes. Because she cares. She's giving us our best chance at a new life for ourselves."

"I know. I didn't believe it at first, but she is right. I hated her for knowing that."

"I did as well."

"Then I learned to love her for it."

"As did I. It made me love her even more."

"Do you think that you have it in you to fall in love with another woman?"

"I don't know. But I must try. And so do you."

"Yes. I worry that I can't."

"So do I. Good luck."

"And good luck with you."

Both men continued to stare at the horizon. She had walked out of their lives, and yet they still clung to the possibility that the ship was faulty, and it would bring her back to them the next day. Dreams were all they had. And they clung to it.

End of Book VIII

Afterword

DUSTING OFF THE CLASSICS

Hello readers!

When I first undertook this entry into the series, I wanted it to focus mainly on the holidays. The reason for such is due to the time this series was first published, in 2020, during the December holiday season, while also because of the time period that took place in this part of the series.

This led to me taking the series back in another direction: home. No matter what we each, individually, believe, one thing can be said for us all: at the end of the year, it naturally feels like we did it. We all succeeded at making our way to the end of the year, and we can declare that we did well. We can easily fall into step and say, in the words of the Doctor from Doctor Who 'A Christmas Carol': we're halfway out of the dark. That's what December feels like, and why; in every culture, there is always some sort of celebration at the end of the year, paying tribute to what we look back on, what we overcame, and what we have to look forward to.

But also, whether it's Christmas, Hannukah, Kwanzaa,

or the Winter Solstice, etc. not only is there a sense of feeling like one is halfway out of the dark, but you also feel the beauty of tradition. As if everything has changed, but also everything is still the same. That's what I wanted to capture when I wrote this, and what I felt that the reader needed.

So much has changed since the first book of the series. But still, we needed to return to older scenes.

We needed to go to Rosings Park.

We needed to go back to Longbourn.

And by so doing, we revisit all those beloved characters from the original novel.

Lady Catherine de Bourgh is back.

Anne de Bourgh is back, and she has her voice.

Mrs. Jenkinson, Mr., and Mrs. Bennet, the Lucases, the Longs, the Collinses, and all of Hertfordshire. It was as if we were returning to older times, dusting off the classics, and doing what occurs at winter festivities: return to tradition after a year of many changes.

Then, when the new year is ushered in, the world moves all around us and the changes begin again.

That was the journey for this book, and for the reader. It was to bring Kitty and the other characters back to familiar shores, dusting off the original text of 'Pride & Prejudice' (and also, I drew a great deal of inspiration from parts of the 1980 BBC adaptation again, which I am one of the few Jane Austen fans who really like that one. I got inspiration from Lady Catherine's scenes). I have taken the reader far away from the original tale, and sometimes, one needs to return to it and retain that tradition before another great change occurs. As it will in the next book. But until then, for a moment the reader could peruse this book and think: 'well done. We did it. We are halfway out of the dark!'

I hope that was the right impulse and that the reader did miss these characters and felt that they needed a return to familiar faces and places that they loved so much.

Regression

While the main theme for this entry was 'finding nostalgia', another theme of the story was the topic of Regression.

When it comes to stories, we writers naturally rely upon the traditional *cause and effect* routine. It means that our characters start out on some sort of journey, be it physical or emotional, they get into trouble, encounter more trouble, and then when the tale ends, their mentality has enhanced, and their full emotional journey has reached its apex. Now they can go boast of reaching their full potential, they can progress onward, going forward with all their beliefs and being the best person that they could be.

This is the proper and correct method of storytelling.

However, it's not always true. We humans are in a constant state of progress and regression. From an individual level to a societal one.

Usually, we humans start out with noble intentions, then at some point, we falter, learn from our mistakes, and we evolve.

And then we do it all over again. That evolution that we have achieved does not always linger with us. Often, we sabotage ourselves, and after we have made the ultimate form of progress, we accidentally regress and must begin the journey—again. With humanity, there is always a constant flow of cause and effects, and we undergo them.

In this entry, Kitty is undergoing a definitive path of regression.

She once had the ability to not let the men in her life dictate her happiness, or for her to be very dependent on their company. Now she is regressing. She needs them. To the point where it affects her judgment on things.

And more than that, in this tale, Kitty is spiraling downward. She is learning that she has no sense of control in some matters, and that, at some point, she took a wrong step somewhere. Even worse, she is suffering under the painful fact of life: even when we have good intentions, and we did everything right, somehow everything has gone so wrong.

When considering where Kitty left with, she began as a woman who did everything right, romantically.

Item 1 – she liked Mr. Bingley. Yet when Jane began to like him, and he reciprocated her feelings, Kitty backed off. She did right.

Item 2 – when Mr. Dixon proposed to her, after the initial shock, Kitty tried to maintain a friendship with him, but offered no encouragement. She did right.

Item 3 – when Lieutenant Finlay wrote her, telling her he loved her, she returned his affections. Yet since he left without offering her anything, she let his love fortify her, but not affect her daily life or happiness. She still lived her life as she always did.

Item 4 – When Colonel Fitzwilliam confessed his feelings to her, she did not seek him out or let that affect her daily habits. She confronted her feelings, that she returned his affections, and then she kept going.

Item 5 – when Finlay returned in her life, she was honest about the Colonel.

At this point, Kitty was on the right path and had all the correct intentions.

Then, in *'Follies & Forgiveness'* that's when everything starts falling apart. Up until that point, Finlay and Fitzwilliam were two different men who always occupied two different spaces and times in Kitty's life. But in *F&F*,

both men had come in, at the same time, and they now occupied the same space. It was no longer one coming in after the other left her, and she was able to transition. But both men came rushing in at one time, and both loves she felt were now warring within her.

This led to Kitty losing control over her own sense of self, unable to rein in her passions, and allowing liberties to both men at the same time. Both men understood, but at some point, her torn heart was not only affecting her own progression, but it was affecting them. While they were unable to release her from their hearts, she could not release them, and this forced all three of them to be torn in two. Thus, all three of them are often submitting to their base natures, and even compromise their dignity, their self-control, and they don't even notice when they are damaging their own image or the image of those around them. It's a complete submission to one's sensibility. It's beautiful, that cannot be denied. It's real and passionate, which is nothing short of exhilarating. But, in that era, it's also socially fatal.

And that connects back to the immortal habit of regression in our lives. Usually, we humans never set out to do wrong. Often, we begin with good principles and walk down the right path. But we do this in a world where things get complicated very quickly. As a result, that path of progression that we were taking gets barred and ends up accidentally going down another pathway. And that path is the wrong one. And sometimes you keep going down that wrong path until one of three things occur:

1. One day, you just realized that you took a step too far, you reflect, and you evolve again. This is usually what happens.

2. You humiliate yourself in a very public way, and you spend many a year trying to undo the damage you have done. Usually, the damage is only repaired when you try to repent, because you knew you were wrong. But if you do it simply to improve your self-image, then it becomes a mission about vanity, and that usually never works out.

3. You stay on the wrong path and continue to burn everyone around you. Usually this is not what often happens, but there will always be outliers. Hence why any society will always have a criminal sector to it, no matter where you go.

The first is what Kitty goes through. She is at the very precipice of that inevitable process that we all undergo; that no matter how right you were, that you could have done everything correctly, and you still end up in the wrong place. It's one of the principal facts of life.

The instinct to me feeling like Kitty needs to undergo this, is because it is a constant and major factor of the human condition. Life is not just one primary *cause and effect*. It's a series of *causes and effects*. And perhaps, it's how it should be. For if our lives were just one cause and effect, where else could we go? Humanity thrives on being a creature that is constantly on the move. By being progressive, then regressive, then realizing that and attempting to be progressive again, is the natural journey that we have to repeat. Kitty's actions are symbolic of this, and it's not something that is confined merely to her age. Mistakes and repentance, flaws overcome by virtue, will always be a cycle that one undergoes one's entire life. A person in their 30s can make the same romantic missteps as a teenager. A person in their 50s can fall into the same passionate misfortunes as a person in their 20s. If you watch one episode of the tv show, *Golden Girls*, they give you plenty of proof of that. That's a darn good show, actually. If you haven't watched it, I recommend it. Especially Season 7. But each to his own, of course.

Either way, since Kitty is not a traditional heroine for JAFF novels, but rather an everywoman/everyman, she must undergo the same experiences, while also being cathartic.

That's why Kitty goes to Australia. It's a physical version of what a lot of us undergo, emotionally. You have that time in your life where you regress, so you find a way to distance yourself from that moment. Kitty does the same, but through leaving England. Either way, what she represents is a successful getting away from such experiences. And while she does that, the reader can undergo that as well. The fact is, everyone in the world regresses. Everyone failed somewhere. If you still feel like your secrets haunt you, and sometimes keep you awake at night, it's time to admit it, acknowledge that you messed up, and put them behind you by trying to fix the problem you caused, or just improve.

Remember, while you are reading this, it's the end of the year in the novel. You made it. You are halfway out of the dark.

The Regression of Mr. and Mrs. Bennet

I know this will seem odd, because after all the Bennets have gone through, you would think Mr. and Mrs. Bennet would have improved at this point. So why did I have them serve as antagonistic and still ignorant of the proper way of looking at Kitty. After all, Kitty has proven herself, many times over, to be an admirable daughter.

Truth is, it's simply that I had to adhere to how Jane Austen ultimately wrote Mr. and Mrs. Bennet to be. Jane Austen specifically implied that Mrs. Bennet never fully succeeded at evolving into a superior person. She kind of always stays as she is. As such, even when I write her to have moments of revelation, I cannot have her remain that way, because it's not fully true to that aspect of the tale. I only add elements when the story has blank spots that can be filled with other ideas. But when something is a staple and cemented as Mrs. Bennet's character, it must be respected. And technically, Mr. Bennet is not said to enhance his character either, by the end of the original book, but loves to take advantage of Pemberley's library. Since this is a continuation of the series, the original idea still must exist somewhere in the narrative.

This did help, however, because it continued the very theme of regression that was what the story was attempting to convey. Mr. and Mrs. Bennet, whether they mean to or not, will have moments of character evolution, but then will revert to their original ways. Then they will begin the whole process all over again.

Uncle Philips, the Mover & Shaker

I just realized that, in all the afterwords that I have written, I don't recall speaking much about Uncle Philips. Unless I did and was mistaken. As the reader can see, he plays a major part in Kitty's character development.

In Miss Austen's novel, Uncle Philips has no lines, and from the one time we do see him, he is not fondly written about. In fact, his description hints at a very uncouth and unimpressive man. He is not considered attractive to look at and it might be implied that his manners are rough.

In this series, he seems to be the epitome of progressiveness, which seems opposite to how it's implied how he is written. I can assure the reader that I did not ignore Miss Austen's description but took the time period into account. In that particular era of history, there were some very liberal habits. But while Uncle Philips's mentality might seem very progressive now, it still would not have been considered proper for a young lady at that time. Uncle Philips would have been regarded as encouraging wildness in a woman, where he was just attempting to allow them to chase down a liberty that would not have been considered acceptable in that era. He would have been viewed as a perverse sort of oddity, at that time. Especially with him being a male.

The second reason is because I used him as a means to convey a movement. As I said before, there were some liberal concepts running around Regency England. For one, there was the School of Romanticism, where people felt that their emotions guided them better than any sort of logic. But there were also the activists such as Mary Wollstonecraft. She was the mother of Mary Shelley and Fanny Imlay. Her first daughter, Fanny, was conceived out of wedlock, and Mrs. Wollstonecraft raised her as a single mother, before remarrying, and then conceiving Mary Shelley, who would go on to write the famous novel, *Frankenstein*.

When conduct books were the rage, Mary Wollstonecraft, a known activist, rebelled against them. She declared that the books, which focused on telling a woman everything she needed to make her a proper wife, was actually stunting the female growth process, and in fact was leading to the woman being a terrible wife. For the book shunned any other form of education that did not focus on making the woman a domestic ideal. Mrs. Wollstonecraft said that, by having ladies focusing solely on strict lessons, it limits her mind, and gives her no chance of having anything in common with her husband. She cannot appeal to him on an intellectual level, and ultimately, it would be an unequal marriage. Mind you, this is the research that I gathered about her. The reader can correct me if I am wrong, or if my source was incorrect.

But if it is true, I took Mrs. Wollstonecraft's beliefs and put them in Uncle Philips's form. He has a natural antipathy of conduct book maxims, and he does not regard the traditional way of bringing up daughters to be the proper way for a lady to be raised.

Naturally, in that era, that would have rendered him to be notorious, but nowadays, his mentality makes all the sense in the world. To this day, I thank Jane Austen for not giving Uncle Philips any lines. This gave me the excuse that I could have for shaping him as my instincts compelled me.

Either way, for those few readers who are still continuing to read this series, thank you so much. I cannot tell you how happy writing this series makes me, as well as how delightful it is to write Kitty Bennet. For some reason, it just feels cathartic.

Either way, friends, I promise, thanks for reading!

—Ney Mitch

THANK YOU FOR READING

Did you enjoy this book?

We invite you to leave a review at your favorite book site, such as Goodreads, Amazon, Barnes & Noble, etc.

DID YOU KNOW THAT LEAVING A REVIEW...

- Helps other readers find books they may enjoy.
- Gives you a chance to let your voice be heard.
- Gives authors recognition for their hard work.
- Doesn't have to be long. A sentence or two about why you liked the book will do.

About the Author

Ney Mitch has been a long-standing Jane Austen enthusiast, having written forty novels that were inspired by her various works. Since stumbling on Miss Austen's books after graduating from college, she has always dabbled in Austen inspired literature, ranging from writing works for teens to adults. Originally, her desire was to adapt Jane Austen's writing in a way to help young adults connect with her, however over time, she has spread her aims to other genres and styles. Having received her BA Degree at Desales University, she is a writer, both literary and dramatic, as well as being a Historic Reenactor.

facebook.com/courtney.mitchell.589

x.com/CMMitchelPsyche

pinterest.com/shebaanna

Also by Ney Mitch

WITH SATIN ROMANCE

Austen Gaskell Series

Curiosities & Contemplation

Resolved & Resigned

Triumph & Tragedy

Woes & Worries (Coming soon!)

~

Kitty Bennet Adventure Series

Vanities and Vexations

Forms & Fashions

Romance & Recklessness

Nuance & Novelty

Doubts & Difficulties

Follies & Forgiveness

Joys & Judgements

~

Romance & Revolution Saga

The First Impression

~

The Memory Series

Moments of Moments Past

Moments of Moments Present

Moments of Moments Future

Moments of Moments Infinite

❧

Pride & Prejudice Reimaginings

Rapture & Rebellion

Fortune & Misfortune

Desire & Destiny

Pride & Peace

Resolve & Revelations

Hope & Hopelessness

Faith & Family

❧

Chances Series

Chances Are

Chances Come

Chances Fade

Chances End

❧

Seasonal Situations

Considearations Near Christmastime

Curiosities at Christmastime

❧